BARBARA ELSBORG

Susie's CHOICE

ELLORA'S CAVE
ROMANTICA®
www.ELLORASCAVE.COM

An Ellora's Cave Publication

www.ellorascave.com

Susie's Choice

ISBN 9781419963148
ALL RIGHTS RESERVED.
Susie's Choice Copyright © 2009 Barbara Elsborg
Edited by Sue-Ellen Gower.
Photography and cover art by Les Byerley.

Electronic book publication July 2009
Trade paperback publication 2012

SUSIE'S CHOICE

&

Chapter One

🔊

On his way back from the bathroom, Joel tripped over three pieces of Christian's clothing. Boxers featuring yellow ducks, a lone black sock and a T-shirt Christian had used to wipe sweat from his armpits. Joel grimaced. Was it so hard to tidy up after yourself?

"Hey, come on, little guys. Giddy up," Joel said.

Christian leaned on one elbow and blinked at him bleary-eyed. "Who are you talking to?"

"Your underwear. You seem to think it can get to the laundry bin on its own, whereas I reckon it needs a bit of encouragement."

"Smartass."

Joel stood in front of the mirror to fasten his tie and caught sight of the devastation behind him. All courtesy of Hurricane Christian.

"We need a cleaner," Joel said, running his fingers through his straight dark hair in an attempt to flatten a wayward lock. "Now. Today. Whoever turns up tonight can have the job."

"What, even if it's shapeshifting werewolf?"

"Especially if it's a shapeshifting werewolf." Joel grinned and then scowled when his foot caught on one of Christian's shirts. "You're going to have to convince them you're not like this all the time. Tidy up the mess."

"I have to do everything."

"No, you don't." Joel put on his jacket. "I just want you to make sure we have a cleaner by the end of the day."

Christian rolled onto his back. "Why do I have to make the decision? Why can't you do it?"

"You're whining," Joel said.

"No, I'm not."

"Yes, you are."

"Shut me up, then."

Joel launched himself onto the bed and pinned Christian down by the shoulders, his knees on Christian's thighs. Joel stared into his lover's dark green eyes, thinking about how to persuade Christian to cooperate and then pressed his lips against his mouth. Christian melted beneath him, his muscles loosening in supplication as Joel deepened the kiss. Strong arms moved around Joel and tugged him down.

Joel pulled back. "Choose someone who looks as though they know how to clean a bathroom."

Christian glared, tried to push him away and didn't succeed. Joel kept him right where he wanted him.

"Christian, come on, you have to sort this out. I'm too busy."

"You could at least show some interest."

Joel sighed. "We're looking for a house cleaner, for Christ's sake, not an interior designer. How hard can it be to pick someone?" Joel licked around Christian's ear and made him squirm. "Talking of hard..."

"It's not fair," Christian said with a gasp.

"What's not fair?" Joel nibbled along Christian's collar bone.

"You've got clothes on."

"That's because I have to get to work. I can't lie around naked all day, much as you'd like me to."

Christian's fingers squeezed between their bodies and tugged at the zipper on Joel's trousers.

"You're gonna make me late," Joel moaned.

"Now who's whining?"

"God, Christian." Joel hissed as Christian's hand pressed against his cock.

"Be late for once."

Joel held himself up on his elbows, allowing Christian to unfasten the button on his suit trousers. The zipper eased over his erection and Christian slid a hand inside the fly of Joel's boxers. Joel allowed Christian to pull off his jacket and maneuver him onto his back. He lay basking in the desire in Christian's eyes. A couple of tugs, Joel's pants slipped down and his cock sprang free. Like an adorable lizard, Christian's tongue flicked out and licked the glistening head of his dick. One drop of pre-cum gone, plenty more where that came from. Only Christian wanted to go slow.

"Christian, you bastard, I don't have time." Joel groaned.

"You don't mean that."

"Cocksucker."

Christian laughed and lowered his head. Kneeling with his legs either side of Joel's calves, he ran his tongue along the underside of Joel's straining shaft, traced the pulsing vein and then licked upward, wrapping his mouth around the delicate tip. The moment Joel felt Christian's lips on the head of his dick, his balls tightened. Christian might be shit at keeping house but he was the best lover he'd ever had. The only one Joel had been tempted to keep. He wished he could make himself tell Christian that. He knew Christian needed to hear it, but Joel clammed up whenever he got close to expressing affection.

The long, hard, wet pulls on his cock drove the worry from Joel's mind. All his concentration lay on what Christian was doing to his body. His fingers slid into Christian's soft, brown hair. When Christian looked up at him with those cheeky eyes, Joel almost lost it. He wanted to roll the pair of them over and fuck Christian in the mouth, but contented himself with pushing his lover's head down harder.

"Oh Christ, you're killing me." Joel closed his eyes as Christian's lips tightened around him.

Then Christian did something he'd never done before. He pulled away. Joel felt his weight shift from the bed. He lifted his head and tried to focus.

"I want you to come home early tonight and pick the cleaner. Someone hot," Christian said.

"You fucker. Finish me," Joel growled.

Christian grinned. He danced around the bedroom, a hard-rock dream, his cock bouncing, and Joel gave in.

"Oh for fuck's sake, Christian. All right. I'll do the choosing. Just suck me."

Joel sighed with relief when he felt Christian's hot mouth tighten around him. He would have agreed to anything at that moment. He'd pick a goddamn cleaner for them. The ugliest and oldest that applied. It would serve Christian right. He was the one who'd be with them in the house all day.

As Christian took Joel deep into his mouth, the orgasm began to build in Joel's lower back, a tightening as though his body were being squeezed between two pieces of metal. He held it in check for a moment, the agony close to bliss before the jolt shot like lightning from his balls and out through the end of his cock, sending his cum pulsing into Christian's mouth. Joel lay there in his Brooks Brothers shirt and his Hermes tie, his pants around his ankles, groaning with the sheer, delicious, wicked pleasure of it. He stroked Christian's head, curling his hair in his fingers.

Christian kept him in his mouth as he softened, licking him as gently as a kitten, cleaning up every trace of his cum. Then he tucked Joel back into his boxers, zipped and buttoned him up and pulled him to his feet. Joel kissed him, tasting himself on Christian's lips, and his hands slid to Christian's backside.

"You cunning little fucker." Joel nipped Christian's ear— hard.

"Ouch. You'll have to get home early. They're all coming tonight between six and eight."

"All? How many are there?" Joel asked in alarm.

"Five."

Joel narrowed his eyes. "I don't like being manipulated."

"Oh yes you do." Christian skipped out of range as Joel reached for him.

"Christian, I have a job that requires me to work long hours. There's no way I can guarantee being home early. It's your house. You should be the one to deal with this."

Christian's shoulders dropped. "You said you'd do it." He leaned against the wall with that determined look on his face, but Joel wasn't going to make this easy.

"Tell me again why you can't?" Joel asked.

"Because I picked the last one and we both know what happened."

"Right."

Joel looked down at Christian's rigid cock and knew he ought to take care of that, but he was annoyed. Christian could do it himself.

"See you tonight," he said, and walked out.

Christian's hand was on his erection before the bedroom door closed. That had sort of gone as he'd hoped. At least there was a chance Joel would pick the cleaner, assuming he didn't get caught up at work or pretend to be. Christian was determined Joel felt like the house was his too. He hoped this would help. Two months ago, when he'd asked him to move in, Christian hadn't really meant as a lodger but Joel insisted on having his own room and paid Christian rent every week, even though they spent almost every night in Christian's bed. And if they weren't in Christian's bed, they were in Joel's.

As Christian's hand moved up and down his engorged dick, he thought about the day he and Joel met. A Saturday.

Four months, two weeks and three days ago. Christian had been walking through Greenwich Park and seen this lean guy staring up the hill toward the Observatory. He was tall, a couple of inches taller than Christian who was six-one, and slim with jeans that hung low on his hips. Those black jeans and the creased white linen shirt, half tucked in at the back, made Christian swallow hard even before he saw the guy's face. Plus his stranger had straight, dark hair and Christian loved dark-haired guys.

When the man began to walk up the grassy slope, Christian followed, held in the inescapable grip of a human magnet. He kept his distance. He didn't want the guy to think he was a stalker. Well, he was a stalker but he only wanted to look, then Christian could have Mr. Tall-Dark-and-Handsome in his dreams. That was the sad story of his love life—imaginary lovers, dream lovers, rarely the real thing.

Christian waited until the guy had picked up a ticket to go into the Observatory, and then stepped forward to get one of his own. He'd lived in Greenwich for years but it had been a long time since he'd been in any museum, let alone the one on his doorstep. The free entrance was a pleasant surprise. The courtyard buzzed with chattering Japanese students clamoring to take pictures of each other as they stood with their feet either side of the Meridian Line. But Christian's guy didn't stop. He went straight into one of the buildings and Christian followed.

Pretending he was a detective on a case, Christian took care not to be spotted. He hung back behind the cover of other visitors, watching the guy check out the exhibits. Christian paid no attention to the displays, his eyes were fixed on the source of his future daydreams. He'd caught tantalizing glimpses of the side of the man's face. A square jaw with dark shadows. He needed a shave. Christian thought of bristly skin against his inner thighs and gulped. A long neck. Christian imagined pressing his lips against it, licking, sucking, and he had to stick his hand in his pocket to disguise his blossoming erection.

Memory of that moment, as Christian lay naked on his bed, made his hand speed up. He wrapped his fingers around the root of his dick and squeezed as his other hand jerked at the tip.

Finally they reached the room with the famous Harris time pieces, the clocks displayed in a long cabinet that allowed viewing from either side. Christian saw his chance to have a full-on gaze at the guy's face. One look and he'd leave. One look would have to be enough. But as Christian raised his eyes, the guy stared straight at him and gave a little smile. *Shit, busted.* Unsure whether to run or walk, Christian found himself doing neither. The stranger had come to the other side of the glass to face him properly. Christian had been relieved he didn't look as though he intended to punch him.

"Like what you see?" the man asked.

Christian liked the American accent. He loved the dark eyes and thick lashes, the slim hips and flat stomach. He relished everything else as well. The guy was straight-to-ten-on-the-hardness-scale gorgeous.

"They're fabulous, aren't they?" Christian choked out the words. "Amazing precision." Then wished he hadn't.

Joel laughed this great, fruity chuckle and Christian knew he was in deep trouble. This was serious, desperate, full-blown, heart-stopping lust.

"Want to make me a coffee?" Joel said.

They walked back to Christian's house. His name was Joel Cooper. Age thirty-five. Four years older than Christian. Born and raised in Denver, Colorado. Christian had been quietly thrilled about that. How many times had he dreamed of meeting an American cowboy? It didn't matter that Joel turned out to be a city slicker. He was a corporate lawyer for a big American firm and on loan to London for eighteen months.

His apartment was in Canary Wharf, the other side of the Thames to Greenwich.

Christian still hadn't been sure about him. Maybe he was straight. Christian couldn't have made the first move to save his life. He was so nervous when he tried to open the door to his house, he'd dropped his keys. He fumbled for them on the path while his mind whirled. Had he tidied? Unlikely. In what state had he left his bedroom? It couldn't be good. What if he was wrong about Joel? Well, they'd have a cup of coffee and a piece of cake and Christian would be a genial British host and chat about the weather, and the moment Joel left, he'd be upstairs, lying on his bed, wanking off. But as soon as the front door closed behind them, Joel had pulled him into his arms and kissed him.

As Christian thought of that first meeting of mouths, he handled his dick with a tighter grip. Hard, wet and warm—the perfect kiss. Joel's tongue explored his mouth as his hands fondled Christian's backside and Christian thought he was going to come in his pants. Then Joel had pulled back and looked at him.

"Well, James Bond," he said with a smile.

"What?" Christian's eyes were fixed on the dimple in Joel's cheek.

"You'd be a hopeless spy."

"Huh?" Christian asked, still on the dimple.

"You followed me all the way from the bottom of Greenwich Park."

Christian groaned. He hoped he wasn't blushing but the heat in his cheeks told him he might be.

"I thought you were kind of cute. I wondered what you were going to do." Joel chuckled.

His hands moved to the front of Christian's pants and cupped his balls. Fingers strayed over his rock-hard erection and squeezed with a gentle touch. Then Joel had taken hold of

Christian's hand and put it on the front of his own pants and Christian felt a cock as rigid as his own.

"One thing," Joel had said.

Christian's heart plummeted to somewhere below his balls. Joel must have caught the look on his face because he grinned.

"Hey, it's not that bad. It's just that I dig chicks as well. I wanted you to know."

"Guess what?" Christian smiled so wide, he thought his face might crack. "Me too."

Joel's eyes had darkened and he'd pulled Christian into his arms.

Christian remembered their frantic first coupling, still standing in the hall, just inside the door. They'd dragged off their clothes and the moment Joel had reached for Christian's cock, he'd come all over his fingers. God, he'd felt such a fuckwit but Joel had whispered in his ear about how hot he was and then he'd come himself.

Christian arched back on the bed, stiffened and spilled onto his stomach, long wrenching bursts of cum spraying over his belly and chest. He looked down at the sticky, opaque fluid and wished Joel was there to clean him up.

Chapter Two

ଔ

Susie Hood looked at the clothes strewn over her bed and sighed. She had no idea what to wear for this interview. One smart skirt hung in the closet but it was unfashionably long, dark gray and boring. Fine for an interview for office work, but she wasn't trying for a job as a secretary, only as a cleaner. She picked up her short pink skirt and then put it down and grabbed her blue pants, only to toss them down and pick up the pink skirt, pulling it on. She yanked a red, hooded top over her head, dragged her fingers through her fine, shoulder-length blonde hair and checked her watch. Seven thirty. If she started walking now, she'd be on time.

She picked her way down the stairs, missing the two creaky steps midway and reached the bottom undetected. The door to the lounge stood half open and she began to tiptoe past.

"Susie? What you up to?"

Her heart thudded in her chest and she put her head around the door.

"I've got that interview for the cleaner's job. Remember?"

Her father Harry sprawled on the couch, one hand tucked down the front of his trousers. Her brothers Pete and Mike sat in the two other chairs, their long legs draped over the arms, staring at the football on the TV. They all held cans of beer. Squashed empties littered the coffee table. When they flattened the cans, they always sprayed beer everywhere and made things sticky. More for her to clean up.

"What are you wearing?" her father asked.

Susie reluctantly moved into view.

"Ooh legs," Mike said. "When did you grow those?"

"Ha, ha. I need to go or I'm going to be late."

"Ten quid an hour or it's not worth doing it," Harry said. "You still have this house to look after."

"How many jobs does this make you've not got?" Pete asked.

Susie's heart clenched with pain. She was trying not to count but the supermarket, library, local leisure center and quite a few others had turned her down. Most without interview. She was desperate for a part-time job to provide enough money that she didn't have to keep asking her father.

"See you later," she called as she left.

"Good luck," Mike shouted.

Within a few hundred yards, Susie realized the heels were a mistake. She usually wore jeans and flat shoes. Every few yards, she found herself turning over on her ankle and she could feel the skin across her toes being rubbed raw. A few more yards and she gave up, retracing her steps. She pulled her bike out of the shed and took off her shoes. Yep, her toes were bleeding. Looping the straps over the handle bars, she set off again, pedaling barefoot. There was no way she was going back to get other footwear.

She really wanted this job. The advert had been funny. She'd laughed out loud when she read it. She was used to cleaning up after three guys so she knew she could do this. Okay, cleaning was not up there with the jobs she'd really like but Susie had to be practical, sensible and honest with herself. Cleaning was the only thing she knew how to do.

* * * * *

Christian was the one who opened the door to the interviewees. That was the deal. Joel sat in the dining room ready to grill them. The first one hardly spoke any English, but she was gorgeous. Christian had his tongue out as he showed her through. Long, glossy brown hair, tiny waist, nice tits, but incapable of understanding a word he said. Although he wasn't sure that mattered.

The second could have been their mother. In fact, the way she'd stared at Christian's bare feet and pursed her lips, was exactly like Christian's mother.

The third was so fat she could barely get through the door and she stank of cigarettes. Neither he nor Joel smoked.

The fourth was a good-looking guy with short white hair and a cheeky smile. He was extremely gay. He'd flirted like mad with Christian until he'd seen Joel and immediately developed a tent in his pants. Christian decided he'd kill Joel if he gave Mr. Q-Tip the job.

Number five didn't turn up.

Joel came out of the dining room in time to see the man who definitely wasn't getting the job turn to blow him a kiss before Christian slammed the door.

Joel rolled his eyes. "I need a drink."

He followed Christian to the kitchen and they grabbed bottles of Corona from the fridge.

"Is that it?" Joel asked. "We have to choose between Goldilocks and the three bears?"

Christian laughed. "So which one was Goldilocks?"

"Which do you think?"

"The Romanian?"

"Fancied her too, did you?"

"Not bad," Christian said. "But can she clean?"

"With breasts like hers, do we care?"

Christian looked around at the dust, the mess and the dirty marks on the tiles. "We need someone to sort us out."

"Apparently, Mrs. Winterbottom has extensive experience of doing for young men," Joel said with a high-pitched English accent. "She'd be delighted to put us straight." He dropped his voice to normal. "I had to bite my tongue to keep from laughing when she said that."

"So what are we going to do? Do we really want one of them?"

They looked at each other.

"We could try the Romanian. I could draw pictures of what we wanted her to clean," Christian said.

Joel stared at him a moment and then burst out laughing.

"Okay, so who else?" Christian asked, irritated.

"If we're being sensible we ought to go for being put straight by Mrs. W."

"I don't feel like being sensible." Christian was reaching out for a slice of the lime when the doorbell rang. "Maybe number five will be the answer to all our problems." Christian grinned.

"I'm still hoping for a shapeshifting werewolf."

Christian was smiling when he opened the door, but when he looked at the pale-faced blonde standing there, the smile fell off his face and he almost dropped the bottle of beer.

Susie still shook. She'd fallen off her bike five minutes away from the house. Her bare foot had slipped from the pedal and somehow the front wheel caught the curb and sent her sprawling into the gutter. A bus barely missed her. It hadn't even bloody stopped, just flared its horn. Her top was smeared with dirt and her knees were grazed and bleeding. She'd wiped off as much dirt as she could with the single tissue in her pocket but she knew she looked a sight. She'd been torn between going home and forgetting the whole thing, or knocking on the door to ask if it was possible to make another appointment. And she knew she was now late. She hated to be late.

She'd struggled into her shoes and pressed the bell. When the door opened, she found herself facing a good-looking, green-eyed guy with a bottle of beer in his hand. He smiled and then didn't, and her fingers rose to pull down the hair at the side of her face.

"Susie Hood?" he asked.

She nodded.

"What happened to you?"

"I'm sorry I'm late. I fell off my bike."

"My God. Come inside."

Susie walked into the hall to see a tall, black-haired man leaning against the wall. He had the darkest eyes she'd ever seen.

"Little Red Riding Hood, I presume?"

And he was the wolf, but with a sexy American accent. His voice felt as if he were stroking her. A shiver went down Susie's spine and she swallowed hard.

"I'm Joel Cooper," the American said. "This is Christian Harris. It's his house."

Susie saw the brown-haired guy flash a glance at the other.

"You're bleeding," Joel said, moving away from the wall.

Susie looked at her knees. Blood trickled down her shins.

"Kitchen." Christian took hold of her elbow and guided her down the hallway into an enormous but incredibly untidy kitchen. "Sit down." He threw a pile of magazines on the floor and pushed her onto a chair before going over to the sink.

He had a snug butt under his well-worn jeans. Susie's gaze dropped to his bare feet. Long, sexy feet with perfect toe nails. She dragged her gaze up. It had to be the most cluttered room she'd ever seen. Piles of paper lay everywhere, newspapers, magazines, sheets filled with writing. Every spare inch of countertop was covered with something. Mugs, plates, cans, packets. There was a line of opened cereal boxes wedged next to the microwave. Ten different sorts. It was as though everything that had been in the cupboards was now out of them. Her eyes met Joel's and she looked at her lap. He'd watched her inspect the mess.

Christian crouched down, peering at her knees. He held a wet kitchen cloth. "Don't worry, it's a new one."

"I can do it," she said.

"Let me."

Susie winced and gripped the edge of the chair as he wiped away the grit and dirt, but he did it with a gentle touch, careful to tend to each scratch until it looked clean. She could feel his breath hitting above her knees and felt a tightening between her legs. Not the time to feel horny, but she couldn't help it. It had been a long while since she'd been so close to a good-looking guy. Two good-looking guys. Oh God, she really wanted this job. The tip of Christian's tongue kept flicking out over his upper lip as he concentrated on cleaning her skin. She imagined what that tongue could do to her, felt a flood of moisture soak her panties and shifted on the seat.

"Sorry. Did I hurt you?" He lifted his head and looked at her.

Thank God he didn't know what was happening between her legs.

"It's okay."

He had sexy lips. Soft and sensuous. Susie pictured herself running her hands through his hair and pulling his head down to bring his lips to her thigh. She wouldn't mind the American attached to the other thigh. Two guys. Big fantasy. She lurched again, eliciting another "Sorry" from Christian. Two of them? Where had that come from? She glanced up. Joel leaned against the counter, watching. His eyes met hers again and for a moment, when his mouth twitched at the edge, Susie believed he'd read her mind. Heat flushed through her. She knew her face was red. *Shit.*

"You'll be down to the bone in a minute," Joel said.

Christian got to his feet.

"Thank you," Susie whispered.

Joel cleared his throat. "We'll let you know."

The hope she'd been nurturing vanished at that point. "Right," she said in a quiet voice.

That was a no, then. Hardly an interview. Maybe Joel *had* guessed what she'd been thinking. She got to her feet, took one step and went straight over in her stupid heels. Christian reached for her and she pulled away. Susie didn't want help. She wanted to run.

"Sorry. Thanks for cleaning me up. Sorry I was late. Sorry for wasting your time."

She turned and rushed for the door, tears of humiliation in her eyes.

Christian heard the front door slam and turned on Joel. "What the hell was that for?"

"You want her."

Christian gave a short laugh. "So what?"

"I mean, you *really* want her."

Christian bit his lip.

"She's exactly your type. Sweet and innocent. You liked her vulnerability. You got off then, just looking after her. I can see the evidence in your pants. You pictured yourself taking care of her. Admit it. You fancied the pants off Miss Red Riding Hood."

"You're right. I do fancy her." Christian breathed out.

"Good, so do I," Joel said. "And she's not my type at all." He grinned.

Christian's eyes dropped to his partner's crotch, Joel's burgeoning erection evident.

"Why do you fancy her if she's not your type?"

"Partly because you do, but you know how I like a challenge."

Christian rolled his eyes.

"The point is, do we want a cleaner or do we want a fuck buddy?" Joel asked.

"I don't think she applied for the latter."

"Well, it was implied in the ad."

"You are such a liar."

"She was cute though," Joel said with a sigh.

"Maybe she'd like both of us." Christian made his way across the kitchen.

"You go looking for trouble."

Christian grinned. "Found you, didn't I?" He slid his hands around Joel's back and pressed his hips against him.

"Did you see that scar on her face?" Joel asked.

"Yes."

"Ran down the side of her cheek to her chin. Wonder how she got it?"

"Car accident, maybe. She had the most kissable lips," Christian said.

"She's a mouse."

"Long legs. Great silver blonde hair."

"Could she be a shapeshifting werewolf?"

"She could be anything you want her to be," Christian said in a quiet voice. "She smelled of honeysuckle. I can still smell her."

"Smoky, mysterious eyes. I think Susie has a secret. I like uncovering secrets."

Christian kissed Joel's neck.

"I'll ring and tell her she's got the job, shall I?" Joel said, and Christian smiled.

Susie put her bike in the shed and locked it. There'd be other jobs. She'd land one eventually, but the sound of that one had appealed. She'd spotted the advert in the local newsagent's window.

Wanted. Dead or Alive. Cleaner-housekeeper-miracle worker for two housework-challenged super-busy guys. Three days a week. Nine to Five. Excellent pay for Mother Teresa. Even better for Keira Knightley. And in case we're called sexist – better yet for Daniel Craig.

Susie didn't actually like cleaning, but without pieces of paper to prove she'd reached proficiency in something useful like Russian, microbiology or urban planning, the only thing she could do was routine stuff like housekeeping or work in a shop. Only, without previous experience no one even wanted her for that. She'd been too ill to do anything for a long while but now she was better, she needed to earn a living. Her father had made it clear he wasn't prepared to keep putting his hand in his pocket. Susie wanted new clothes, a haircut, to go out and enjoy herself. She couldn't reclaim her life without money.

She closed the front door as gently as she could but her eagle-eared father in the lounge heard her, even above the noise of the TV.

"Susie?"

She put her head around the door.

"You got it," her father said.

"Got what?"

"The job, you twit."

"No, I didn't," she muttered, not understanding.

Pete sniggered. "Some American guy called and said you can start tomorrow. Nine o'clock."

Her heart fluttered. It had to be a joke. Joel had barely looked at her and when he did, it didn't look like approval in his eyes.

"If you're going to be out all day, make sure we have something ready for us to eat when we get back from work." Her dad spoke without taking his eyes off the TV.

Susie went into the kitchen and lifted a large, homemade lasagna out of the freezer. It would be defrosted by morning and she could put it in the fridge before she left. She went up to her room with a smile on her face. Her first job and for two of the best-looking guys she'd ever seen. Maybe she'd end up going out with one of them. She imagined herself at the cinema, snuggled up to Christian, his hand up her skirt, her hand in his pants. Then in a restaurant, with Joel's dark eyes gazing at her across the table, his fingers playing with her where no one could see.

The smile had gone by the time she stood in front of the bathroom mirror. Susie pushed her hair back to look at the thin white line than ran all the way down the side of her face. What good-looking guy would want her with a face like this? And if her father hadn't got there in time, it would have been much worse. Maybe she wouldn't have had a face at all.

Chapter Three

๛

"I think I should stay home from work today," Joel muttered into the pillow.

Christian wriggled his ass into Joel's groin. "Why?"

Joel wrapped his arm around Christian. "I need to keep an eye on you."

"You afraid I'll whisk Little Red Riding Hood into bed the moment she arrives?" Little chance of that, no matter how much Christian might fancy it.

"Well, that was my plan."

Christian laughed. "And how were you going to manage that?"

Joel slid his hand down Christian's chest. "I thought I'd ask her to start in the bedroom. I'd lead her upstairs and suggest she lie down for a while to look around and see who— I mean what needed...doing."

Christian groaned as Joel grasped his cock.

"Of course, I might have to unzip my trousers to give her a hint," Joel said.

"And what were you going to do to her, once you got her into bed?" Christian gasped as Joel squeezed gently just below the head of his cock.

"Fuck her in the ass then the cunt and then the mouth. Maybe the mouth first, let those pretty lips suck me off." Joel groaned. "I shouldn't have said that. Now I have an image in my head of Miss Red Riding Hood kneeling at my feet, looking up at me with her cute, soft eyes."

"You're supposed to be thinking about me, about how my cock tastes and feels."

Joel licked his lips and continued his tease. "A creamy pussy, yum, think about it."

"Shut up."

"She was turned on when you were wiping her knees."

"She was not."

"You calling me a liar?"

"Yes," Christian said. He knew Joel was trying to encourage him to make a move on Susie. He couldn't.

Joel's eyes darkened. "Seems like I need to teach you a lesson in manners." He released Christian's cock. "Turn around and bend over."

Christian threw off the duvet and swiveled round. He pressed his face into the pillow and stuck his butt in the air. Joel slapped his backside with the flat of his hand. Hard.

"Ouch."

"I like your ass all rosy and hot." Joel smacked Christian again.

Christian groaned his pleasure into the pillow. Each blow wound him a little tighter. An icy-cold dollop of lube slid down the crack of his butt and Christian flinched. "Shit, has that been in the fridge?"

Joel laughed. "It was in my glass of ice water."

"Bastard."

Christian sighed when Joel's fingers slid over his ass and spread open the cheeks of his butt. His asshole contracted as the cold jelly hit it then relaxed as Joel's fingers began to massage in the lube, rubbing in circles, pressing at the pucker without pushing inside. Christian groaned deep in his throat. Finally Joel nudged a little harder and his fingertip slipped inside.

"That's so good," Christian moaned.

Joel was slow and careful, easing his way into Christian's body, pulsing his finger with a steady in and out as he stretched the tight passage, readying it to receive his cock. One finger became two and Christian lurched as Joel breeched the restrictive muscle barrier and his fingers sank deep.

Christian hissed through his teeth when Joel began to push harder, sliding his fingers in a fixed rhythm, curling as he withdrew to tease the walnut-sized prostate gland—a maneuver guaranteed to bring Christian off in no time. Joel's free hand reached for Christian's cock but Christian caught his wrist and turned to look at him.

"I need you in me now," he gasped.

Joel squeezed more lube onto his hand and rubbed the glistening jelly along the length of his cock. So fucking beautiful, Christian thought. A long, thick shaft rising out of black curls. As Joel positioned himself, Christian turned and wedged his face in the pillow. He felt the tip of Joel's cock press and then ease its way in as Christian bore down, encouraging his body to accept the intrusion. Joel continued to push until his balls were pressed up tight against Christian's backside. He waited for Christian to get used to him and then began to move in a slow, careful dance.

That wasn't what Christian wanted. "Harder, please."

Joel leaned over Christian's back and began to drive forward in long, powerful thrusts. Christian's hand slid to his cock, jerking himself off in the same rhythm as Joel fucked him. Each forward shift had Joel's heavy balls slapping against the sensitive triangle of skin between Christian's ass and the root of his cock. Bodies slick with sweat, both panting, both groaning as they moved together. Joel kissed Christian's shoulder, his arms sweeping under Christian's body as he pounded into him.

Christian knew Joel was close and his own orgasm built inside him as he yanked at his cock. It was like an imminent volcanic explosion, the friction on his dick sending him on a one-way path toward eruption. As the ache started behind his eyes, Christian knew this was going to be a big one. Part of his mind imagined Susie there with them, Christian driving into her as Joel drove into him.

"Harder, harder," Christian gasped.

He pushed back as Joel rammed himself into his ass. Christian's balls drew up, tightened in their sac and separated. Christian pictured his lover's cock inside Susie's ass while Christian fucked her cunt and he came with a long sigh of pleasure. His cum shot from his dick and sprayed over the sheets. Joel stiffened against Christian's back and then burst inside him with long, wrenching spasms.

When the last delectable contraction faded away, the two men collapsed, Christian in the wet spot as usual, but still linked, chests heaving as they dragged air into their lungs.

Joel pressed his face into Christian's neck. "Oh God, you fucking wear me out."

"I love you," Christian whispered. He hoped Joel could say it back but didn't expect to hear it.

There was silence for a while and just as Christian thought he ought to break it, Joel spoke. "What the hell got into you back then? Harder?"

"Nothing."

Disappointed Joel couldn't say something loving, Christian swallowed his insecurity rather than tell the truth. Not a good idea to tell Joel he'd been thinking of their newly appointed cleaner while they'd been fucking.

As Joel's cock slipped out of Christian's ass, Joel leaned over and kissed him. A long, slow, soppy kiss that sent tingles down Christian's spine. His heart hurt at the thought of losing Joel. They both knew he wouldn't be in London forever. At some point, he'd be called back to New York, maybe before the eighteen months were up. They never talked about it.

Christian wrapped his arms around Joel and watched as his loose-limbed, satiated lover closed his eyes and slid into a light sleep. Joel could have ten minutes, no more, and then Christian would have to wake him, otherwise he'd be late for work. Christian watched as he slept, thinking even if Joel couldn't tell him that he loved him, Christian felt he did.

Before Joel, Christian's love life had been composed of a series of short and ultimately unhappy relationships. In his late teens and early twenties, he'd been a sexual mess. One moment he'd have a crush on a girl, the next a guy. For a while, he'd been sure he was gay. Christian hooked up with a few men and then fell for a waitress. He dated Lisa for six months before she dumped him after she caught him ogling a guy's backside. All he'd done was look, but it was enough. He'd gone back to guys then, though finally realized he swung both ways.

Research on the internet had shown Christian he wasn't alone, that the way he felt wasn't wrong or perverted, just different. It didn't make life any easier. Christian had no problem with being bisexual, but he hadn't yet met a girl who felt the same way. They might start off saying they were okay, but they inevitably got jealous and it all fell to pieces. Similarly, in the end, jealousy had driven away the gay men he'd taken up with. The irony being they were okay with him liking other guys just not women. Nothing seemed to work.

Christian stopped telling people he was bisexual and never let a relationship go on for too long because he always became frustrated. Things got too complicated. Not knowing what he wanted made his head and heart ache. This relationship was different. He loved Joel. It was Joel he needed to be with, and while they both wanted a woman in their lives, it hadn't become a problem between them. Christian wouldn't let it. He would not lose Joel.

"Time to wake up." Christian kissed him on the lips.

"Just gone to sleep." Joel eyelids fluttered and closed.

"I might have something planned for the shower."

Joel opened his eyes and gave a slow smile. Never failed, Christian thought.

* * * * *

When the bell went unanswered, Susie knocked on the door. She'd been too nervous last night to take in the size of the house, but the place was huge. A double-fronted, three-story detached house on one of the best streets in Greenwich. It had to be worth a fortune. She reached for the brass knocker. It needed polishing. Susie smiled, she could do that.

The door flew open and the one with green eyes, Christian, stood there grinning at her.

"Hi, come in. You're just in time for a coffee."

"Hi." Susie stepped over the threshold.

Christian wore faded denim jeans, a white T-shirt and he was barefoot again. Every muscle was outlined beneath the tight tee, the gentle curves of his pecs, and the ridges of his abs. He had a great physique. He was a little broader than the American, though not quite as tall, but they were both over six foot. Susie liked tall men, especially tall, good-looking men. *Huh, who didn't?*

Christian cleared his throat and Susie blinked. *Oh God, did he catch me staring?*

"Come on. Try to ignore the dirt as you walk through. It's not going anywhere until you tackle it."

She followed him down the hall, tripped and stopped walking. Susie stared at an imaginary crack in the wooden floor. Two good-looking guys living together. They had to be gay. Was that sexist? Bigoted? Prejudiced? She didn't mind them being gay. Well, she did a bit but only because it meant they were unavailable.

Christian turned. "Are you okay?" He smiled at her again. It was a cheeky, suggestive smile and Susie swallowed hard. Maybe not gay.

"Fine," she croaked.

She followed him into the kitchen. It looked no better than the previous night.

"I tried to tidy a bit," Christian said.

"What did you do, wash a couple of mugs?" She slammed her hand to her mouth, mortified she'd said that out loud, but he laughed.

"Three actually. How do you take your coffee?"

"Black, no sugar."

"Like Joel."

He poured her a mug from the filter machine and motioned for her to sit at the table. Susie watched him stir three heaped spoonfuls of sugar into his drink.

"How are your knees?"

"Fine, thank you."

"You're wearing trousers so I can't tell if that's the truth."

"Really, they're fine." Sore, but she'd live.

"So tell me something about yourself," Christian said, and took a sip of his drink.

Susie began to worry. "I thought I had the job."

"Yeah, you do. I just want to know a bit about you. You got short-changed yesterday. I bet you had all sorts of interesting things to tell us."

Oh God, not really.

"Well, er...I'm twenty-four. I live with my dad and my two older brothers Pete and Mike. My mum's dead. My dad works for a printing company. Pete's a fireman and Mike's a plumber." She stopped.

"Is that it?" Christian asked.

Susie nodded.

"Pets?"

"No," she said.

"Bad habits?"

"I don't smoke."

"Boyfriend?"

Why do I have to blush? "I'm not very interesting. What about you?" *Oh God, did that sound too eager?*

"I work from home. I'm a freelance writer. While you're slaving away cleaning up Joel's mess, today I'm going to be struggling with an article about adrenaline junkies for FHM."

"Not your mess?" Susie asked, and raised her eyebrows.

Christian coughed. "Caught me in a lie already. Okay, I admit I'm the untidy one. Joel would be neat and perfect if I let him."

"What does Mr. Cooper do?"

"God, don't let him hear you call him that. He's Joel. I'm Christian and you're Susie, unless you'd like to be Miss Red Riding Hood?"

"Ms."

She was relieved to hear him laugh. Christian had a lovely smile. His whole face lit up, his eyes twinkled and creased at the edges, and little dimples appeared in his cheeks. Susie felt a tingling in her pussy and swallowed a groan.

"Right, Ms. Hood. Well, please start on the kitchen. There are loads of cleaning products under the sink. Mostly in pristine condition, having been bought with the best of intentions and never used. Make a list of what else you need. You can go anywhere in the house, but if you disturb me when I'm working, I'm afraid I'd have to kill you."

"So you don't want me to bring you coffee every now and again? Or a slice of cake?"

"Did I say kill? I meant kiss."

Shit. Susie was helpless to stop the flush spreading across her face, so she turned away and hid. Which was what she always did.

* * * * *

Susie was looking forward to working on the kitchen. She'd brought a few things from home—a pair of rubber gloves, a couple of disposable clothes and some anti-bacterial spray, just in case, but when she looked in the cupboard under the sink, she saw Christian was right. They had every cleaning product going—sprays for wood, stainless steel, ceramic tops and tiles and most of them were unopened.

The dishwasher needed cleaning before she loaded it. She hadn't realized they could get that dirty. The rest of the pots and dishes she did by hand. Before Susie put anything away, she cleaned the cupboard it belonged in. The kitchen units were a pale beechwood with white ceramic handles. Well, the handles turned out to be shiny white and not matt brown once she'd wiped them. Dark slate tiles covered the floor, though there was so much rubbish strewn everywhere, it could hardly be seen. She sorted everything and made neat piles on the table. Most of the sheets of paper seemed to be jottings made by the same person, presumably Christian. The subjects covered a wide variety of topics—allotments in London, sex toys, Yosemite National Park and sheep shearing.

Susie read the sex toys one with an ear cocked for Christian reappearing. She hadn't heard of some of the things he wrote about. She could guess what butt plugs were but not pocket pussies, vibrating harnesses and jelly love beads. Susie couldn't help wondering if Christian or Joel had tried any of the stuff and a surge of damp warmth wet her panties. Feeling guilty, she tucked the sheets of paper under the rest and sprayed cleaner on the stainless steel cooker hood. Fantasizing wasn't a good idea. Sexy thoughts needed to be confined to her bedroom when she was on her own.

She brought a chair over to the sink and knelt on the counter so she could reach to clean the window. One wipe left the cloth black. Susie gasped in disbelief. Had no one ever cleaned? She turned the cloth over and was reaching up again when she sensed someone in the room. Susie turned to see Christian staring at her. The look in his eyes was unmistakably carnal but gone in an instant. She clambered down.

"I wondered where my coffee was," he said.

"Sorry."

"Hey, I'm teasing. I wanted to check you were okay, that you'd not given up in disgust, choked to death on dust or been attacked by woman-eating bacteria."

Susie laughed. "I'm fine. I'll brew a fresh pot of coffee and bring it up, shall I?"

"Great." Christian nodded and disappeared.

He walked back upstairs with his heart hammering and his hard-on throbbing. When he'd seen her kneeling on the counter, that tantalizing strip of bare flesh at her waist had sent him rigid in an instant. There was a hint of a luscious, rounded backside under her jeans, the kind of curve he loved on a woman. Her blonde hair hung to her shoulders, looked silky and soft and he wondered how it would feel brushing against his skin, especially the skin between his legs, or wrapped around his dick and balls.

That was a mistake. After a further rush of blood to his groin, his cock seemed capable of breaking through his zipper. Christian sighed. He wanted to bend her over the kitchen table and fuck her 'til she screamed. How about demanding she strip and then let her strip him before he ate her for lunch? His mind sizzling with erotic fantasies, Christian had done the sensible thing and dashed upstairs. What the hell had he and Joel been thinking, picking someone they fancied? This was going to end in tears, only Christian wasn't sure who'd be crying.

He'd just settled back into his article when he heard Susie calling.

"Christian, I've got your coffee but I don't know where you are."

He thought about letting her find him then remembered the state of the bedroom and leapt to his feet.

"I'm in here." He yanked open the door.

35

She stood there smiling. Christ, she could light up a room. He'd forgotten her scar, drawn to her lovely eyes and sweet mouth with those Cupid's bow lips.

"One coffee, three sugars." She handed him a mug.

"I'm impressed."

"Well, I said three, but I only put in one."

"Ah, looking after my eating habits already?"

Jesus, another blush. Christian stood watching her backside as she walked off. Joel was wrong about her. He'd thought she was a mouse but Christian suspected she had a caged lioness hiding inside. He grinned, took a sip of his barely sweetened coffee and winced. He'd have to tame that out of her.

Chapter Four

ജ

Christian was deep in thought when Susie brought him a sandwich. He registered that food had appeared at his side, mumbled thanks and carried on working. He was no longer writing the adrenaline article. He'd started another erotic fantasy. One featuring a very sexy cleaner called Josie Sweet and two extremely horny guys, Xan and Jack. Christian gave a long, lazy smile. He'd had fifteen erotic books published under a pen name, Raphael Strange, four of them written since he'd been with Joel. The guy was an inspiration. So, it seemed, was Susie.

He became so entrenched in the story, he lost track of time. Christian had set up the guys to meet for the first time when Jack knocked Xan down with his car while he was out jogging. Jack had been trying to avoid hitting a woman on a bike. Christian smiled. He had no problem writing the sex scenes between two men. He and Joel had done enough to keep him going for a book the length of *War and Peace* but it had been a while since he'd fucked a woman.

Joel's hand on his shoulder jerked Christian back to reality.

"Shit, you made me jump. What are you doing home?"

"What time is it?"

Christian looked at the wall clock and sprang to his feet. "Eight? Christ."

"What have you been doing?" Joel unfastened his tie and tried to see the screen.

Christian reached back to click off the document. "You can read it later."

"Ah, right. Porn." Joel laughed.

"It's not porn." Christian bristled. He knew Joel only said that to annoy him. He was annoyed that it did annoy him.

"So how did you get on with Miss Riding Hood?"

"Oh my God, I forgot she was downstairs. Has she gone?"

Joel pulled off his tie and walked into his room to change. "I presume so. I didn't see or hear her. You forget to do anything for dinner? Do I have to get take-out again?"

Christian didn't miss that dig. The deal was Christian cooked four days of the week. Two of the four usually ended up as take-outs.

"I'll go and look while you get changed."

Christian bounded down the stairs, wondering if he could throw together an omelet and salad, so long as the lettuce hadn't liquefied. He couldn't see that Susie had done much in the house. His socks were still draped around the newel post. Several pairs of shoes lay in a heap in the hall. But when he opened the kitchen door, Christian gasped. He expected a drum roll. It was the wrong house. It was next door. A parallel universe.

Every surface gleamed. The floor looked a different color. The sink shone. She'd even polished the fucking kettle. Christian opened the fridge and his mouth fell open. Gone were the haphazard clingfilm wrapped packages. Everything was neat and tidy and on the middle shelf sat a shallow dish covered with foil. He took it out and peeled off the top. Some sort of cheese and potato thing. There was a note with it.

Thought you might be hungry. Two hundred degrees for twenty-five minutes. I wasn't sure if you were vegetarians so I played safe. I'll cook braised gizzards another time. Susie.

Christian switched on the oven. God, the oven. The knobs no longer stuck to his fingers. All the baked-on marks on the top had gone. He could see through the glass door. The shelves were silver. Christ, he'd always thought they were meant to be black. He stuffed the dish inside and opened a cupboard to get a couple of glasses. She'd cleaned in there as well. The glassware had lost its grimy look and was arranged neatly in rows. The kitchen drawer was another revelation. He could see what he was looking for. He triumphantly pulled out the corkscrew on the first attempt.

Joel came in and stopped short. "Fucking hell."

Christian beamed. "Hey, you asked for a Mother Teresa and we got one."

Susie sat eating lasagna with her father and brothers, wondering if Christian and Joel had found the soufflé and enjoyed it. There hadn't been much of a choice over what to cook. Most of the food in the fridge appeared to be on the point of moving on its own. Though while she'd peeled the potatoes she'd wondered if they expected her to cook. Maybe she was taking on more than they intended.

Although Susie felt tired, she'd had a great day. The kitchen looked fabulous after she'd finished. They had some expensive pieces of cooking equipment, though they hadn't looked after any of them. She found four containers of oven cleaner. A job they saw needed doing but had never got round to tackling. Only trouble, Susie thought she might be working her way out of a job. Once the place was clean, it wouldn't take three full days a week to keep it looking nice.

"You're very quiet," her father said.

"Bit tired."

"You sure looking after two houses won't be too much for you?" he asked.

"No." Susie's response came fast. She knew full well which house she'd have to give up if he thought it *was* too much.

"I don't want you to overdo things," he said.

Susie nodded.

"What do they do for a living?" Mike asked.

"Joel is a lawyer. Christian's a writer."

"Oh, Christian and Joel," Pete mimicked.

"Not poofters, are they?" Harry asked, and Pete snorted.

"No, Dad," Susie said. The only answer he'd accept.

"Just because two guys live together doesn't mean they're gay," Mike said. "I suppose you'd assume two women living together were lesbians?"

"Yes," said Harry.

"Point them out," Pete said. "I'll try and convert them."

Mike laughed. "One look at you and they'd swear off men for life."

Harry glared at Mike and turned to Susie. "How are you going to be paid? Cash?"

"I don't know. I didn't ask." Susie hadn't liked to disturb Christian when she'd left.

"Well, you better sort it out. Cash would be best."

"Okay."

"Have they given you a key?" Harry suddenly asked.

"No, why?"

"How do you get in?"

"Christian works from home. Are you at work tomorrow?" she asked Pete, trying to change the subject before her father decided he didn't like the sound of that.

"Yeah, early shift."

The three men started to talk about Pete's new boss at the fire station and Susie breathed a sigh of relief. She didn't want to discuss Christian and Joel. They belonged to her.

* * * * *

"That was delicious," Joel said, putting the fork down on his empty plate. "A woman who can cook and clean, who isn't going to nag about the toilet seat being left up—we're not letting her escape."

Christian put the plates in the dishwasher. "God, she's even cleaned this. All that crap down the sides has gone. She must think we're real slobs."

"You are," Joel said, and finished his wine.

"I've turned over a new leaf."

Joel made sure he kept his face straight. The chances of Christian developing a tidy streak were about as great as Susie turning out to be a fairy. Joel caught Christian's thigh with his hand and pulled him close.

"How about you let me see what you've written today."

"It's only a draft. I'd rather you wait."

"Then maybe I'll make you wait." Joel slid his hand over Christian's crotch.

Christian trembled.

"Like the idea of that?" Joel asked, rubbing his palm the length of Christian's cock and feeling it hardening under his fingers.

"Yes," Christian choked out.

"Thought you might. Upstairs. On your back on the bed. Naked. Arms and legs spread. Twenty seconds. Go."

Christian fled.

Joel smiled.

By the time he walked naked into Christian's bedroom, having stripped off in his own, Christian was exactly where Joel wanted him, his body stretched out, his cock long and thick. The foreskin had pulled back from the swollen, blood-filled head and Christian's dick began to twitch as though it knew what was coming. Maybe it did. Joel opened the bottom drawer and took out the restraints. Spreading Christian's legs, he tied each ankle to a wheel under the bottom corners of the bed. Joel leaned over Christian's mouth while he fastened his wrists to the metal headboard, dangling his cock near his lips. Christian knew better than to risk a lick.

"Good boy," Joel said as he stood again.

He watched Christian's eyes track his hands as he picked up the leather cock ring.

"Don't I get one?" Christian asked.

"Want me to douse that with a bucket of ice?"

Christian shuddered. "No."

"Then no, you don't. You'll have to control yourself."

There was no way he'd get a ring on Christian in that state. Joel slipped his balls through the loop, bent his cock and pressed it down, pulling everything up so it hung over the band. He adjusted the fit and sighed.

Joel slipped a couple of pillows under Christian's head so he could see and then sat at the bottom of the bed with his legs hooked over Christian's thighs.

"Fifteen minutes," Joel said.

"No, I—"

One look and Christian closed his mouth. Joel picked up a bottle of oil and dripped it over Christian's cock, a slow dribble from the tip to the balls. One smooth stroke of his palm to coat the shaft and Joel wrapped one hand around the base and the other higher up. Each fist gave a gentle twist in opposite directions and Christian's breathing became ragged.

"That feel good?"

"Yes."

"Want me to do it again?"

"Uhuh."

"I'll take that as a yes."

Joel slid his hands up and down and then twisted again in alternate directions. Christian groaned and a large bead of pre-cum oozed from the head of his shaft. Blood surged into Joel's cock and he flexed his hips. The tide wouldn't go out so easily.

The ring around his cock and balls would keep him primed, ready to shoot. Joel wrapped his hand around the base of Christian's dick and squeezed hard. With his other hand, he teased the sensitive head using his thumb and index finger, pressing them together and then pulling back to rub around the ridge below the crown. Joel released his grip on the base and then squeezed again. He varied each touch, each movement after a couple of repetitions, never letting himself fall into a rhythm.

"Christ, Joel, I'm not going to last five minutes let alone fifteen."

Joel palmed the whole length of Christian's shaft in a twisting, up-over-and-back- down-to-twist movement that had Christian's hips cantering off the bed. Joel tightened his grip on the base so Christian couldn't come.

"Steady, tiger," Joel said with a laugh.

"My balls," Christian gasped.

"What about them? Need bouncing?"

"Don't you fucking dare. God, they ache."

Joel kept one hand tight at the base of Christian's cock and used his other hand to gently stroke the swollen sac. Within seconds Christian was groaning and whining. He pulled at the restraints but there wasn't a chance in hell of him getting free.

"God, Joel, I can't take much more."

"Want me to stop?" Joel took his hands off him.

"You do realize I'll come just from looking at you. It isn't only your hands that drive me crazy, it's you, the look of you, smell of you, taste of you. Oh fuck."

Joel grabbed the base of Christian's cock with one hand and pulled down on his balls with the other. The noise Christian made was a cross between a groan and a wail. Once Christian had stopped moving and his breathing calmed, Joel began to tease him all over again. Fast, slippery jerks that had Christian gritting his teeth, followed by slow twists that Joel knew would bring him off. His breathing changed, his body tensed and Christian's cock swelled in his hand.

"Arrggh, don't stop," Christian gasped, and Joel pumped him to oblivion.

He watched as the slit at the tip of Christian's cock opened to release a jet of cum, closed and then released another. The sticky fluid was all over Christian's chest. The first jet had almost reached his chin. Christ, the guy could shoot.

"Fuck, fuck," Christian groaned as Joel milked him dry.

Joel couldn't wait much longer. His balls were on fire. He reached back, unclipped the restraints at Christian's ankles and pushed his legs to his chest so his asshole sat waiting. Joel grabbed the lube and squirted as if he were firing at a target. Christian yelped and his puckered entrance tightened and then relaxed.

Pressing the blunt head of his cock against the dark hole, Joel took a deep breath at the exact same time as Christian and they both laughed. As Christian made the internal adjustment to let him inside, Joel pushed hard and slid straight in. Having Christian helpless below him, his arms outstretched, his face taut with concentration, sent a pulse of pure lust to Joel's groin. He withdrew almost to the point of falling out and then drove back into Christian's ass.

"Oh Christ," Christian groaned.

Sweat dripped down Joel's face, his arms forcing Christian's legs back against his chest, and he drove into him, a hard slamming motion that wound him like a clockwork train. Tighter and tighter because he knew when he let go, he was going to race into action and zoom round the track. The sensation of Christian's tight, hot passage clasping him sent his balls into a frenzy. The cock ring ensured the orgasm had to wait but, boy, did it make it worth waiting for. Joel's eyes closed as the spike hit his brain, shot down a million nerve endings to his balls, which fired a machine gun splatter into his dick. The explosive release of his cum made Joel cry out in a combination of relief and pleasure. He groaned through every spurt. When the last spasm had faded, he pulled back far enough to let Christian lower his legs.

"Oh God, that was so good." Joel collapsed on top of Christian and reached down to pull off the cock ring.

"Let me hold you," Christian said.

Joel unclipped his wrists and fell back on the bed. Christian wrapped his arms around him and pressed his lips against Joel's. They kissed gently, a contrast to the hard fucking that had gone before. Joel knew he could do anything to Christian. He'd never hurt him but Christian trusted him implicitly and that fucking scared him more than he could ever admit.

Chapter Five

ෙ

When Christian opened the door for Susie the next morning, he pulled her straight into his arms.

"Thank you, thank you, thank you," he said then let her go, realizing he might have overstepped the mark. "Sorry, I just had to give you a hug. How did you do that to the kitchen? Are you a witch? Got a nose wiggle you'd like to tell me about?"

Susie laughed.

"Joel says thank you too. Only one from him and three from me. But we both want you to cook for us again and again and again. That thing you made yesterday was delicious."

Susie blushed, the red tinge on her cheeks making her look even more appealing. "If you tell me what you like to eat, I'll cook it."

"We'll start off with coffee. You'll be pleased to see we haven't wrecked our new kitchen yet."

Christian led the way down the hall.

"What would you like me to do today? The bathrooms?"

"Please."

Christian wasn't about to admit that after their hot and steamy bout of sex and the long hot shower, he and Joel had spent an hour trying to get both bathrooms into a state they dare let her tackle. Although part of that hour had been spent spraying water at each other. Christian grinned as he remembered.

He poured two mugs of coffee and put them on the table.

"Look, one sugar," he said, and put a heaped tablespoon into his mug.

Susie rolled her eyes.

"And don't disappear today without saying goodbye."

"I did shout but I guess you were so involved with your writing you didn't hear me."

"Well, come up and k...kick me." He'd nearly said kiss. He had the word on the brain.

When Christian gave her that unexpected hug, Susie drew in his warm, masculine smell. Now she was in his bathroom, she breathed in the aroma of his soap and aftershave. Out of curiosity, she went straight to Joel's bathroom. The smell was different, spicier. She smiled. As she cleaned their bathrooms, Susie imagined herself with each of them. She could see that they'd made an attempt to clean up. The toilets weren't too bad but Susie wanted everything to be spotless.

She washed the mats and the towels, polished the curved glass wall of the shower in Christian's bathroom until it gleamed and did the same to the glass-framed mirror. When she opened the cupboard on the landing, a deluge of towels slipped toward her. She tried to catch them but everything fell out. Susie laughed. She pulled the rest of the contents onto the carpet and sat down to sort them into neat piles of different colors. It had to be something in men's genes that made them unable to fold. Even when her brothers tried — which wasn't often — they made a hash of it.

Susie had a thing about textures. She loved the feel of the towels. The newer ones were softer. She rubbed a yellow one against her cheek, picked up a blue one and compared the feel. Then she closed her eyes, swapped the towels over until she didn't know which was which and tried to tell them apart by touch. Easy.

It had been a towel that had given her the very first orgasm. She'd been drying herself in the bathroom and pulled the towel between her legs, felt an odd tingling and done it again. Susie remembered dragging the material backward and forward over her soft folds, occasionally catching something that sent a frisson of pleasure rushing through her loins. She pulled harder, faster and her body had tightened. Muscles clenched inside and there was a strange feeling of something taking over, creeping through her body with nothing she could do to stop it. And she'd wanted to stop it, just for a moment, because she'd been frightened. Then there was a sensation of something breaking and she'd gasped as the contractions caught her, held her and finally let her go. She'd slumped to the bathroom floor in wide-eyed wonder, desperate to have another go.

Unlike the day before, Christian found himself unable to concentrate. He kept thinking about Susie, picturing her in all sorts of poses—on her hands and knees with her cute little butt in the air, on her back with legs spread or pressed against the wall with her leg over his hip. Every time his mind slipped, he'd find his hand down his pants. Two seconds later, he'd jerk it out again. Twice he'd been unable to resist temptation and had nipped to the downstairs toilet for a bit of quick relief. She was going to think he had a weak bladder. His bathroom was nearer but he was worried she'd guess what he was doing.

When his hand wrapped around his cock yet again, Christian decided to slip into Joel's bathroom. He knew she'd finished working in there, whereas she hadn't yet started on his. When he came out of the study she sat on the landing with her eyes closed, surrounded by towels, rubbing two of them on her cheeks. Christian felt the spurt of pre-cum shoot from the end of his dick. *Fuck.*

Susie dropped the towels and opened her eyes at the same time.

"Fabric softener," she said.

"We already have some." *Oh God, did that come out strangled?*

"You're not supposed to use it on towels."

"Right, excuse me."

Christian slammed the lock across the door and pulled down his pants. Then he looked at the shining bathroom and his cock wilted. Joel's bathroom had never been as bad as his, but now the tiles gleamed, the bath shone and the taps looked new. How could he jack off when she'd done all that? But then Christian thought about her face and the towels and his hand was working at his cock almost before he knew it.

He wanted her so much he ached. What would she do if he tried to kiss her? That was a damn fool question because there was no chance of it happening. Christian squeezed harder, moved his fist faster, pictured himself coming on Susie's breasts, spurting onto her face, and the orgasm surged from his balls. Christian bit his lip and grabbed the toilet tissue. He leaned back against the wall. If he carried on at this rate, he was going to wear his cock out in a day.

By the time he emerged, she was on the floor in his bathroom, bent over as he'd imagined, not waiting for him to fuck her, but scrubbing the grout between the tiles with a toothbrush.

"Come and have some lunch," he said.

Susie stood up and pulled off her rubber gloves. Christian looked round and sighed. "How come we can't get it to look like this?"

"You're probably using a soft toothbrush."

He saw the glimmer of a smile on her lips. "I hope that one's not mine.'

"No, Joel's. Don't worry. I'll wash it afterward. He'll never know."

Christian laughed. "I'll make us a sandwich today. What would you like?"

"Anything, I don't mind."

Christian followed her downstairs, his gaze fixed on her backside. He wondered what she'd do if he reached out and grabbed it. Slap him, probably. He wasn't very confident with women. He tended to let them take the lead. Actually, that was true with men too. If Joel hadn't walked around to the other side of that display case, Christian would have watched him waltz out of his life. Joel was so confident, it was scary. If he wanted something, he simply went for it.

But since the two of them had met, neither of them had brought a woman back to the house. They'd danced with them in clubs, but there was a sort of unspoken rule that they didn't bring one home unless the other did as well. And since Christian was about as brave as a bowl of custard, there had only been the two of them in the relationship right from the start. At least as far as Christian was concerned. Christian wasn't certain about Joel. He pulled some late nights at work and sometimes Christian wondered if he really was at work or at some club or maybe in a hotel room. Christian hadn't asked him directly because he hadn't wanted to know. He trusted Joel not to fuck another guy but women were different.

The last cleaner had nearly wrecked everything. Christian had picked her. She'd been all over him from the first morning, but for some reason she hated Joel. Not that she met him that often, but she flinched every time he went near her and it pissed Joel off. Christian had wondered if she somehow sensed how dominant Joel was and felt frightened. There was no denying Joel was a powerful alpha male but he was gentle too. Christian had never been scared Joel would hurt him. But Kate hadn't been able to see the real man under Joel's cool exterior. Christian liked Kate a lot but when the three of them were in the house at the same time, the tension was stretched tight as a violin string. Christian knew Joel was jealous. He didn't even try to be nice to Kate and in the end, because Christian couldn't bring himself to do it, he asked Joel to sack her. They had huge row about it because much as Joel was delighted to see her go, he'd wanted Christian to tell her.

Susie started to make a drink while Christian cut the bread. He liked the way she seemed at home in the kitchen. Of course, now that she'd been through every cupboard, she probably knew it better than him.

"Where did you work before," he asked. "Were they as untidy as me? No, don't answer that, no one is as untidy as me."

There was a little pause.

"I haven't," Susie said.

"Haven't what?"

"Worked before. I used to look after my mother and then I was…sick for a while, so I've never had a proper job, only minor stuff like handing out flyers and delivering newspapers. Does it matter?"

Anxiety flared in her lovely eyes. *Damn.*

"Well no, of course it doesn't. It's only cleaning." Christian swallowed. *What a stupid thing to say.* "Sorry, that came out wrong."

Susie put the drinks on the table and sat down.

"I've lots of experience with housework. I do everything at home for three men. Cleaning, washing, ironing, cooking. My brothers are far messier than you and Joel. I like your house. I like working here."

Christian put the sandwiches on the table and sat opposite her.

"Didn't you want to go to college or anything?"

She blushed. "I'm not smart enough. I barely finished school."

He hesitated. "What do you want to do?" That hadn't come out right either and he winced. For a guy who made a living out of manipulating words, he was making a mess of this.

"You mean—how could I possibly want to devote my life to cleaning guys' toilets?"

Christian blushed, heat flooded his cheeks.

"I need the money. If I could work in a bank, I would. If I could persuade people to change their energy provider, I—well, no I probably wouldn't want to do that. Nor convince people to sue when they had an accident that wasn't their fault." She wrinkled her brow. "Come to think of if, there are loads of jobs I don't want."

Christian jumped in. "I wouldn't want to clean windows on a skyscraper."

"Don't you like heights?"

"Don't like cleaning windows," he said with a smile.

Susie laughed. "Yep, I'd noticed."

She took a bite of sandwich.

Christian wondered why she hadn't gone to college. He didn't believe she wasn't smart enough. Maybe her mother had been sick for a long time and she'd been roped into caring for her. He knew all about sick parents.

"How long was your mother sick?"

"All her life."

"What was the matter with her?"

She picked at the crust on her sandwich. "She was an alcoholic."

Christian's heart did a little skip. "So was my father."

Susie raised her eyes to his. "Really?"

He nodded. "This was their house. Four years ago, Mum came home and found Dad in the garage. He'd had a heart attack. He died on the way to the hospital. And you know what? In a way we were glad. I could stop worrying about him killing someone when he drove home from the pub, and Mum got her life back. She lives in Spain now, with her sister. They're having a great time."

He took a deep breath.

"It's hard, isn't it?" Susie whispered.

He stared straight into her eyes and saw the same pain he knew had been in his for so many years. He wanted to sweep her into his arms and hold her tight. Not fuck her, just hold her, and make everything right.

"Do you have any brothers and sisters?" she asked.

"No, only child."

"I wish I was. My brothers drive me crazy. Particularly Pete."

"Are they older than you?"

"Yes, Pete's twenty-nine, Mike's thirty-one."

"And they still live at home?"

"Why bother getting a place of their own when they have me as a resident slave? I don't think they'll ever settle down. They're too interested in having a good time."

"You can still have fun after you settle down," Christian said.

Susie smiled. "Ah well, you've grown up, they haven't."

"Do you have a boyfriend?" He'd asked her before and she hadn't answered. Christian's heart thumped hard behind his ribs, not sure he could accept a yes.

"No." She toyed with her sandwich. "What about you?"

That served him right, Christian thought. If she'd asked him if he had a girlfriend he could have said no. He would never deny Joel. "Sort of," he muttered.

"And she's seen your bathrooms?"

Christian laughed.

"Well, by the end of today they'll be fine. She'll be really impressed," Susie said, and smiled.

Christian wanted to tell her that there was no woman in his life, only a guy, but he couldn't get the words out.

* * * * *

53

Joel came home early. A meeting at a client's in Dartford had been cut short. There was little point going all the way back into the city. When he opened the front door, he heard the sound of male and female laughter and smiled. He found Christian and Susie in the kitchen, drinking wine. She was preparing food while Christian leaned against the countertop next to her.

"Hey, you're back early," Christian said with a smile. He stood up, took one step toward Joel and stopped.

Joel tightened his mouth. "A pissed-off client, so I thought I'd come home." He turned to Susie. "Hello again. Something smells good."

"Beef stroganoff. A casserole though because Christian didn't know what time you'd be back."

They'd thought he wasn't going to be back yet. What had he interrupted? Knowing Christian, nothing.

"Apart from pissing off the client, did you have a productive day?" Christian asked.

"Very, thanks."

"It's good to have you back early for a change."

"Good to be back early for a change."

Joel felt awkward with Susie there. Normally he and Christian would have a kiss, sometimes a fast fuck, but they stood making inane conversation. Joel's eyes slipped to Susie's backside as she bent to put the dish in the oven. He licked his lips, heard Christian laugh and looked up to see his lover wink at him. Joel sighed. He was being stupid. Christian wouldn't try anything with Susie, he was too scared of rejection. This plan was going to go wrong.

"I'd better be going," Susie said. "Um, I don't suppose you could, um…"

"Give you a lift? Yeah, I'll run you back," Christian offered.

"No, I don't need a lift. I've got my bike. I didn't mean that, I, er…"

"Money," Joel said.

"Pay you. Christ, I forgot. And here I am, thinking you're doing it for love." Christian pulled out his wallet. "Is cash all right or did you want a check?"

"Cash would be great, thank you."

Christian counted out a hundred and fifty pounds and offered it to her.

Her hand twitched. "This is a lot. Are you sure?"

"You've earned it. You should see the bathrooms, Joel. I'm not sure I'm going to let you use them. You can take a leak in the garden. By the way, your bathmat is blue not gray, and the towels are fluffy again."

"Can you turn water into wine?" Joel asked.

"Only on Sundays," Susie said, and shoved the money in her pocket.

Chapter Six

&ᑐ

Christian closed the door after Susie had gone and padded back to the kitchen. Joel pulled him into his arms and kissed him.

"Do you think she has any idea we're a pair?" Christian asked.

"Depends on whether you've been flirting with her while I was at work or telling her what a lovely butt I have."

Christian sighed. "She's cute."

"And she's got a sense of humor."

"Wait until you see the bathrooms. They fucking glitter. But I think it's our duty to make everywhere untidy again so she has to keep coming back."

"What did you have in mind?" Joel asked.

Christian rolled his hand down Joel's crotch. "You could take off your clothes and toss them on the floor."

"What about your clothes?"

"You know how much they love being on the floor."

"But is dinner ready?"

Christian's stomach rumbled loud enough for Joel to hear and he laughed.

"Maybe you'd better get your strength up," Joel said. "Eat first, fuck after."

They ate in virtual silence. One mouthful and they'd looked at each other and smiled. The beef melted in the mouth, the mushrooms still tasted of mushrooms, the entire meal seasoned to perfection. Christian looked in disappointment at his empty plate. A few stray grains of rice and smudges of sauce remained, smeared in circles where he'd chased the last drops with his fork. He was tempted to lick the plate and if he'd been on his own, he would have. He looked at Joel and wondered if he'd notice. Yeah, he would. Christian pushed his plate away.

"I could get used to this," Joel said. "A clean house and well-cooked meals. Three days a week enough?"

"Do you think it's too soon to ask her to move in?"

"What? Into your bed?"

Christian went hot. "I was joking."

Joel pushed his chair back from the table. "You didn't make a move on her?"

"No. We talked a bit. Her mother was an alcoholic. Dead now like my dad. I got the feeling she's not treated well at home."

Joel leaned forward. "What sort of feeling?"

"Not sure. She's expected to look after her father and two brothers. She's in her mid-twenties yet never had a proper job. There's something a bit odd."

Joel furrowed his brow. "You don't think she's being hit? That scar..."

"No, I don't think that's it. She seems repressed somehow, as though she's been hiding in a shell and only just decided to peek out. Sometimes she's chirpy and funny and other times she's shy and withdrawn."

"Did you make even a tiny move on her?" Joel pressed.

Christian squirmed. "I was tempted—several times, but I sort of let her think I have a girlfriend."

Joel laughed. "You've actually got a boyfriend, but I didn't think that would stop you." He ran his finger round his plate and licked it. "This is so good."

Christian swallowed. "She's a nice girl—woman."

"Nice? Do we want nice?"

"Naughty and nice."

Joel laughed. "So how many times have you had a wank today?"

Christian's shoulders dropped. "God, am I that obvious?"

"I can read you like one of your books."

Joel got up and cleared the table. He put the plates in the dishwasher then pulled Christian to his feet. "I need to distract you from thinking about Susie Hood and you can distract me at the same time. Time to toss those clothes on the floor."

With an expert flip, Joel opened the button on Christian's jeans and eased down the zipper. He pulled them open at the waist and tugged so they fell, pooling around Christian's ankles, leaving him in a pair of his fruit-decorated underpants. Christian's erection tented the loose green cotton shorts. There was a wet patch over one of the yellow lemons. Joel kept his eyes on Christian's as he slid his hand under the elastic waistband.

"Thinking of her or me?" Joel asked, squeezing Christian's erection hard.

"You." Christian groaned and closed his eyes.

"Then look at me," Joel said, and Christian's eyes snapped open.

His boxers followed his jeans to the kitchen floor. Joel licked his lips.

"Dessert," he muttered, and dropped to his knees.

Christian stiffened as Joel's mouth enveloped his balls. His fingers tightened on the edge of the table as he felt the heat of Joel's breath and the rasp of his tongue. Joel rolled the delicate sac around in his mouth, separating the balls, pressing with his tongue until Christian whimpered. Then his lips began to tease their way up the length of Christian's cock. Joel's tongue paused in the shallow dip below the plum-like head, and then he engulfed almost the whole of Christian's shaft in one swift movement. Christian cried out and his legs tensed. Joel's fingers moved up the back of his thighs until they reached Christian's ass and then he tugged him forward so that he sank deeper into his mouth.

"Oh fuck," Christian gasped.

He knew Joel liked him to keep still when he deep-throated him, but it was almost impossible not to move. Joel pulled back to work on the very top of his shaft while his hand twisted the root below. Short, super-fast sucks on the swollen head of Christian's cock dragged him to the tips of his toes. He wanted it to stop. He wanted it to never stop. Joel was so good at this, teasing him beyond the point of endurance, stretching out the pleasure until Christian wanted to scream.

Christian dragged one hand from the table to stroke Joel's hair, rubbing the soft strands in his fingers as Joel ran his tongue over the crown of his cock. Each wet caress sent a spasm of ecstasy shooting into Christian's gut. When Joel tightened his mouth around the tip and twisted the base, Christian gave a deep groan.

"Oh Joel, shit, Jesus, that's so good."

Christian tried to push back the desire to come but it was a hopeless task. Joel was relentless, sucking him, licking, and teasing with his teeth. Short, fast sucks to long, leisurely laving and then Christian was so deep he felt the tip of his cock touch the back of Joel's throat. Joel swallowed against him and Christian moved beyond the point of return.

The tingle started in the back of his head and curled down his spine like tornado. The surge came so fast, Christian was overwhelmed. Shockwaves twisted through every part of him and Christian made a strangled sound. He spurted into Joel's throat, jet after jet of his cum spraying from his dick as he gasped. He grabbed the table and arched his hips forward.

"Fuckfuckfuckfuck," he groaned.

If Joel hadn't stood and taken him in his arms, Christian thought his legs would have given way. Joel held him while Christian's breathing eased and his muscles came back under control. When Joel kissed him, Christian could taste his cum and felt a tug of longing in his butt. Joel deepened the kiss, exploring Christian's mouth, mapping a path, licking his teeth and Christian clutched him tighter, felt the hard ridge of Joel's dick pressed against him and sighed.

Joel pulled back with a smile. "Going to let me read what you've been working on? And when I get over-excited, you can calm me down."

Christian didn't bother putting his jeans on. He shucked off his T-shirt, retrieved his clothes and went upstairs naked. Joel flicked his ass all the way up.

"Are the drapes closed?" Joel asked.

"No."

"You're going to freak out that nice old lady who lives across the street. Again."

Joel slipped into Christian's bedroom at the front of the house and drew the curtains then did the same in Christian's study. Christian stood naked at the door, watching him, his cock already beginning to reinflate.

"Pull up what you've done," Joel said.

Christian sat in the chair. He'd not been so productive today, but he knew what he'd written would make Joel hot. It always did. When he turned to tell Joel he had the screen up, Joel stood naked behind him with something else up. He had an impressive erection, strong and hard, hugging tight to his stomach. Christian loved the way Joel could go from puppy soft to solid steel in seconds.

"You haven't even read it yet," Christian said.

"I just like what I'm looking at."

"Sit down." Christian gave up the chair.

He stood behind Joel and reread it over his shoulder. Christian had to restrain himself from reaching forward to make corrections. He knew Joel wouldn't say anything until he'd finished. He massaged the knotted muscles in Joel's neck and those at the top of his back, and felt him relax under his fingers. Finally, Joel reached the end. He swiveled round in the chair and looked up at Christian.

"So which one am I? Xan or Jack?"

"Which do you think?" Christian asked.

"The good-looking one. Jack. The extremely sexy one. Jack. The insatiable one. Jack."

He edged Christian forward so his legs moved either side of the chair and then pulled him down to straddle his lap. Christian kissed Joel on the shoulder and moved his mouth up his neck, blazing a trail of hot, moist kisses until he reached his lips. As he slid his tongue into Joel's mouth, Joel caught the back of Christian's neck, pressing their faces together. Christian's cock lay alongside Joel's and Christian inched his hand between their bodies, rubbing the two heads together. They moaned into the other's mouth.

Joel fumbled in his desk drawer and his hand came out with a tube of lubricant. Christian hissed as cold fingers slid between the valley of his buttocks, pressing against his asshole before slipping inside him, twisting like a corkscrew, pushing deeper. The burning sensation dragged a whimper from his throat.

"It's time you did some work," Joel said, maneuvering Christian so his feet were pressed against the desk behind the chair and his hands rested on the chair arms. Christian lifted his hips so he could slide down on Joel's tumescent cock. Joel grasped the base of his dick and held it while Christian lowered his body.

As Christian slowly impaled himself, they both gasped, making exactly the same sound and then laughed. Once Christian had the whole of Joel's cock inside him, he stayed motionless for a moment, enjoying the sensation of having his ass crammed full by his lover. When Christian began to lever himself up and down, using the chair arms, Joel grabbed Christian's hips and helped. Christian's swelling cock bobbed against his stomach as he pumped. Joel's eyes closed.

"That is so good," Joel groaned. "Fuck it, Christian. I can't believe how great that feels. Geez, you blow my mind almost as good as blowing my dick."

Christian laughed and Joel grunted.

"I just can't get enough of you. We're gonna wear our cocks out," Joel gasped.

Christian's thighs and arms ached from the strain but he continued to clench and shunt as Joel built to a climax. He heard Joel's breathing grow fast and choppy, saw his eyelids fluttering. Christian wanted to grab his aching cock but he couldn't take his hands off the chair. The sensation of his cock slapping his stomach as Joel surged into him had Christian panting. Finally, Joel rammed Christian down hard onto his dick and at the same time, semi-rose from the chair driving as deep as he could. Christian cried out and his cock shot one thin spurt of cum over Joel's stomach. He hadn't even thought he could come again so soon.

"Oh God, Joel," Christian gasped.

Joel pulled him against his chest, their hearts beating furiously.

"How was that, Xan?" Joel whispered.

"You're the best, Jack," Christian whispered back.

* * * * *

Susie's father confronted her the moment she walked in.

"I've been waiting to eat for twenty minutes. Where's my dinner?"

"Sorry, Dad. I had to walk back. I got a puncture."

She ached with exhaustion. It wouldn't take long to run out of the meals she'd prepared and frozen. Still, tomorrow was Friday and she wouldn't be going back to Christian and Joel until the following Wednesday. Plenty of time to cook and freeze a variety of dinners.

"Have they paid you yet?"

"Yes."

"You should ask to be paid each day in case they try to cheat you."

"I'm going to be paid at the end of each day. They wouldn't—"

"Let me have half of it. Cover your board here. Your brothers pay me, I don't see why you shouldn't now that you're earning."

"But I'm not going to earn that much, couldn't I—"

His hand was out, his face plastered with the it's-no-use-arguing-with-me look. Susie pulled the notes from her pocket. Her father snatched them from her hand and counted them.

"That's a hell of a lot. What did you have to do for all that?" he demanded.

"I cleaned and did some cooking. Eight hours a day, Dad. It's a long time."

He handed back eighty pounds. "Owe me the five."

Susie's heart twisted. Pete and Mike earned more than three times the amount she would be paid and she had a feeling this job wasn't going to last long.

Pete arrived as she put out plates of chicken casserole and baked potatoes for herself and her father.

"Let your brother have that. He's been working hard all day."

Susie bit her lip and did as she was told. It was highly likely she'd have had a clip around the ear if she'd argued. She retreated to her room, deciding to eat with Mike, although she felt so tired, her appetite had vanished. It was a good sort of tired, though, because she was bringing the guys' house to life again. Susie slumped on her bed. She never thought she'd derive any pleasure from cleaning a couple of bathrooms, but there was a real sense of achievement in making a house shine. But maybe the greater pleasure was in impressing Christian and Joel.

Unfortunately, she suspected she was working herself out of a job. Once the place had been thoroughly cleaned, it wouldn't need three full days a week to keep it looking nice. But maybe they'd need laundry doing—washing and ironing. And she could cook. She liked cooking. Susie resented doing anything for Pete and her father, who rarely stirred themselves to make her a drink, let alone say thank you. Mike was different. He was much kinder but he wouldn't be living at home for much longer. He was already looking for an apartment. Susie had no choice but to stay. There was no way she could afford even the cheapest room.

Susie wanted to please Joel and Christian, wanted them to like her. She thought Christian already did, though she wasn't sure about Joel mainly because she'd hardly seen anything of him. As she thought about the pair of them, their great bodies and handsome faces, Susie's hands slid inside the front of her trousers.

Who was the better-looking? She wasn't sure. Joel was dark and gorgeous with thick black eyelashes and smoky eyes. But Christian's green eyes were beautiful and he was fun. She'd relaxed around him and they made each other laugh. Sometimes when he looked at her, she thought she saw something in his face that looked like desire but then convinced herself she'd imagined it. Neither of them would be interested in her. She had nothing to offer. No sparkling conversation, witty jokes or fabulous bedroom technique. Christian had already said he was sort-of going out with someone and there was no way Joel would be unattached. He must have women lining up to go out with him.

But she could have them both in her mind. Susie imagined Christian's hands sliding under her shirt onto her breasts, twisting her nipples in his fingers. He'd lower his mouth and brush his lips against hers. Joel eased down her panties and lifted her skirt. Susie's fingers played with the delicate petals between her legs. She was already wet and dipped her fingers inside to gather her cream and spread it over her folds, stroking herself gently. Christian's mouth on her breast, Joel's lips traced a path down her body. Spreading her fingers either side of her clit, she squeezed the hard bud and a shiver of pleasure gripped her pussy.

Susie wanted both of them. Christian licked and sucked at her breasts and Joel kissed her clit, teasing it with the tips of his teeth. Tremors of pleasure spread from her gut. They looked up at her, Christian's green eyes and Joel's dark navy eyes, and Susie came with a gasp of pleasure, her back arching off the bed.

Chapter Seven

හ

The following morning when the bell rang, Susie knelt in the hall cleaning the skirting boards. She stood up, peeled off the rubber gloves, pulled her hair forward to cover her scar and opened the door. She expected to see the postman but found herself facing an attractive blonde wearing bright red lipstick, her eyes hidden behind large, dark sunglasses. Her suit looked expensive and her heels so high, Susie was amazed she could walk. The sunglasses came off to reveal unfriendly brown eyes above a disapproving frown. Susie took an instant dislike.

"Who are you?" the woman snapped.

"Susie Hood."

The woman arched one eyebrow. "Perhaps I should have said — what are you?"

Susie bristled but kept her mouth shut.

"Is Christian in?"

"Yes, he's upstairs working."

The woman pushed past. Susie rushed around her and took up a protective position at the bottom of the stairs.

"Who shall I tell him is here?"

The blonde looked at her as though she'd sprouted donkey ears. Susie was tempted to lift her hand to check. When the woman moved to the side, Susie blocked her path.

"What the hell are you doing?" the intruder demanded, and then her gaze slid to the bowl of water on the floor and the pile of cloths. Her scowling face morphed into a laugh. "So they got a cleaner. About bloody time." She stared at Susie. "Well, get on with it then. Clean."

Susie didn't move, stunned by the woman's aggressiveness.

"Christian, get down here!" the loud-mouth yelled.

Susie's spine stiffened. "Excuse me, if you'd like to wait, I'll go and tell him that you've come to see him. What name is it?"

"He's expecting me, you idiot. Get out of my way."

She grabbed Susie's shoulder and pushed her aside. Susie fell against the wall and watched her go up the stairs. She thought about following and changed her mind. Hopefully the bitch wasn't a mad axe murderer. Susie gave a little smile and headed for the kitchen. *Yeah, you barge in, Ms. Tight Suit and Jimmy Choos, but you know what they say about getting to a man's heart? And I've got it covered.* Susie grabbed ingredients from the cupboards and switched on the stove.

It took moments to get the chocolate chip cookies prepared. Susie set the timer and went back to the hall. She heard the blonde laughing upstairs and glared. Susie didn't want to imagine either Christian or Joel with girlfriends, particularly not nasty pieces of work like that.

At least the dust and dirt needed her magic touch even if Mr. Gorgeous upstairs didn't. Susie dropped to her knees, slipped her hands inside the yellow gloves and continued to scrub. Ten minutes later, the smell of cookies permeated the house and the woman came back downstairs.

"You missed a bit," the bitch sniped.

"Be care..." Oops, too late.

Susie watched as her heels went from under her and the woman slipped, taking the bucket with her.

"You stupid fucking idiot. Look what you've done. Why did you put the bucket just where I was going to walk? I'm soaked. Christ, my fucking backside."

She struggled to her feet and Susie reached out with one of the dry clothes to wipe her sudsy shoes.

"Leave them alone. These are Jimmy Choos."

Oh God, I guessed right. Susie had a pang of guilt but a drop of water wasn't going to hurt leather. Christian came bounding down the stairs.

"Your cleaner just stuck a bucket in my path and ruined my shoes."

Christian looked down. "Don't be such a drama queen, Bella. It's a couple of spots and I'm sure it was an accident."

Susie watched the expression on her face change from fury to simper. Bella sidled up to Christian. "Bye, sweetie, see you soon."

She gave him a kiss on the lips, entirely for Susie's benefit, Susie was sure, and then waltzed out with a large wet circle on her bum. Susie bit her lip, looked at Christian who just managed to close the door before he released a choked laugh.

"Right," he said. "Is it too early for alcohol?"

"Much too early. I'll make coffee but I better clean this up first in case any more beautiful women come calling."

By the time she got to the kitchen, Christian sat at the table, scribbling on a sheet of paper. His face was screwed up in concentration and Susie had an urge to put her arms around him. But since that first morning when he'd given her a hug, she felt as if he'd gone out of his way to avoid touching her. She took the cookies out and Christian's head came up.

"Is that what I can smell?"

Susie lifted them onto a cooling tray and Christian came up behind her.

"Can I have one?"

"Let them cool a bit."

"Nope. I like things hot."

Susie rolled her eyes and slid two onto a plate. When she turned with the coffee, both cookies had gone.

"Hey, one of those was for me."

"Too tempting. You're trying to fatten me up."

"This, from someone who has three sugars in his coffee?"

"I need something sweet after speaking to that sour-faced…" He paused. "What did you think of Bella?"

Susie felt like he'd asked her to pet a rattlesnake. "I tried to make her wait downstairs but only a machine gun would have stopped her."

Christian laughed. "Ha, Bella doesn't wait for anyone."

Susie hesitated and then asked the question anyway. "How long have you been going out?"

Christian groaned. "We're not going out. She's my agent. She's the last person in the world I'd go out with. She'd screw me to kingdom come. I'd be lucky if I still had balls after she'd done with me. I don't like power-dressing, power-hungry, loud-mouthed women. I like—"

He stopped so abruptly, Susie looked up in surprise. He was staring straight at her. She dropped her gaze to her coffee. She knew she was blushing. Oh God, he'd think she was flirting.

"I like someone softer, someone gentle," he said.

"Does she know that?" Susie asked.

"I couldn't give a shit. She can try as hard as she likes but I wouldn't touch her with a barge pole. Unfortunately, I have to meet her in Covent Garden for lunch. She has a publisher she wants me to meet. Are you going to be okay on your own?"

Susie nodded. She laced her fingers through her hair, trying to pull it further over her scar while she pretended not to. Christian reached out, caught her hand and tugged it from her face.

"Susie."

"Please don't." Susie lurched away, knocking over her chair. Her face averted, she set the chair upright and bolted.

She was back on her hands and knees in the hall when Christian came past.

"Susie, I'm sorry," he whispered.

Too mortified to answer, she didn't take another breath until he'd gone upstairs. Susie sighed. She'd not handled that very well. Christian had scared her when he'd tried to look at her scar. She didn't like people seeing it because it made her think about how it had happened.

She'd been asleep, lying in bed and dreaming of snow falling from a leaden sky as she stood at the top of a mountain. Susie lifted her face, let the flakes drop on her eyelashes and tried to catch them in her mouth. Then she'd felt an odd pressure on her face, something pushing her down, back into bed, her head on her pillow. But her face was wet and it hurt. Her eyes flickered open, she saw the gleam of a knife blade, and had thrown herself the other way.

Mike heard her scream, rushed in and bundled her in his arms. He'd pressed a towel to her face, put her hand against it and driven her to hospital. Susie remembered how he'd kept telling her she'd be fine, that it was just a scratch and not to worry, a few stitches would sort her out. Even if his pale face and tight grip on the wheel hadn't told her it was a lie, the state of the towel did. It changed from pale green to deep red, soaked with her blood. She kept asking him what had happened because she wanted it not to be what she thought. He kept saying it was an accident and Susie knew it wasn't.

She shivered. That night, the knife hadn't just cut her face, it had sliced away her confidence. No matter what she did or wore or said, the scar was always there, reminding her of how much she'd lost.

Christian changed out of his relaxed writing gear into a smarter pair of pants and a button-down shirt. He didn't want to go into the city but had no choice. Bella would string him up if he didn't show. His erotic novels were currently being published by a fairly small company but she'd made contact with one of the big boys who liked Christian's sense of humor and was interested in him writing some chick-lit. Bella had warned him not to use that word. It was out of fashion. He'd been scribbling some ideas about two guys after the same girl when he'd been distracted by Susie.

It was very easy to be distracted by Susie. It happened to him all the time. One look and his cock purred. Christian had become so desperate to pull her into his arms and kiss her that it was making him ill. She'd worked in the house for two and half days and turned his world upside down. He was horny and frustrated. Even worse, Joel knew exactly what was wrong. Joel had teased him and said the sex had never been so good and that made Christian feel guiltier. It was a good thing he was going out, out of temptation's way, only it wasn't a good thing at all.

Why the fuck had he reached for her face? She was self-conscious about her scar, always using her hair to cover it. Drawing attention to the damn thing had not been one of his more intelligent moves, particularly since he was trying to make her feel more comfortable around him. Christian wanted to tell her she was beautiful in spite of the scar, that he didn't even notice it, and instead he'd frightened her. Telling her that now was going to freak her out only he had to tell her he was sorry. No getting out of that.

She was in the kitchen, emptying the dishwasher.

"Susie?"

One word and she dropped the cutlery tray. It clattered to the floor, spilling the contents. She was as skittish as a deer.

"Oh God, sorry, I made you jump." He bent down to help her pick up the knives and forks. "I'm sorry I upset you earlier. I wish—"

"You startled me, that's all. You should see me when the telephone rings. I practically leap in the air. You'll have to whistle if you come up behind me."

"Not good with scary movies then?"

Susie gave a mock shudder. Christian wanted to say that she'd be all right with him, that she could hide her face against his chest while he stroked her hair, but he couldn't get the words out. There was some irony in the fact that he could make money writing about guys seducing women, playing around with words until he found the right thing to say, but in real life he found himself tongue-tied.

"Bella always puts me in an odd mood," he said. "I want to keep her as an agent, while she does everything she can to make us an item. I don't want to go out with her. I have to tread a fine line, trying to keep us both happy."

They reached for the last spoon and their fingers touched. They both wrenched their hands back as if they'd touched a live wire.

"I don't have a girlfriend," Christian blurted. "Neither does Joel."

"Oh."

Susie put the tray back in the dishwasher and lifted the door to close it.

"Could you...do the ironing before you leave?" Christian asked.

"Okay."

He stared at her for a minute. "I...maybe...if..."

Christian slid out the kitchen, disgusted with himself. Had he left his brain in bed when he got up this morning? Ironing? What the fuck was he thinking? That hadn't been what he'd meant to say at all. How many ways could he mess up asking a girl out? Was he so out of practice?

He grabbed his jacket and stamped out of the house. Well, yes, he was. In the days when he'd picked up women, it had usually been in clubs and bars. The sex came before the getting to know them and consequently he never did get to know most of them. He didn't really know Susie, only the snippets she'd revealed, but he wanted to get to know her. He wanted to touch her, feel her hair, stroke her skin and kiss her lovely lips. More than that. Christian sighed as his cock twitched. He held his jacket strategically as he strode toward the station. If he thought too much along that path, he was going to get arrested for indecency.

* * * * *

Susie missed having Christian in the house. Even though he spent most of his time in the study, it was still nice to have him around. He tended to come down every hour or so to talk to her and sometimes she felt he'd rather she sat and chatted than did any work. Susie decided she might as well clean Christian's study while he was out. When she pushed open the door, she decided it was too much of a mess for her to know where to start. Apart from the stuffed bookcases lining the walls, there were books all over the place and magazines piled up in what looked like random heaps but probably weren't. Susie was intrigued to know what Christian was working on. Each time she brought him a coffee, he was quick to click to a different screen.

She picked her way over to the bookshelves and looked at the titles. They didn't seem to be arranged in any order. Susie itched to sort them out but knew she'd have to ask Christian about that. He had a book on Texas cowboys next to one on snowflakes next to one on British trees. There was a thin paperback slotted on top. Susie pulled it out. *Seducing Alice* by Raphael Strange. The picture on the cover was a profile of a naked woman, her hands tied behind her back so her breasts jutted forward. In front of her was a guy dressed in black leather, a whip dangling from his hand.

A couple of pages, no more, Susie told herself and opened the book. One paragraph in and she was damp between her legs. She stuffed the book back where it had come from, took a step toward the door and turned. Would Christian miss it? She could put it back on Wednesday. It seemed an odd thing for him to have anyway. Before she could change her mind, Susie grabbed it, ran downstairs and stuffed it in her purse.

Chapter Eight

ဢ

Joel came home late on Friday night, stressed, tired and irritable. Christian kept his mouth shut because he knew, in this mood, Joel would explode at the slightest thing. The enchiladas Susie had made cheered him up, the wine mellowed him further and Joel fell asleep on the bed as Christian gave him a back massage. He'd mumbled about going in to work the next day because they were finalizing some mega-bucks deal and when Christian woke, Joel had gone.

Having the day to himself gave Christian time to finish two writing commissions ahead of schedule, but without Joel to tell him he'd done well, he felt restless. By five o'clock, Christian had talked himself into calling Susie. His heart pounded in his throat as he worked out what he was going to say but there was no answer. Christian chuckled and put the phone down. As he walked away, it rang. Christian grabbed it, thinking it might be her.

"Hi, gorgeous," Joel said.

"Hi, handsome." There was a pause and Christian sensed bad news. "You're not coming home, are you?"

Joel sighed. "Sorry. It's going to be another late night. Someone's been sticking commas into the document and the other side has freaked out."

Christian laughed.

"The good news is I'm on my own in the washroom on an empty floor and I'm thinking of your cock," Joel said.

Christian's brain reacted at once, sending signals shooting down his spinal cord to his groin, telling his arteries to expand to allow blood in, veins to constrict to stop blood flowing out.

Inside his pants, Christian's cock swelled like a sponge, trying to find room to unfurl.

"Are you thinking of me?" Joel asked.

"Part of me is." His cock grew harder by the second.

Joel chuckled. "Where are you?"

"In the doorway to the living room."

"Visible to the road?"

"Just about."

"Pull your pants and shorts down to your ankles. Now."

Christian shivered at the tone of Joel's voice. He caught the phone between his cheek and his shoulder then unbuttoned, unzipped and pushed both items of clothing down together.

"Pull your T-shirt up so it's over your eyes."

His cock was stone-hard, jutting out, his foreskin pulled back to reveal the plum-shaped head. Christian lifted the T-shirt to cover his eyes and clamped the phone back to his ear.

"Hold your balls in your left hand and squeeze."

Christian's fingers wrapped around the delicate sac and he groaned.

"Harder."

A gasp jerked out of his mouth.

"How many times have you wanked off today, Christian?" Joel said in his ear.

"Three." In fact Christian had jerked off so many times, he thought he was in danger of pulling the skin off his dick.

"Only three?"

"Maybe I lost count."

Joel laughed. "Thinking about cock or cunt?"

"Both."

"You're not going to get both unless you do something about it. Stop stroking yourself."

Christian's hand came off his cock. He knew Joel was guessing what he was doing but it made his heart pump faster.

"You want to taste Susie's sweet pussy?" Joel asked.

"You know I do."

"I want to push your face into her cream, make you lap up every drop. I want to fuck her and then make you lick my cum out of her."

Christian's breathing accelerated. He could feel pre-cum sliding down his dick.

"Please let me touch myself," he said.

"Shuffle into the room."

Christian hesitated. If he did, he could be seen by anyone passing the house.

"Do it," Joel said. "Put your hand on your cock and move your feet."

Christian groaned but edged forward. He could vaguely see through the T-shirt, well enough to avoid tripping.

"Jerk yourself off. Slowly."

Christian tightened his clasp on his dick and swept his hand up to the head to collect pre-cum on his palm before he rolled his fist down his length. Christian gritted his teeth and hissed.

"Slowly," Joel repeated.

"You fucking bastard."

Joel laughed.

"I hope you're doing this too," Christian said.

"Short, fast jerks," Joel said. "Are your balls tightening? You feel that ache in your head, the trembling in your thighs?"

"Yes."

"If I told you to stop, would you?"

Christian gasped into the phone. "Yes." He pumped faster, hoping it was an academic question.

"Stop."

"Fuck, fuck," Christian gasped, but he took his hand off his dick.

"Pull your T-shirt from over your eyes."

Christian dragged it off his head and dropped it on the floor. It took a moment for his eyes to focus.

"Look out of the window."

Christian already knew what he was going to see. Joel with his mobile pressed to his ear.

Joel smiled. "Good boy."

Christian shuffled back into the shelter of the doorway and exhaled. He switched off his phone and stepped out of his pants and shorts. By the time he'd put his phone down, Joel was in the house.

"Don't move," Joel said.

Christian leaned against the wall, his breathing ragged.

Joel unfastened his tie and tossed it over the banister. He hooked his jacket onto the acorn newel post and smiled. Christian knew that look. It was one of Joel's—you're-not-going-to-come-until-I-say-you-can faces. Christian felt a shiver of excited anticipation streak up his spine. He risked a joke. "Bad day?"

"It was. Not now. Get on the stairs on your hands and knees."

They didn't play these games often. Neither of them was into heavy BDSM stuff but dabbling on the fringes turned them both on. Christian gripped the edge of the carpet with his hands and spread his knees on a step a few stairs lower.

"Don't move. Don't touch your dick."

Christian watched Joel go into the kitchen and closed his eyes. He didn't want to know what he was bringing back. The stinging blow on his buttocks knocked him onto his face and gave him a mouthful of carpet.

"Shit, that hurt."

"Quiet. Each strike, you can crawl up one step. If you call out, you go down a step."

Christian pressed his lips together. His hips jerked forward at the next slap. He had no idea what Joel was using but that time hadn't been so hard. Slowly, smack by smack, he ascended the stairs and by the time he got to the top, his cock was weeping pre-cum like a leaky tap. Christian stayed on all fours at Joel's feet.

"Did you like that, Christian? Your butt did. It's all red and shiny."

Christian shuddered as Joel ran his hands over his backside.

"Put a beach towel over the bathroom floor and kneel on it like you are now."

Christian's pulse jumped with excitement. His balls already ached. He dragged the large blue towel out of the airing cupboard, wincing when he dislodged the neat stack Susie had made and raced for the bathroom.

Joel came in naked, carrying two plastic bags. His cock was as rigid as Christian's, rising out of a wreath of dark curls.

"Reach further forward," Joel said. "Eyes closed."

Joel approached him from the front. Christian felt the brush of Joel's cock against his head and then down his back as Joel leaned over. Christian yelped when the ice cube touched the top of his backside. Joel rubbed it along the crease of his butt and then drew it slowly up his spine. Tingling bursts of sensation shot over Christian's back. Joel drew patterns on his skin, traced his ribs, occasionally trailed the ice cube around to his nipples and Christian quivered with every touch.

The whole action was repeated but this time Joel held the cube in his mouth. Christian could feel warm lips and the cold ice melting, dripping over his skin, rolling under his body and onto his chest. His nuts were ready to burst, desperate to release their load, but he knew Joel would make him wait.

Christian shuddered when a hot tongue caressed his balls. Joel pushed Christian's legs farther apart and took his sac in his mouth, his nose pressed up against Christian's perineum. When Joel's mouth moved away, Christian braced himself. His fingers curled around the towel.

Joel laughed. "What's wrong?"

"I know what you're going to do, so just do it."

"No, you don't," Joel snorted. "And I'll do it when I want, not when you want."

Christian felt oil dribbling down his butt. He gave a groan as Joel's fingers began rubbing it in, pressing along the crease, spreading his cheeks, circling his anus. Christian's cock jerked and a louder groan tore through him. Joel's finger pressed at the entrance to his body, an insistent nudge to make Christian relax his muscles and push forward, and then it wasn't a finger but an ice cube that slipped inside him.

"Oh Christ."

Well, Joel was right—he hadn't known that was coming. The sensation was weird, but great weird. Christian could feel the ice melting, water sliding down to his balls and cock, running along the length of him, dripping off the tip. Then came what Christian *had* expected, Joel's lips around his balls, an ice cube in his mouth. The combination of fire and ice had Christian shaking in sensory overload. Hot felt cold then hot again. The ice smooth then sharp then smooth. Joel's tongue hot and cold. Christian could hear himself whimpering. Lips clamped together didn't help.

"On your back," Joel said.

Christian's legs had locked. Joel had to help him turn over. Christian's cock looked pissed off. He wasn't surprised.

"You're so sexy." Joel almost growled the words. "While I sat bored to tears at work, wanting to strangle the wankers who thought the world would end if we didn't do this deal today, I started to think about what I'd like to do to you. I planned it out in great detail and did some shopping on the way home."

Joel wrapped his hand around the base of Christian's cock and pulled his fingers up, milking a large pearl of pre-cum from the slit at the head. Joel used his thumb to wipe it over the head of Christian's cock.

"I want you to lie still and trust me."

Joel took another ice cube between his fingers and lay on his side next to Christian. He traced the contours of Christian's face, around his eyes, the line of his hair, down his nose and along his lips. He held the ice at Christian's mouth, let him suck for a moment before he continued down his neck and across his collarbone. Joel picked up a new cube to torment Christian's nipples. Christian tried his best to keep still but he was torn between agony and ecstasy. His nipples were so sensitive he wanted to scream.

When Joel ran the ice around his navel and over his belly, a hoarse cry erupted from Christian's throat. His eyes closed and he let the sensation carry him onto another plane. He lost track of whom, when, where, and only felt...the touch, the caress of hot lips on one leg, of cold ice on the other. Christian was helpless under Joel's teasing torment. One brush of anything against his dick and his spunk would shoot so hard and high he'd likely hit himself in the mouth. But Joel was careful not to touch his dick. Instead, he drove Christian crazy by touching everywhere else, his fingers trailing the ice all over Christian's body and his mouth moving after, licking and kissing the water away as the ice melted.

"Joel, I can't take any more." Christian didn't care if he had to beg. "I need you to check my balls haven't fallen off in disgust."

Joel laughed. "I've not finished with you yet."

He squirted oil onto Christian's groin and rubbed it in, coating his wiry pubic hair, pulling the strands through his fingers. Christian wanted to ask what he was planning but knew Joel wouldn't tell him. He heard the match strike and his dick whimpered. When Christian saw the candle he wasn't sure whether or not to be relieved.

"I—"

"Trust me," Joel said. "The higher up I hold it, the less painful the hot wax."

"Try hanging off the ceiling and dropping it from there."

Joel's mouth twisted and he tipped the candle, letting the wax fall from about three feet onto Christian's chest. It spattered and solidified to white spots.

"Oh shit," Christian gasped.

An intense burst of sensation flared, pain that quickly morphed to pleasure. He closed his eyes and grunted as he felt the hot wax hit him in a steady stream across his ribs. A pause while the flame melted the wax and it began again. Joel held the candle lower, the sensation was more intense and Christian moaned and squirmed. When the splashes of heat hit his nipples, his fists clenched so tight at his sides, Christian felt the towel tear.

"Maybe I should have tied you down," Joel said.

Christian couldn't speak. His chest was covered in wax. Joel had dripped different colors over him.

"You look like a work of art. I should exhibit you in the Tate Gallery."

"A picture or me?"

"You."

Joel twirled a candle in his hand, letting the melted wax collect. Christian saw his gaze drop to his groin.

"Christ, Joel. I don't…"

"You saying no?" Joel asked.

Christian never said no, but he was considering it now. The first blue splash against his cock had his hips cantering but the burning sensation faded to leave a pleasurable heat. Christian never moved his hands but the rest of his body writhed under the onslaught. He closed his eyes and let Joel do what he wanted. He knew he was coating his balls and dick, adding layer upon layer. Strangely enough, Christian had lost the urge to come. He was still hard as a poker but in a weird hanging limbo.

"Oh fuck, you look sensational."

Christian risked a glance. He almost didn't recognize his body.

"I am so hot for you. My cock's never been this desperate," Joel moaned.

Joel pushed Christian's legs up to his chest. Christian felt the lube hit his butt, Joel's finger slipped inside and he opened his eyes. Joel's face was taut with strain, his breathing noisy. His wide eyes had grown very dark. Christian was desperate to tell him how much he loved him but he was scared of ruining the moment. This was the nearest Joel got to telling him, showing him how much he loved to fuck him, play with him, be with him.

One long, slow slide into Christian's butt and Joel gave a deep sigh of satisfaction.

"You feel so good, all tight and hot and sweet."

He moved slowly at first in deep lunges. Christian's hand slid to his cock and for a moment he thought it had come off in his hand. "Jesus." He looked at the multicolored wax mold and laughed.

"Could we sell it?" Joel asked as he pumped into him.

"Make a model and you could have me up your butt all the time."

"You're already a pain in the butt."

Christian gasped as Joel began to drive into him more forcefully. He dragged Christian up from the floor and pounded into his ass.

"Fuck, fuck," Joel gasped.

Christian was jerking at his cock and the moment he felt Joel spurt into him, Christian's cum flew across his wax-covered chest, jet after jet until he was left gasping. The pair collapsed into each other's arms and lay shuddering on the floor. Now Christian had to say it. He stroked Joel's cheek.

"I love you."

There was no reply, but at least Joel didn't pull away. Christian had to be satisfied with that.

Chapter Nine

ஸ

"There's something I need you to do for me while I'm at work," Joel said as he stood in the kitchen, eating a slice of toast.

"Apart from clean up all that wax?"

Joel laughed.

"It isn't fucking funny. I'm going to be picking it off my body for days," Christian said.

"I'll give you a hand when I get home."

"Do you *have* to go in again today? It *is* Sunday."

"Yeah, sorry. I'll make it up to you."

Christian frowned. "So what is it you want me to do?"

"You have to promise to do it first."

Christian hesitated and then nodded. "Okay."

"Call Susie today and ask her out."

Christian tried not to let his face change. Joel swept a hand around his back and pulled him close.

"It's not that difficult. Listen, repeat after me—Hi, Susie, like to go for a walk?"

"Okay, okay."

Christian closed the door behind Joel and sighed.

By lunchtime he'd gone through a million ways of asking Susie if she'd go out with him and come up with nothing he wanted to say. The problem was not the opening sentence, it was what followed, when she asked him why, what, how and Christian knew all that was still just an excuse. In reality, he was scared shitless she'd say no, because if she did, that would wreck everything. Joel would be pissed that he'd fucked up and Christian would be even more pissed because he'd have wrecked the relationship he and Susie had developed.

Knowing Joel's reaction if he failed to call her, Christian picked up the phone. A guy answered. He guessed it was one of her brothers.

"Could I speak to Susie, please?"

"Susie! Phone!" the man yelled.

Christian waited, his pulse pounding in his head.

"Hello?"

"It's Christian." Then he couldn't speak. He was such a dick.

"Hi," Susie said.

One short word, but she sounded so pleased to hear his voice that Christian felt his cock twitch against his denims and had to repress a groan.

"I wondered if…er…if you'd like to go for a walk?"

"Now?"

Christian panicked. "You're probably busy, sorry."

"No, I'd love to. Shall I meet you somewhere?"

"How about the Leisure Centre on Trafalgar Road?"

"Thirty minutes?" Susie asked.

"Great."

That should give him time for another wank. It was a good job masturbating didn't make you go blind.

* * * * *

Christian was waiting when Susie got there. No way would he have been late. He felt his heart give a little jump when he saw her coming. She wore a yellow sundress and sandals with flowers on the toes and looked so cute his breath caught in his throat.

"Hi," Susie said as she reached his side.

Christian wondered whether to give her a peck on the cheek. But maybe it would make her think about her scar. He hesitated too long and the moment passed.

"I hope I haven't dragged you away from anything important," he said.

"Only washing the dishes. They'll be there when I get back."

"Shall we wander up to the Cutty Sark? We'll find a bar and I'll buy you a drink."

"Sounds good. So what's Joel up to?" Susie asked.

Did she wish Joel was there and not him? Christian sagged. How insecure could he get? "Working. He's been involved in a big deal all weekend."

"Wow. I think I'll take lawyer off my list of jobs I'd like to do. Mind you, my brother Mike, who's the plumber, got called out at eleven last night when someone's toilet overflowed. That's not a job I want either."

Christian chuckled. He cheered up. Susie was chatting to him and he was walking next to her. He'd be happier if he could bring himself to take hold of her hand, but he was so frightened she'd pull away, he stuck his own hands in his pockets to avoid the temptation. He then had to avoid the further temptation of fiddling with his dick.

They shared a bottle of wine at the Trafalgar Tavern and sat overlooking the Thames. Christian knew he was talking too much but he couldn't seem to stop. When she laughed at his jokes, it was as if she'd poured petrol on his fire. He burned for her.

When they left the pub, Christian caught her hand almost by accident, felt her soft fingers curl around his and his heart stuttered.

"Shall we walk around the indoor market?" he asked.

"Okay."

It was packed and Christian tightened his grasp. He'd
never been interested in the market before, but now he found
it fascinating because Susie made it so. She spotted what he'd
missed, the artistry in handmade clothing, the quirky animal
jigsaws, the chunks of wood carved into castles that with one
flick became a log again. Christian wanted to buy one for her,
but she grew so embarrassed, he bought one for Joel instead.
He did manage to persuade her to accept a hat. It was a
flowery thing and it made her look like an angel. Christian
gave up trying to hide the bulge at his crotch. It was a
permanent fixture.

They walked and talked and finally, reluctantly, Christian
took her home. He realized he'd uncovered very little about
Susie. He'd chattered far too much about his writing and the
places he'd seen when he worked for the *Times* as a foreign
correspondent. But she was a good listener and made him
laugh with her comments. She was far brighter than she gave
herself credit for. She'd read everything Christian had, though
all the books had been borrowed from the library. He told her
to help herself to books from his shelves and made a mental
note to move all of those by Raphael Strange. Christian felt
he'd uncovered a hidden treasure in Susie. *Oh Christ, I want to
keep her.*

"This is where I live," Susie said as they reached the top
of a street of terraced houses. "I think I can manage the last
few steps on my own."

"But a T. rex might leap from the bushes and bite off your
head. I'd feel dreadful."

Susie laughed. Her face lit up and her eyes sparkled.
Christian was desperate to kiss her. One little peck, enough to
last him until he saw her again because it was going to be two
very long days. If he didn't do it now, she'd walk away and
he'd undo all the good work of that afternoon. Or maybe that
was exactly what he'd do if he kissed her. He'd scare her off
and she wouldn't even come back on Wednesday. Oh shit, he
had to kiss her. Christian leaned forward and pressed his lips

against hers. He didn't do anything stupid like ease his tongue into her mouth, though he wanted to. Her lips were so soft and sweet and she tasted of the wine they'd drunk. She didn't pull away and he ached to edge a little further. He could just...

She pulled back and Christian couldn't mistake the confused look on her face. It wasn't "take me home and fuck me". Her face said "what the hell did you do that for?"

"I have to go." Susie glanced at the house. "Thanks for a lovely afternoon and my present. Bye, Christian."

She practically ran away from him. Christian watched as she crossed to the other side of the road. He wanted her to look back, but she didn't.

Susie saw her father watching through the bay window as she walked up to the front door. He had a scowl on his face and she realized with a sinking stomach that he might well have seen Christian kiss her. Twenty-four years old and her father couldn't let her go. She knew he just wanted to protect her, particularly after all that had happened but how much more could life throw at her? Susie had wanted Christian to yank her into his arms and kiss her senseless but now she was glad he hadn't. She didn't need a lecture about guys using and abusing her. She went straight past the lounge and into the kitchen to do the washing up. It would have been a lovely surprise to find it had all been done, but Susie never had lovely surprises. Nothing had been touched. The pile of saucepans was still heaped next to the cooker and the dirty plates sat on the draining board. She started the water running in the sink and bent down for the dish liquid.

She sensed rather than heard someone come into the room.

"Sorry, Suze. I meant to do them but it was football on the TV. I'll give you a hand."

She turned to smile at Mike. "I wish Dad would buy a dishwasher."

"He won't bother while he's got you."

Mike dried as she washed.

"So who were you out with this afternoon?"

"A friend."

"What friend?"

"None of your beeswax," she said.

Mike laughed. "I'll tickle it out of you later."

"My lips are sealed."

"That'll be the day."

"Any plans to move out yet?" Susie asked, rinsing a handful of cutlery.

"Why, will you miss me?"

She turned to face him and nodded. Mike kissed the top of her head. She really would miss him. He was the only one who was kind to her.

"Will you iron my blue shirt so I can wear it tonight?" he asked.

Though he still took her for granted.

"If you ask me nicely."

"Please, will you iron my shirt?"

"Okay."

"You're a star."

"She's a dirty-minded little slut."

Both Mike and Susie froze. Her father held the copy of *Seducing Alice* she'd borrowed from Christian.

"Where did this come from?" he asked.

"I bought it," Susie said.

"It's pornography." He ripped the book down the spine and tossed it on the table.

Susie ground her teeth.

"Never bring anything like that into this house again. Do you hear me?"

"Yes."

He took a beer from the fridge and walked out. Susie's shoulders sagged.

Mike picked up one half of the book and looked at the cover.

"Do you fancy this, Suze?" he asked.

She wasn't going to answer that.

"You need to find a better hiding place," he said in a quiet voice. "Pete and I kept our magazines behind the water tank in the airing cupboard. Probably still there."

He ruffled Susie's hair.

"I don't want you to move out," she blurted.

"You'll be fine."

Susie knew she wouldn't.

With the washing up done and Mike's shirt ironed, she took the ruined book to her room. She'd have to buy another. First thing tomorrow, she'd go to the bookshop in Greenwich and order one. In fact, Susie thought she might find out what else Raphael Strange had written and order another. She'd read *Seducing Alice* three times and each time her pussy had tingled and her mouth had gone dry. She was both excited and appalled at what the men did to Alice. She couldn't help wondering what the book was doing in Christian's study.

* * * * *

By the time he'd walked home, Christian's erection had gone down. He worried he'd blown everything with that kiss. He wouldn't tell Joel. As he opened the front door, he heard Joel call him from the kitchen.

"Christian? That you?"

"No, I'm a burglar," Christian shouted.

Joel appeared in the hall. "And here was I, hoping you were a crazy rapist."

Christian laughed. "I could be."

Joel came forward and kissed him, sliding his hands onto Christian's backside. Christian loved the feel of his lover's tongue in his mouth, slightly raspy but strong and sweet. Not like Susie's but… He pushed the image of her face away.

"Are you tired?" Christian asked.

"Physically, no. Mentally, yes, I'm fucking exhausted. My eyes are sore from checking documents and my head buzzes from listening to a guy who likes to use fifty words when five would do. Plus, it never ceases to amaze me how people can get so riled up about punctuation. I thought we'd hashed all that out yesterday, but no, they had to go over it again."

"Hey, you're talking to a writer. Words and commas are my lifeblood."

"Right. Get a life—comma—idiot, are the words and comma that come to mind. So where's my meal? Not been slaving away in the kitchen, eagerly anticipating my return?"

"I've been out all afternoon," Christian said.

Joel raised his eyebrows. "No shit, Sherlock."

Christian swallowed. "With Susie."

For the first time in a long while, he knew he'd shocked Joel. Christian waited for his reaction. Joel held him in suspense for a moment and then gave a slow smile.

"Get past the hand-holding?"

"Almost."

Joel rolled his eyes and headed back to the kitchen. Christian kicked off his shoes and padded after him.

"I kissed her," Christian blurted. He hadn't meant to tell him but somehow that seemed unfair and unfaithful.

"Exchange body fluids?" Joel had his back toward him.

"No, just a quick kiss. Then she ran for it."

Joel turned and didn't even try not to laugh. He was unable to speak for several moments. "It was that bad?" he choked out.

"No," Christian said in indignation.

"So you ran after her? Asked her to give you another try?"

Christian shook his head.

"You are such a wuss," Joel teased.

"I'm not."

"Are so."

Christian leapt on his back. "Take me upstairs and I'll prove I'm not a wuss."

"I'm not carrying you upstairs. You'll cripple me. I'll count to three and then I'm coming after you. One."

Christian fled. He adored being chased. He didn't know why, but the rush of adrenaline that flooded his body, knowing Joel was on his heels, was an incredible high. He took the stairs three at a time.

"Two," Joel shouted.

Christian was near his bedroom door when Joel brought him down onto the carpet with a thump. Christian felt Joel's teeth in the back of his neck and he melted, his muscles relaxing, instantly submissive. Joel's hands slid under his body, unfastening his jeans, yanking them over his hips to expose bare buttocks.

"You went commando?" Joel said.

Christian cringed. He felt Joel's hands skim over his backside and then felt his breath on his lower back.

"Start the day like this or did you take off your pants before you went out?"

Christian knew there was no point lying. "The latter."

"Bad boy."

Joel yanked off the jeans and forced Christian's knees apart. He brought the flat of his hand down hard on Christian's backside and won a yelp.

"Bad Christian, bad boy," Joel repeated, striking Christian each time he spoke.

Christian's dick strained against the carpet, the rough texture rubbing him into a higher state of arousal. He whimpered at each slap but in pleasure not pain. Then Joel's tongue was on him, licking along the delicate line between his balls and his anus. Joel sucked gently on Christian's sac and pressed his mouth against his ass. The sensation of Joel's slick, invading tongue drove Christian into a frenzy. He groaned into the floor.

"Christ, Joel. You have to let me up. I'm going to come all over the carpet."

"Get your new girlfriend to clean it up."

"You know she's not my girlfriend. Shit, please. I want you to fuck me."

Joel moved off and Christian got to his feet, pulling his foreskin back over the end of his dick.

"Are you going to think of her when I fuck you?" Joel whispered in his ear.

"No," Christian lied.

"My room," Joel ordered.

Christian threw the cover off the bed and stripped off his T-shirt. When Joel emerged from his bathroom, he was naked except for a thin ring of black leather pulled tight around his balls and dick.

"I thought you were tired," Christian said.

"Only mentally, I told you. I want this to last."

Christian knew it would, well, for Joel anyway. He thought he'd come the moment Joel penetrated him. Joel slid onto the bed and kissed his lips so tenderly, Christian felt his eyes tear up. They explored each other's mouths, softly then more forcefully until Joel started to slide down his chest. Christian caught hold of his shoulders.

"I love you," he said quietly.

"I know," Joel told him, and continued his downward journey.

Christian reached for his shoulders again, stopped him. "Just because I want her, doesn't mean I want you any less."

"I know," Joel said more quietly, and wrapped his lips around Christian's cock.

As Joel licked and sucked at Christian, he wondered if there was anything he could do to precipitate Christian and Susie getting it together. He fancied her himself, he hadn't lied to Christian, but he knew Christian liked her a lot and if only one of them was going to make it with her, he wanted it to be Christian. Joel had received a request to go back to the States. The eighteen months was nowhere near up, but his firm had lost a senior guy to a heart attack and wanted Joel to fill the gap. They weren't forcing him to return but Joel wasn't sure how well it would be taken if he insisted on staying in London. Well, he couldn't insist. If they ordered him back, he had to go.

So Susie was going to save him because Susie was going to take Joel's place in Christian's heart. There was no way Joel could cope with Christian seeing another guy, but a woman was different. Joel had a feeling Christian was usually more dominant, but because Christian was aware that most of the time Joel liked to be the one in charge, that's the way their relationship had developed. They weren't a clear-cut Dom and sub. They liked to switch. Joel was quickly turned on by Christian taking control but it didn't happen that often. With Susie, Christian had a chance to be the strong one.

Christian groaned and Joel concentrated on what he was doing, teasing Christian's shaft, nibbling around the crease below the head until Christian's fingers pressed so hard into his head, it hurt. He loved the taste of Christian, that salty edge, the little spurts of pre-cum that oozed from his slit. Joel dipped the tip of his tongue into the tear-shaped slit to gather another drip and Christian's hips jerked up.

Joel let Christian's cock slide from his mouth. He held it and slapped it against the side of his cheek several times while Christian grunted and groaned, then took the shaft between his lips and pushed his mouth down hard. Christian swelled even more as his orgasm neared.

"God, I love you," Christian gasped and Joel felt the warm spill of Christian's seed in his mouth.

Joel felt guilty that he hadn't really been concentrating. Not that Christian had noticed. In any case, Joel knew a lot of Christian's horniness over the last few days had been due to Susie. And if Joel was being honest with himself, she'd been in his mind too, not just picturing her as Christian's partner. Images of the three of them playing together, their mouths all over each other kept slipping into his head. Joel shuffled up the bed and pressed his mouth against Christian's. When his lips parted, Joel let the cum slide into Christian's mouth. Christian moaned and wrapped him tighter in his arms.

Chapter Ten

ജ

Wednesday couldn't come soon enough for Susie. She'd ordered a replacement copy of *Seducing Alice*, hoping she could put it back before Christian noticed, and another by Raphael Strange called *The Club*. Five days before delivery. Susie thought all the time about the kiss Christian had given her, replayed it in her mind, turned it into a passionate snog and back to a goodbye peck. He'd held her hand all afternoon—still, the kiss didn't have to mean anything. She wanted it to, wanted him to repeat it. Again and again.

But he didn't. In fact, he seemed nervous around her, not willing to stay in the same room. Susie came to the reluctant conclusion that he wanted to forget about it, so she had to do the same. She concentrated on cleaning—washed the windows outside and did their ironing, taking special care with Joel's shirts. There was a load of wax in the bathroom and in the bottom of the shower. What the hell had Christian been doing? Susie cooked salmon *en croute* for their dinner and went home feeling let down, not just by Christian but by herself.

Christian was out all day Thursday and asked her to make sure she locked the door when she left. She washed and ironed the sheets, tried not to look at the dried stains and smears, thought about girlfriends sleeping with them and wondered if anyone would ever want to sleep with her.

Now that Christian had given her permission to borrow his books, she searched his shelves and found another Raphael Strange called *Owner*. She lay on the newly made bed to read it. Susie only intended to have a break for half an hour but the book was hard to put down. It was about a guy who was sold by his girlfriend to another man. The sex scenes between the men had Susie panting. She slipped her hand under her skirt and into her panties. She was dripping wet. As she slid one finger over her clit, the door bell rang. She jerked her hand out and sat up. The bell rang again. Susie thrust the book under the bed and rushed downstairs.

Christian's agent Bella stood on the doorstep in a low-cut, tight pink dress.

"Christian's not in."

Bella's shoulders sagged. "Damn. I've been trying to phone him but his mobile's off. I assumed he was working. Since I'm here, I'll have a coffee."

She pushed her way past Susie and made for the kitchen. Susie figured the quickest way to get rid of her was to make her the drink.

"What's it like working for these two?" Bella asked.

"Great."

Susie lifted a jar of instant coffee from the cupboard. Faster than making fresh. Books to read. Bitches to push out of the door.

"Do you have a boyfriend?" Bella asked.

"I'm working on it."

Bella grinned. "Me too. Saturday's the night."

"Oh?"

"They're having a party, didn't you know?"

"Why would they tell me?" Susie hid her disappointment behind a shrug. She placed the cup in front of Bella.

"That's true. You're only the cleaner."

"Would you like a slice of cake?" Susie asked. "Oh, maybe you better not. It's rather fattening."

Good job verbal daggers didn't draw blood, Susie thought.

Bella pushed the untouched coffee to one side and got to her feet. "Better go. People to see."

Susie followed her to the door. Bella turned as she was leaving, her mouth twitched and Susie knew the question she was about to ask was the one she really wanted answering. Maybe she'd known Christian wouldn't be here and this was all some ploy. Susie waited.

"Do you think they're gay?" Bella asked.

"I know they're not," Susie said, and closed the door.

She leaned back against it and listened to Bella clip-clop down the path. She didn't know any such thing but Bella's face had been a picture of amazement. Were they gay? The kiss Christian had given her suggested he wasn't but since he was pretending it had never happened, maybe she was reading too much into it.

* * * * *

Susie was in the middle of a pile of ironing on Friday afternoon when Christian asked his question.

"Are you doing anything tomorrow night?"

"No." When did she ever do anything on Saturday night? Apart from watch TV.

"We're having a few friends around for supper. Eight o'clock. Could you come?"

Susie forgave him everything. Forgave the fact that he'd kissed her once and never kissed her again. Forgave the fact that he reacted like a rabbit whenever she walked into a room. Her heart launched into a tango with her lungs, dancing merrily round her chest.

"Yes," she said.

"There's a load of cooking to do. It might go on late, stay over if you like."

And the dancing stopped because the music ended. For a long while Susie didn't say anything. Christian just stood there. She carried on ironing, imagining Christian's neck under the collar she pressed flat.

"What sort of thing did you want me to do?" Susie asked finally, still nurturing a tiny hope that she'd misunderstood.

"I'd intended to get the ingredients from Marks & Spencer, but I don't know when I'll have the time. Maybe you'd do that for us? There'll be ten of us. Two are vegetarians." He took two hundred pounds out of his wallet and gave it to her. "Will this cover it?"

"I should think so." Susie put the money in her pocket. She tried to swallow her disappointment. He only wanted her to cook. "By the way, I forgot to tell you something." She hadn't. "Your agent Bella came round yesterday."

"What did she want?"

"She asked me if you and Joel were gay."

Susie kept ironing, didn't look at him.

Christian tapped his fingers on the doorframe. "What did you say?"

"That I know you're not."

Now Susie looked at him. Christian dropped his head and avoided her gaze. He mumbled about something he had to do and rushed out of the room. Her shoulders slumped. Maybe Christian wasn't sure if he was gay or not. That was why he'd kissed her.

Christian was still working when Joel got home.

"Shit! She left without telling me—again."

"I expect you were in your own world—again," Joel said with a laugh. "So did you do what I told you? Did you talk to her?"

"Er..."

"What does er mean?" Though Joel guessed it meant no.

"We did talk a bit. She said Bella had come here and asked if we were gay."

Joel froze. "What did Susie say?"

"That she knew we weren't."

Joel exhaled. "And your response? Did you sweep her into your arms and show Susie she was right?"

Christian rolled his shoulders. "Not exactly."

"What did you do?"

"Nothing. I was so dumbfounded I didn't know what to say."

"Jesus, Christian."

"And I think I upset her," Christian said.

"How?" Joel massaged the muscles at the back of Christian's neck.

"I did what you suggested and asked her to come tomorrow. I said she could stay over."

The hands left his neck. Joel moved round to sit on the edge of Christian's desk.

"So how did that upset her? Isn't she coming?"

"She said yes."

Joel beamed. "That's great."

"I gave her two hundred quid. She's going to help with the cooking."

Joel reached out and flicked Christian's head with his thumb and middle finger.

"Ouch. What was that for?"

"You know what for. Does she think she's coming to do the cooking or to join us and our friends for an entertaining dinner party?"

Christian hesitated and Joel shook his head. "For a writer who's supposed to be able to think inside a woman's head, you sure can be dumb as shit sometimes."

Christian growled. "Care to repeat that?"

Joel smiled. "Dumb as shit, dumbass."

Christian leapt at him and knocked him to the ground amidst a shower of papers from his desk. The two tussled, taking turns to pin each other down until Joel wrapped a choke hold on Christian and pressed his face into his lover's hair.

"Now say after me. I am an idiot," Joel panted.

"You are an idiot. Owww."

"Try again."

"I am an idiot. I did ask her to join us, Joel. I'm sure it's all right. I mean, I asked her to help, not do it on her own."

"So do you still like her?" Joel asked.

"Yeah. She's funny and sweet. And I found something else out."

"What?"

"She's been reading one of my books. I found it under the bed. Unless it was you?"

"No. Which one?"

"The one where the woman sells her boyfriend into slavery. I can't find *Seducing Alice* either. I said she could borrow what she liked. Maybe she liked the look of it."

"Christ, Christian. She only needs a push. Can't you even manage that?"

Christian bristled. "I'm not hopeless."

"Okay, so explain to me how you're going to get her into bed."

Joel felt Christian stiffen and released him. Christian sat up and the two of them exchanged looks.

Christian flopped like a fish. "I have no idea."

Joel sighed. "You're so slow. I'm going to have to do this myself." Maybe he could taunt Christian into action.

"I want to do it."

"Whining again."

"She's only been here two weeks."

"Exactly," Joel said. "Two whole weeks and you've been thinking of fucking her all that time and not done anything about it."

He got to his feet and pulled Christian to his. By the time they'd reached Christian's bedroom, Joel's cock was trying to force its way through his zipper. Joel stood behind him, rested his chin on Christian's shoulder and cupped his groin. Christian was fully erect, his cock a rigid length of engorged tissue.

"What the hell are you thinking about?" Joel asked. "You're like a fucking nightstick."

"Sex."

"Who with?"

"You."

"Right answer." Though Joel wasn't sure it was true.

Joel stroked Christian's erection through the ridge of his jeans and Christian arched back into him, reaching up to link his hands behind Joel's neck. Joel's heart was hammering. He barely had to look at Christian before he wanted him. Joel unfastened the button on his lover's jeans, and then eased them over his hips, pushing them down his thighs. Christian turned and his fingers fumbled with the buttons on Joel's shirt and Joel reached for Christian's. Too slow, they wrenched off the rest of their clothes and Christian pressed his mouth against Joel's. They rutted against each other, rocking their hips, gasping into the other's mouth, hands clutching arms as their cocks banged and surged together.

Christian kept his mouth connected to Joel's and forced his hand between their bodies. He grabbed Joel's cock and pumped his fist up and down. Joel pried him away and pushed him back onto the bed, watching as the muscles in Christian's chest flexed as he breathed. Joel knelt at his side and trailed his fingers from the dip at the base of Christian's throat, through the depression between his rounded pecs, circling the tight nubs of Christian's dark copper nipples and then back to the center of his body to follow the trail of golden hair to his stomach. As Joel ran his nail along Christian's hip bone, his partner turned into his touch. Joel was fascinated by Christian's skin, warm and soft yet muscles like stone. His fingers slid to Christian's cock, satiny smooth and burning hot, and traced the pulsing vein on the underside. Joel dropped his head and licked from Christian's balls to his purple-headed tip. One long, slow, wet slurp that had Christian cantering off the bed.

Joel wrapped a tight fist around Christian's dick and then slid higher to lick one of his nipples while the fingers of his other hand teased its mate. One nipple was caressed and kissed, the other pinched and nipped. Christian groaned and gasped, his hands slotted in Joel's hair. Joel felt Christian's cock surge with a fresh shot of blood and his pulse spiked.

Moments later they were top to tail on the bed, each working the other's dick. Joel gasped around Christian's cock as Christian mouthed his balls. For a change, Christian was the one on top. Joel felt Christian's finger pressing at his anus and a spiral of heat twisted down his spine. Joel liked to be in control when he was giving head and even as Christian began his games with his cock, Joel felt Christian running too fast. He was fucking Joel's mouth, pressing his dick deeper and deeper with each thrust. Joel tried to push his hips up because he couldn't breathe but in the end knew he'd have to let Christian do what he wanted.

Christian tensed and his cum flooded Joel's mouth. He pulled off Joel's dick and swiveled round.

"Shit, Joel. I'm sorry," Christian mumbled.

Joel wiped his mouth with the back of his hand.

"You're a liar, Christian. You weren't thinking of me. You were thinking of her."

"That's not true. I'm sorry. I just forgot what I was doing."

Joel gave a short laugh. "Yeah, you forgot it was my mouth you were fucking and not her pussy."

"I want both of you," Christian blurted.

Joel stood, looking at him for a moment, and then pulled Christian into his arms.

"So do something about it," he whispered. "But first, do something about this." He took Christian's hand and put it on his cock.

Chapter Eleven

ഇ

"I'm not happy about this," Harry said.

"It's a chance to earn some decent money." Susie had her fingers crossed behind her back. There was no way she wasn't going to Christian and Joel's to help with the dinner party but she didn't want to upset her father.

He narrowed his eyes. "Sure you're not spending the night with your boyfriend?"

"I don't have a boyfriend."

"So who was the guy I saw you kissing?"

Susie's heart thumped.

"A mistake," she muttered.

"I'm just looking out for you, Susie. I don't want you to get hurt."

"Joel and Christian already have girlfriends. They just need me to cook. You know I'm a good cook."

He huffed and picked up his newspaper. Susie made him a cup of tea.

"I'm going to the market to pick up a few things. Shall I bring you some fish and chips?" she asked.

"And mushy peas."

For a moment Susie thought he said please. She laughed to herself and slipped away. She went to collect the two books she'd ordered and buried them deep inside her shopping bag. She picked up four cartons of strawberries from the market and fresh asparagus but really needed to go to the supermarket. How she was going to carry everything was another issue.

She'd just stepped back inside the house when her father yelled that someone was on the phone.

"It's the fourth time he's called. A Yank," he said. He handed her the phone and lifted her lunch from her hands.

"Hello?"

"Hi, Susie, it's Joel. I was calling to see if you needed a hand getting the food. Christian tells me he lumbered you with the whole thing."

"I'd love some help. I need to go to the supermarket."

"Shall I come and get you?"

Susie glanced at her father putting vinegar on his chips. "It's okay. I've got my bike. I'll be there in fifteen minutes."

She put a change of clothes in a backpack along with her toiletries, plus the two books, and went to tell her father she was leaving. Harry sat in front of the TV, his lunch on a tray. Saturday night he always went out with his mates for a curry, so she didn't have to bother cooking. Pete and Mike would be out drinking.

"What time will you be back?" her father asked.

"I'm not sure."

"Make sure it's in time to cook lunch."

And that was it. That was all she meant to him. Susie's heart ached as she cycled to the guys' place. She didn't think her dad meant to be so selfish, but he took her for granted and after all that had happened to her, it seemed cruel.

By the time Susie put her bike in their garage, she'd cheered up. The idea of being near Christian for a whole evening and sleeping in his house made her fizz with excitement like a huge bath bomb. Even if she was only acting as a maid, it could be fun. And shopping with Joel. It would give her chance to get to know him a little. It had been a long time since she'd been this excited. She rang the bell.

Joel opened the door and beamed at her. Susie's heart did a cartwheel and slammed into her stomach. She'd forgotten how gorgeous he was.

"Hey, ready to take off?" he asked.

"Fine."

"Let's stick your bag inside."

He took her backpack and dropped it inside the door. "Right, your choice. A long and tedious trip into the city or the local supermarket? And be careful what you say."

"Local supermarket."

"Good choice." He bustled her into the car. "Now keep reminding me which side of the road to drive."

Susie glanced at him in horror and saw him smile.

"It took a lot of convincing to get Christian to put me on his insurance. He's a terrible passenger, but I love to drive. If it wasn't for the fact that the thing would only get taken for a spin on weekends, I'd buy a car."

They'd only traveled down a couple of streets before they came to a halt.

"Or maybe not. Geez, this traffic is worse than in New York," Joel said as they waited to pull right onto Trafalgar Road.

"Is that where you're from? New York?"

"No, ma'am. I was born and raised in Denver, Colorado. Went to college in Boulder."

"The foot of the Rockies."

Joel glanced at her. "You've been there?"

"Only in my dreams. I've never even been on a plane."

"You're kidding me?"

"No."

"Christian says you didn't go to college?"

"No." Now he'd think she was stupid.

"Why not?"

"I…I just didn't." Susie couldn't bring herself to tell him the truth.

"Would you like to go?" he asked in a gentle voice.

"Yes."

"What would you like to study?"

Was this an interrogation? "Molecular bioscience."

"Holy shit." He turned to look at her. Susie tried hard but she couldn't keep her face straight. "Very funny, Susie."

She giggled and then frowned. "Hey, why shouldn't I want to study molecular bioscience?"

"Tell me what it is."

"If I study it, I'll find out, won't I?"

Joel chuckled. "Assuming that class is full, then what would you take?"

"English."

"Well, why don't you?" he asked.

Susie twisted her hands around the seat belt. "I'm not clever enough. You aren't allowed to go to university unless you've passed a whole load of exams and I didn't. It doesn't matter."

"Of course it matters. You should follow your heart. It always knows the right thing to do. If you want to go to college, find a way."

Easy for him to say, Susie thought. She suspected everything worked perfectly for a guy like him.

"So what would you do after college?" he asked.

"I think I'd like to run Microsoft."

Joel laughed. "I didn't realize you were such a smart-a…alec."

"Were you just going to call me a smart-ass?"

"Maybe, but I need a better look at it."

Oh God, he was flirting. I'm flirting. Susie took a shaky breath.

Joel pulled off the main road into the supermarket car park. "I hope you made a shopping list."

She pulled a long piece of paper from her purse.

"Ah, you're organized. A woman after my own heart." Joel sighed.

Susie had never found shopping so much fun. Joel was like a big child. He kept putting stuff in the cart and Susie kept taking it out.

"We don't need liquorish bootlaces," she said. "Or flying saucers."

"Spoilsport."

"Okay. One or the other. I'd hate to deprive you."

It didn't escape Susie's attention that he snuck both packets in under bags of salad.

"We better get one of these," he said, pointing to the cakes.

"Is it Christian's birthday?"

"Yep."

He didn't look at her, and for some reason Susie thought it was a lie.

"How about this one?" Joel pointed to a Barbie cake, the upper half of a doll sitting atop a pink dome.

"I think he might kill you. The football?" she suggested.

"Then I think you'd be the one he killed."

Susie laughed. "Okay. Compromise. The boobs."

"I was hoping you'd say that. I wouldn't have dared, in case you thought I was being suggestive."

Susie could feel him watching her, but she wouldn't look his way.

Joel piled the second cart with champagne and wine and made for the checkout. Susie saw the looks that Joel attracted from women and men, though he seemed oblivious. He was breathtakingly handsome. Better-looking than Christian really, though Christian was cuter. She wanted to ask Joel if he had a girlfriend coming that night, but knew the words would never get past her lips. If he had a girlfriend, Susie had never seen any sign of her at the house.

She handed him the two hundred pounds Christian had given her.

"Did he pay you for yesterday?"

"Not yet."

Joel sighed. "You'll have to remind him. Christian gets lost in him own little world." He gave her a hundred back.

"That's too much."

"You're helping tonight, aren't you?"

They piled the purchases on the belt.

"Can I help you cook some of this," he asked.

"Can you cook?"

"Not well."

"Can you follow instructions?"

"To the letter. I'm a lawyer."

"Then yes, you can help."

Joel couldn't remember the last time he'd actually enjoyed shopping. He'd revised his opinion of Susie. He had this image of her as a little fawn but she was perfect. Like a new flower beginning to open, she needed a bit of teasing by the sun. Joel felt particularly sun-like today, his blood simmering with anticipation. She was kind of shy, a bit innocent but in an appealing way. The whole point of him taking her to the supermarket had been to press Christian's case because Joel knew Christian would never make a move on her. Only something had changed. Make that some*one* had changed. Joel grinned.

As they carried the bags in from the car, Joel yelled out, "Hey, we're back."

Christian came pounding downstairs.

"Help us carry the groceries in. Susie bought the whole store," Joel said.

Christian slipped on his shoes and followed them out. It took several trips before everything was unloaded.

"Christian, one of those bottles of champagne is already chilled. Open it and stick the others in the fridge. Susie, if you find the bread and cheese, we'll have a sandwich before we start."

"Music," Christian said. "We can't work without music. What do you like, Susie?"

"The Spice Girls."

Joel jumped at her and Susie fled to the other side of the table. "Oh no you don't," he said.

"Beethoven?"

"Try again." Joel edged around to grab her and Susie went the other way. She looked scared and excited in equal measures.

"Beach Boys," she blurted.

He stopped. "Good choice."

She laughed. Joel whipped around the top of the table and caught hold of her hand. He gave it a quick squeeze before he let her go.

"You have a lovely smile. I wish you'd do it more often."

Joel knew Christian was staring at him but he couldn't take his eyes off Susie. She was blushing and he wanted to feel the heat of her cheeks against his palm. Christian pushed a glass of champagne into his hand and handed one to Susie.

"To us," Christian said, and nudged Joel with his knee.

"To a trio." Joel smiled.

He and Christian looked at Susie.

"The three amigos," she said.

They clinked glasses.

After lunch, the three of them prepared food together and Susie forgot she was disappointed she hadn't been properly invited and that she was merely the cook. The two guys were like a comedy double act, competing over who could make her laugh the loudest. Christian launched into a karaoke version of a Beatles' track, brandishing a cucumber microphone, and Joel stuck radishes in his ears and then stuck them in Susie's. Susie would have been quicker making everything on her own, but it wouldn't have been half so much fun.

Finally everything was ready, either to eat or to heat up at the last minute. The dishwasher hummed and the kitchen was temporarily restored to its spotless state. While the guys worked outside, Susie grabbed *Seducing Alice* from her bag in the hall, nipped upstairs and put it back on Christian's bookshelf. Then she froze. She saw *The Owner* on the next shelf, the book she'd been reading when Bella had come on Thursday. Susie had stuck it under Christian's bed and forgotten to retrieve it. *Shit.* Was that the same copy? Susie checked. No book under his bed. *Fuck.*

Not much she could do about it. She went back downstairs, threw a white cloth over the dining table and set it with sparkling glasses and the guys' curly-handled cutlery. She folded ten serviettes into the shape of little bows and arranged flowers from the garden in a couple of vases. Through the French doors, she saw Christian had turned the patio into an outdoor lounge, set out with cushioned seating and multi-colored lanterns. Joel had hung lights in the trees and put on music. Susie did a final run with the vacuum cleaner and returned to the kitchen.

Joel opened another bottle of champagne. He poured it into three delicate glass flutes decorated with blue glass swirls. "A toast. To Susie, without whom all of this would not have been possible."

"Thank you and a happy birthday to Christian, whenever it may be," she said, and stared straight at Joel.

Joel glanced at Christian but neither said anything.

"So what have you brought to wear?" Christian asked. "I should have said that we'd be in tuxedos. Joel wanted this to be smart."

"Me?"

Christian made a play of looking over her shoulder. "Yes, you. I don't see anyone else."

"Well, does it matter?" Susie asked. "I didn't think you wanted me to serve. I suppose I could go home and get my dark skirt. I haven't got a white blouse, though I could..."

Her voice trailed off when she saw them staring at her. Then Joel glared at Christian, his fists clenched.

"I fucking told you, you idiot. What did I say?"

Christian turned to Susie. "I thought you realized. I asked you to do the food but I wanted you to come and eat with us. There's a place at the table for you. You're one of the ten."

"Me?" Susie clutched her glass.

"I'm sorry," Christian said. "Joel wondered if I'd made it clear and I thought I had, but obviously I hadn't. Of course we want you to eat with us. You know more about our revolting habits than anyone else. You're practically part of this dysfunctional family. Now what have you got to wear?"

"I only brought jeans and a spare T-shirt."

Christian looked her up and down. "I have an idea. Come on."

He took hold of her hand and Susie's heart leapt as he dragged her out of the room and up the stairs. Joel followed with her bag.

"Hey, that's my room," Joel called.

"Put Susie's bag in the guest room and come and tell us what you think."

Christian sat Susie down on the bed and slowly drew his hand away before turning to Joel's chest of drawers. He opened the first and slammed it shut so fast, she wondered what was in there. Christian left the second open and began rummaging through the contents. Susie turned to see Joel leaning against the doorframe. She felt a sudden shiver of pleasure at the thought that she sat on his bed. She ran her hand over the duvet and looked up to find him watching her. Susie had an uncomfortable feeling he knew exactly what she'd been thinking.

"Voila," Christian declared and held up what looked like a black vest.

"It's a black vest," Joel said.

"It's a very long black vest," Christian corrected.

He disappeared into his own room and left Susie and Joel staring at each other. She couldn't tear her eyes away from his. It was like looking into deep black pools, ones she wanted to dive into. His mouth twitched and Susie's nipples hardened. The air grew thick and Susie struggled to breathe.

"Like my bed?" he asked in a gruff voice.

She gulped and Christian burst in, waving a wide silver belt.

"Christ, Christian. You have a silver belt?" Joel gawped.

"Don't ask. Long story and I don't come out well. So what do you think?" He turned to Susie.

He was so excited, bubbling over with enthusiasm, that she didn't have the heart to say no.

"The tennis shoes'll go real well," Joel said.

"She can go barefoot," Christian snapped.

"Or I could cut down a pair of my very expensive flip flops," Joel offered.

The two men smiled at each other.

"Change in here. You can wash up in the main bathroom, Susie. I'll use Christian's shower," Joel said.

And that, Susie thought, was how easily she'd been bamboozled into wearing a vest for a dinner party where the guys would be wearing dinner jackets and the women would probably have spent a week's wages on their dresses.

Chapter Twelve

ຽນ

Susie leaned back in the bath, luxuriating in having a full tub of hot water and no one banging on the door, yelling at her to hurry because they needed a crap. She'd tipped some of Joel's bath gel under the taps and had fun playing with the bubbles, giving herself huge boobs that kept slipping south. Then her fingers slipped south. Susie closed her eyes. She knew it wouldn't take much to bring her off—she'd been on a knife edge of control since Joel had smiled at her on the doorstep when she'd arrived. As her finger circled her clit, she let out a moan of relief. Susie hadn't misunderstood the look in Joel's eyes, or the one in Christian's. No way were they gay. But maybe that was as far as they'd go with her—looks.

She bent her legs, spread her knees and lifted her heels onto the sides of the tub. She brought both guy's faces into her head, arched her pussy out of the water and her fingers rubbed faster. Pinpricks of sensation blossomed throughout her body, swarmed along nerve endings and focused on her core. Tighter, harder, faster and Susie cried out when the orgasm burst, ripples of pleasure flooding out from her center, bliss seeping into every cell. She relaxed into the water and dipped below the surface.

Joel had Christian pinned against the shower wall, the water pouring over them. "You are a fucking stupid bastard, you know that?" he hissed in Christian's ear. "What the fuck do you think she must have thought when you asked her to do the food?"

He dropped to his knees, spreading Christian's butt cheeks with his hands. He pressed his face into the dark cleft and rimmed him, licking around the wrinkled opening. He was rewarded by a loud groan from Christian. Joel's tongue pressed inside and his hand moved around to play with Christian's balls. He knew Christian would only be able to stand this for a moment.

"God, Joel, that's enough. Fuck me, please."

Joel stood, slathered lube all over his dick and pushed Christian hard into the tiles. He positioned his cock over the entrance to Christian's body and nudged, pressed and pushed until he forced Christian's muscles to relax and allow him in. As his cock was suctioned inside Christian's dark passage, Joel dropped his head to Christian's neck, mouthed down the taut, corded tendons to give his shoulder a gentle bite.

Now Christian had adjusted to the intrusion, Joel bent his knees and began to drive into him, hard, ramming thrusts that almost lifted Christian off his feet. The feel of Christian's slick channel, tight as a glove around his cock, sent coils of pleasure whipping through Joel's gut. He reached for Christian's cock, and the moment he began to pump, Christian went rigid and then groaned. Jets of cum hit Joel's hand and spurted onto the tiles. A few hip canters later, Joel came in a sharp, intense orgasm that flared behind his eyes and shot spunk from his balls in a fiery flood.

The two men leaned against the shower wall, faces inches apart, the water still pouring down.

"Thinking of me?" Christian whispered.

Joel laughed. He couldn't speak.

"If we don't do something soon, we're going to explode," Christian said.

"Think...we just did."

Christian chuckled. Joel dragged his breathing back under control.

"What was your book *The Club* about?" Joel asked.

"Why?"

"Tell me."

Christian blinked water out of his eyes. "It's the one about the place where women are trained to service two men at the same time."

Joel smiled. "I thought it was. There's a copy in Anna's bag."

"My book? What were you doing in her bag?"

Joel could almost see the cogs turning in Christian's head.

"It fell out when I tossed the bag on the bed. I put it back. It's still in the wrapper. Looks like she's only just bought it."

"She can't know I wrote it," Christian said.

"I think you're safe, Raphael. But it's an interesting choice, isn't it?"

Christian nodded.

"Our cute little kitten's not so sweet and innocent. I think she needs a push, a bit of teasing," Joel said.

"I don't know, Joel. She's—"

"Do you want her or not?"

"Yes, but what if she doesn't want both of us?"

Joel's heart fluttered. He'd wanted her for them both then just for Christian and now just for him. Both of them was too much to hope for.

"It won't change things between us," Christian said.

"Never." Joel kissed him.

Susie stood in front of the mirror in the guest bedroom and stared at her reflection. Her hand rose to her mouth and she began to chew her nail. There was a problem. Not the vest. It worked quite well as a dress, short but not too short and the hip-slung belt made it look feminine.

The problem was her bra. It was clearly visible at the shoulders and arm holes. A bright pink bra. Susie wasn't sure if she was brave enough to take it off, but she didn't see she had a choice. She looked ridiculous with it on. Black she might have got away with but not pink. Finally she just did it, unfastened the catch and slid it over her arms without removing the vest. Now, so long as she didn't bend over, reach up, lean too far to the right or too far to the left, or get too cold or too excited, she'd be absolutely fine.

Doomed then.

A knock on the door and she gulped in response.

"Can we see?" Christian asked.

"Come on in," Susie called and turned.

Three jaws dropped in unison. The two men entered in bow ties and dinner jackets, looking so James Bond gorgeous, Susie thought her heart would stop. And they were staring at her as though it was the first time they'd seen her, but definitely liked what they saw. Susie's fingers rose to her damp hair and pulled it over the side of her face.

"Wow, you look so great in that," Joel said.

"Better than you do." Christian laughed.

"You fill it out in an…interesting way." Joel stepped into the room and bent down at her feet. "Your plastic slipper, Cinderella."

He took hold of her ankle to slide her foot onto the flip flop and Susie heard a little whimper escape her throat. She hoped Joel hadn't noticed, but he hesitated so maybe he had. He put the other flip flop in place and stroked her ankle with his finger. The touch was so gentle Susie wasn't sure whether it was an accident. Then he stood up.

"You really do look stunning." Joel's gaze swept her from head to foot.

"I need another drink," Christian muttered and fled.

Susie glanced after him.

"Don't mind him. I think something just came up." Joel grinned and took a step toward her.

Susie gulped and ran after Christian.

"There's nowhere to hide, Susie," Joel called.

* * * * *

Joel watched as Susie busied herself in the kitchen, never coming near him. There was a major problem, Houston, and he had no idea what to do about it. He wanted her. *Shit.* Desperately. *Double shit.* Joel was pretty sure Susie was feeling hot and sexy. She had a telltale flush across the top of her chest, but which one of them had set her off? Hardly both. That would take a leap of faith wider than the Grand Canyon. Joel knew that if he waited for Christian to make a move, he'd be able to see hell freezing over in the distance. But if *he* made a move, how badly would Christian take it?

What if he walked up to her and wrapped his arms around her? How loud would she scream? He laughed to himself. Then swallowed as he pictured her underneath him in his bed, her heart racing, her cheeks flushed, screaming in ecstasy. Unfortunately, the next image was of her screaming in fury and slapping his face. But how about if he put her somewhere she couldn't react to his touch? The beginnings of an idea began to form and this time the smile stayed put.

"So who's coming?" Susie asked as she removed foil from the *hors d'oeuvres.*

You, if I have anything to do with it, screaming my name and kicking.

She turned to look at him.

"Christian's agent, a couple of his writer friends and a bunch of lawyers from Horton and Standish where I work."

He poured more champagne into her glass.

"Are you trying to get me drunk?" she said.

"I don't know. What are you like when you're drunk?"

"I fall asleep."

"Definitely not, then."

He wished she wouldn't try to hide behind her hair. He knew she was self-conscious about her scar but he didn't even see it when he looked at her. If he got her naked, he could show her it didn't matter. Maybe one kiss before dinner, before Christian gathered his courage and puckered his lips. Joel took a step then paused at the chime of the front door bell.

Everyone congregated in the kitchen. Joel stayed close by Susie's side and introduced her. He knew it would be assumed they were an item and felt a little guilty using her in that way. He and Christian were careful about how they behaved in public. Whilst it didn't matter if people in Christian's world knew Christian was bisexual, it did matter in Joel's. He wanted promotion. He'd worked hard to make sure he was the one who got the eighteen months in London, even if it did look as though it would be cut short.

The senior partner over here was a fucking bigot. He spent all his time staring at the chests of the female trainees but made his views on shirtlifters perfectly clear. Joel hadn't even heard that expression before, but he'd collected quite a few over the few months he'd been here. He knew he had to be careful. He'd selected a couple of women to go out with on single dates, letting them spread the rumor he had a girlfriend in the States. It had been enough to quell any murmurs about his sexuality.

Bella was all over Christian like a nasty rash, linking her arm with his, giggling into his neck. Christian was making a half-hearted attempt to get away but the woman was like an octopus. Joel didn't know why Christian didn't just fuck her and have done with it. Except he did, because once wouldn't be enough for Bella, and sweet, kind-hearted Christian would be incapable of walking away.

Susie was relieved when everyone sat down to eat. Christian and Joel had put her between them at the head of the table. They seated Bella next to Christian and a woman called

Laura on the other side of Joel. There was only one other woman, Rachel, who worked with Joel. She was going out with the man she sat next to, whose name Susie had forgotten. Strange, she thought, that she remembered the women's names and not the men's. Was that because the names of two men occupied her every thought?

Almost everyone was complimentary about the food, which made Susie relax a little and begin to enjoy herself. A mistake.

"So what do you do, Susie?" Laura asked.

"She looks after property," Christian said before Susie could speak.

Laura smiled. "Really? Whereabouts?"

"Greenwich." Christian answered for her again.

"She's a ventriloquist too," Joel said, and everyone laughed.

"Do you have a large portfolio?" one of the men asked.

"Christian's being economical with the truth," Bella said. "Susie is their cleaner."

"Our part-time housekeeper," Joel said. "Not cleaner. Susie's a fantastic cook. She prepared all this food. She's organized Christian, who can now see his study floor in between the piles of crap. She's found the mates for all my socks and she's also about to start studying for an English degree."

His tone of voice made it clear Bella had overstepped the mark, but it was Susie Bella glared at. The chatter began again and Susie began to breathe.

"What sort of books do you like, Susie?" Laura asked.

"I read almost anything. Classics to modern thrillers."

"The trashier the better for me," said Rachel. "After spending all day on legal contracts I need light relief."

Susie felt on safer ground and made them laugh talking about the weird messages she'd found in library books. "I began to think I'd stumbled on some spy ring and everything was in code. I mentioned it to the librarian and she said it was some local nutcase. Then I worried because we were reading the same books."

Everyone laughed and Susie felt her face heat up.

When the desserts were on the table, homemade *pear tarte tatin, crème brûlée* and a bowl of strawberries, Bella attacked again.

"So how did you get your scar?" she asked, and the table went quiet.

Susie felt Joel's hand creep onto hers beneath the table. She let him take her fingers.

"What?" Belle exclaimed, looking around. "It was just a question."

"A rude one," Christian said.

"Was it in a car accident?" Belle pressed.

"No."

"You don't have to answer, Susie," Joel said quietly.

She didn't have to, the woman was out of line, but now Susie wanted to shock her into silence.

"While I was sleeping, my mother tried to cut off my face."

Susie stared straight at Bella, whose eyes opened wider and wider. *Drop out of her head,* Susie thought, *roll off the table and onto the floor.*

"Jesus." Joel clutched her fingers.

"That's terrible. How old were you?" Laura asked.

"Nineteen."

"Oh my God, how awful," Rachel said. "Is she in prison?"

"No, she's dead." Susie paused. "I didn't kill her."

"I fucking would have," Joel whispered.

Susie turned to look at him.

"What made her do it?" asked a guy next to Laura.

"She wasn't thinking straight. She was an alcoholic and…well, my father said I was prettier than her. He was trying to get her to stop drinking and clean herself up but it backfired."

There was a long pause.

"Bloody hell," Christian muttered. "I think that tops my story about dead-dog dancing in Greece."

"What's that about?" Joel asked, continuing to squeeze her hand, and Susie knew they were trying to deflect attention away from her. She felt bad. She'd depressed the mood of the party.

"Me and a couple of mates were on holiday in Crete. We'd gone out for a stroll and this pack of dogs followed us. They snapped at our heels and it began to freak us out. We picked up some stones in case they decided they wanted to take a chunk out of our ankles. Then we saw this dead dog lying by the side of the road, and one bright spark started going on about rabies — not me — and when these damn dogs started to surround us, we began to panic. Suddenly, for no reason that we could see, they peeled away and vanished."

"So you started to dance with joy?" Laura asked.

"Not yet. We had to come back the same way and the bloody things picked us up again, at more or less the same point. I suppose we were in their territory. A rival pack. One idiot, again, not me before you all come to the wrong conclusion, chucked a stone and the mangy things attacked us, so we all had to chuck stones. Thank God the buggers ran off, otherwise I wouldn't be here to tell the tale. We'd been seriously scared and feeling lucky none of us got bitten. I was whooping and hollering by the side of the road, jumping on this mound of sand and that was when I saw this little paw flapping up and down by my feet. My bare feet. Someone had used sand to cover the dead dog we'd seen earlier. So that holiday is always referred to as the one when Christian went dead-dog dancing."

Everyone laughed and Susie was safe again. Joel's hand slipped away. He kept filling her glass and Susie told herself not to empty it, but the slightest sip and Joel topped it up. When she felt his hand on her thigh, she dropped her dessert fork onto her plate with a clatter. She risked a glance at him, but he faced away from her, talking to Laura. His fingers ran round the lower edge of the vest and he slid his thumb underneath onto her bare skin. Hormones raced through her body, zinging every erogenous zone into a state of readiness. Her pulse rocketed. Her breath shortened. Her mouth went dry.

"What do you think? Susie?"

Christian laughed. "Joel's talking to you."

"Sorry. What did you say?"

"I asked what you liked to do in your spare time."

Joel's hand slid higher up her thigh and he trailed his fingers along her skin. Too close to her wet panties. Susie tried to move back and his grip tightened.

"Kite surfing," she blurted.

"Wow, really?" Joel said.

Susie gave an audible sigh as Joel removed his hand and she began to talk about the one time she'd had a go, trying to make it sound as though she were an expert and did it every week.

"What about you?" she asked Joel, desperate to change the subject.

"I like all sorts of things."

Susie felt his stocking foot on hers, rubbing her calf. His hand moved back to her knee and she lost all ability to think, let alone string together a coherent sentence.

Christian's dessert fork flipped onto the floor. He bent down to get it and Susie felt his hot breath on her thigh as he pressed his lips just below the line of the vest. For a moment, she had Christian's mouth on one thigh and Joel's hand on the other and then they were both gone.

Susie tried to swallow the piece of pear she'd been chewing. It stuck in her throat and refused to go down. They were teasing her. Her eyes filled with tears and she had to blink furiously to stop them spilling down her cheeks.

She leapt up to clear the table despite Christian's protesting he and Joel would do it. Susie really wanted to run home, only even as the thought came to her, she knew it wasn't true. She'd liked it when Joel's hand held hers, loved the feathery touch of Christian's lips. She adored the fact that it was both of them, but neither of them knew about the other. This was beyond awkward.

Chapter Thirteen

ঝ

Susie watched as Joel brought out coffee and Christian carried in the cake. There was some hooting from the men when they saw it.

"Whose birthday is it?" Bella asked. "It's not Christian's."

"Nearly mine." Joel winked at Susie.

"No candles?" Bella said.

Joel shook his head. "And no singing either."

"Christian, did you pick that cake?" Rachel asked.

"No, Susie did," Joel said.

Susie thought she could have warmed the room with her cheeks, they were so hot.

"Christ, I don't know where to cut it." Joel hovered over the cake with the knife.

"Cut—tit, that's funny." One of the men guffawed.

Joel rolled his eyes and then pressed down with the knife. He handed slices to everyone, but he gave the sections with the nipples to Christian and Susie. She didn't think it was a coincidence. She left that piece of icing at the side of her plate. A puckered raspberry-colored circle stared up at her.

"Don't you want that?" Joel asked.

Susie didn't dare eat it.

"I'll have it then." Joel opened his mouth.

Susie's fingers shook as she picked it up. Joel's lips closed around it and she felt a momentary suck as he pulled it into his mouth. Her gaze was glued to his.

"Delicious," he said. "I do like nipples."

"Stop teasing the poor girl," Bella said.

Susie was so wet between her legs, she suspected there'd be a damp patch on the vest when she stood or, worse, on the chair. Her breasts strained against the vest as if they'd been pumped. She didn't dare look down because she knew her nipples were hard spikes beneath the material. When she breathed in, the rasp of the cotton over them sent tremors racing through her, straight to her core. Every time Joel looked at her, her womb clenched in response. She wanted to kiss him, wanted to drink champagne from his mouth while he kissed her. Susie turned away from him before she exploded but Christian was staring at her as if she was the only person in the room. She sizzled.

"Shall we sit outside," Joel suggested.

Did he know she was burning up?

Christian opened the French doors and everyone spilled into the garden. The lights in the trees were already on but when Joel lit the lanterns, the breath caught in Susie's throat. It all looked so pretty. Joel worked his way back to her side.

"You look hot," he said.

Susie shivered and he laughed.

"Is that Gucci?" Bella said at Susie's shoulder.

Susie wondered what she was talking about. "What?"

"The outfit," Bella said.

"Calvin Klein." Joel nodded at the hem.

Susie looked down and saw a little tag she'd not noticed before.

"Where did you get it?" Bella asked.

"It's an…old thing," Susie said.

"Very sexy," one of Joel's colleagues whispered as he walked past carrying a bottle of brandy.

"Hands off, Brad." Joel put his arm over Susie's shoulder.

When he pulled her closer, a rush of arousal swept over her like a hot tornado. *Oh God, I'm going to come.* Susie pressed her thighs together and it made matters worse. Joel's fingers trailed over her shoulder, playing with the strap of the vest, but when Christian approached with a tray of liqueurs, Joel let her go. Susie didn't miss the glare Christian gave Joel, but she missed Joel's touch. Her shoulders slumped. What were they doing? Playing a game she didn't understand?

Susie hadn't known what liqueur to ask for so Christian had brought her a *crème de menthe.* It was one of the most delicious things she'd ever drunk. Bright green, but like soft, smooth fire running down her throat. Susie finished the glass and winced when she realized everyone else was sipping.

"I'd like to have a kiss right now," Joel murmured at her ear.

Susie surprised herself and gave him a quick kiss on the lips. Judging by the stunned look in his eyes, she'd surprised Joel as well.

"You little minx," he whispered. "As if that swift brush was enough."

Susie sank onto a seat, her legs suddenly boneless. Joel smiled and moved away to talk to Laura.

It was nearly one thirty before the last guest left. Bella. She'd clung to Christian like a leech but when he'd called her a taxi, she begrudgingly took it and glared at Susie. Susie glared back.

Joel and Christian came inside to find Susie clearing up.

"Leave it," Joel said.

"I'm only putting the food away. It's okay. You go to bed."

She was a little disappointed when they didn't offer to help, but she wrapped up the leftovers and placed them in the fridge. The dishwasher clicked as it finished its cycle, so Susie decided to empty it and put in another load.

"What the fuck is she doing?" Christian whispered. "See if you can hear her."

Joel padded naked to Christian's bedroom door. He shook his head.

"I want to sleep," Christian whined.

"Stay hard or else," Joel snapped.

"Like that's going to make me."

Joel gave a quiet chuckle.

"You really think this is a good idea?" Christian asked.

"It's going to turn her on."

"I'm not sure about that."

Christian thought Joel wasn't certain either, but knew he wouldn't admit it. If Susie had read *The Club* then she had to be interested in sexual experimentation. He knew she'd read *The Owner* after he'd found it under his bed. But reading about kinky sex, getting off reading about it and actually doing it, were not the same thing. On the other hand, maybe this had to be settled one way or the other. She was either with them or not. And it had to be both of them. That was the deal.

He hadn't liked the way Joel had spent most of the evening talking to Susie, standing close to Susie, putting his arm over Susie, paying far too much attention to Susie. The fact that Christian had a pet parasite to deal with was beside the point. He'd thought he would be the one to make the first move on her, but Joel was pushing so hard, Christian felt things slipping out of his control. A little bit of him wanted Joel to give this up and come to bed, rather than bring things to a head. Christian grimaced. Maybe that was an unfortunate turn of phrase.

"What were you up to when you ducked under the table?" Joel asked suddenly.

Christian grinned. "Kissed her thigh."

"She had my hand on one side and you on the other."

"And she didn't slap our faces?"

"See, she does want us both," Joel said.

Christian thought that was a bit of a leap. "I guess we're going to find out."

There was a creak on the stairs and Christian grabbed hold of Joel. "Bend over."

"Why me?"

"Don't argue. There's no time." Christian slapped lube on his cock. "I'm harder than you anyway."

Joel gave a loud groan as Christian's cock slid inside him.

"This time, don't come too soon, and if you do, fucking fake it," Joel muttered.

Susie yawned as she reached the top of the stairs. As her jaw closed, she heard what sounded like Joel groaning. She kept walking, thinking he'd drunk so much he was probably about to throw up. Oh God, she hoped he didn't make a mess. Then she froze. Through the open door of Christian's room, she saw Joel and Christian and they were both naked. Christian was pressed up against Joel's back and Joel was grunting.

Susie knew she should have kept moving, gone inside her room, shut the door and closed her mind but she couldn't. Her heart hammered in her chest. No longer tired, her eyes were wide open, adrenaline surging around her bloodstream. There was no way she could ignore strong, firm men's bodies united in an act of pure passion. She watched as Joel's hand wrapped around his long, thick cock. Oh God, it was beautiful. What he was doing was beautiful.

He stroked himself as Christian drove into him. In the light from the bedside lamp, Susie could see the tip of Joel's cock glistening, pearly pre-cum coating the head. Christian held Joel's hips, fingers digging into his flesh, keeping him in place. Susie swept her eyes over each man. Joel's lovely dark hair flopped forward, one hand on the bed, the other jerking his cock while his muscular legs strained to keep him upright.

Christian's eyes were closed. His dimpled ass flexed and contracted as he rammed forward, plunging into Joel. They were both moaning, groaning and each slap of sweaty flesh made Susie clench inside.

"Oh fuck, fuck," Christian gasped.

A moan erupted from Susie's throat as a shudder of pleasure ripped through her. She tried but couldn't completely smother it. She doubted they'd heard they were so wrapped in the pleasure of each other's bodies. Then she was gripped by another thought, one that drove the pleasure straight into pain and sent her heart plummeting to her stomach. They were gay. How could she be watching them and not even think of that? They weren't interested in women. They'd played with her and flirted but they didn't want her. They just wanted others to think they did.

She turned away.

"Oh Jesus," Joel gasped.

Christian changed the angle and speed of his penetration. Joel loved it when he turned on the jackhammer and he knew Joel was going to be pissed Susie hadn't come into the room. Christian could have told him she wouldn't, but there was no arguing with Joel sometimes.

"Oh God, Christian. You're killing me."

It was killing Christian. He couldn't keep it up for long. Moments after Joel stiffened beneath him, Christian came with a growl and yanked Joel upright in his arms. It felt as if his cock were shooting jets of fire. He pressed his sweaty chest against Joel's back and gulped air. They were both shaking.

After a moment, the two of them disentangled. Christian gave Joel a tender kiss and they went to the bathroom to wash.

"Sorry it didn't work out," Christian said.

Joel rubbed Christian's shoulder. "I really thought she'd come in."

"Me too," Christian lied.

Joel sighed. "Liar. You just went along with it. Why the fuck would I think she'd join us? I reckon I'm beginning to believe what you write."

Christian pulled a face.

"Though maybe I didn't get this so wrong," Joel said.

Christian looked into his lover's eyes and wondered what Joel was talking himself into now.

"I heard her give a little moan. I think you had your mind on other things," Joel said.

"You were supposed to have your mind on my great technique."

"I did." He kissed Christian. "You know I like it when you go supersonic but while you were fucking my socks off, I also had one ear on Susie and the sound she made was not— 'ugh, that's disgusting' but more 'I want some of that'."

Christian perked up. "Really? So should we knock on her door?"

"What, and stand there with our dicks in our hands, asking if she wants some?"

And all at once, Christian knew what Joel wanted to do, knew what this demonstration had been about. He wanted Susie under no illusions about their sexuality, but he wanted to be the one who approached her. Joel had given him a chance and he'd not taken it. Christian wasn't sure if he ever could.

"She has to want both of us," Christian said, but that felt weak even to him.

Joel's nod didn't reassure him.

By the time Susie had closed the door of her room, she wished she'd carried on watching them. She'd like to have seen the cum shoot from Joel's dick. Even if they'd been using her to deflect attention, they'd unwittingly made up for it with what she'd just witnessed. Susie had never been more turned-on in her life. Even if they didn't mean the little touches and the smiles they'd given her, she'd still enjoyed them. So what that it wasn't going to go any further—that was the story of her life.

She stripped off the black vest and looked down at nipples that were as hard and round as little pebbles. Her pants were soaked. She yanked them off and hid them in her bag. She had a moment's pause when she saw the erotic book *The Club* at the top because she thought she'd pushed it farther down. She'd save that for another time. She had plenty to imagine tonight. Joel kissing her. Christian stroking her.

As Susie washed her face and cleaned her teeth, all she could think about was how Christian and Joel had looked as they'd fucked. So hot and excited and sexy. She wished she'd been between them. The very thought of it, sent a spiral of desire swirling through her body, setting fire to her nerve endings like a flame thrower. The breath caught in her throat and she smiled into the mirror, wondering what she'd do if she saw one of them behind her now.

Susie's head dropped. It wasn't going to happen. They were gay and loved each other. Maybe they hadn't been using her tonight. Maybe they'd flirted, thinking they were being kind. They were probably trying to cheer her up after the comments from Belladonna. God, she was a poisonous bitch.

Susie crawled into bed naked and curled up. Why hadn't they closed the door? She thought about that for a while. Had they been too caught up in the act to remember she was around? They wanted her to understand they were gay? To see and be turned-on? Whichever was true, she was certainly turned-on.

She pushed herself up onto her hands and knees and pressed her forehead into the pillow. Susie trembled with arousal. She had a feeling she'd come the moment she touched herself, but she wanted to try to make it last. Susie slid one hand down from her breast, over the scar below her ribs and onto her stomach, nicely rounded from all the food she'd just eaten, and then, even as she told herself to hold back, her fingers crept into the damp curls between her legs.

Susie snuck one finger over the wet lips of her sex and was gripped by a powerful orgasm. For a moment she froze rigid as waves of pleasure set off on a rippling surge through her body and then she groaned and collapsed facedown. So much for making it last.

As her breathing returned to normal, she rolled onto her back and stared up into the darkness. Joel and Christian. She thought about the way they'd looked at her in the vest dress and the way they'd touched her. Maybe they weren't gay. Maybe they liked women too. Could they be bisexual? Were they both interested in her? Susie sighed. That was even worse. She didn't want to cause problems.

She was making all sorts of leaps here, making things up in her head that she wanted to be true. The absolute truth was she was about as naïve as she could be sexually and she had a horrible scar on her face. She should have said she'd been in an accident—her normal response. There was the other scar too. She touched her stomach. Susie couldn't tell the truth about that. She wanted to forget that part of her life.

Susie slipped off to sleep, thinking about her mother. A huge mistake to let her be the last conscious thought, but there was nothing Susie could do. Every time she tried to force her mind to take a different path, she found herself on the same one.

It hadn't just been an excess of alcohol with her mum. Mary Hood was a little crazy too. A lot crazy. Her dad had given up on her. He never knew what he was going to find when he came home from work and so he used to delay coming home and leave Susie to deal with everything.

Her mum had become obsessed about her fading looks. "Then stop bloody drinking!" Susie wanted to scream but never did because she knew it would make no difference. She didn't even know why her dad had said she was prettier than her mum. It was cruel. But he'd planted the seeds and her mother fed them, growing more and more unkind in the way she spoke to Susie and treated her. Mike tried to reason with her, but how can you fight madness with reason? Then one night her mum snapped and came at her with the knife.

When Susie and Mike had reached the hospital, Mike abandoned the car and bundled her inside. He pushed her through to the reception desk and the woman told them to take a seat. Mike had pulled the towel from Susie's face, and said, "No. Get a doctor. She needs seeing now."

The result was over two hundred stitches, and scars inside that she'd keep for the rest of her life.

Chapter Fourteen

ഇ

Joel sat bolt upright in bed.

"What the fuck was that?"

"What?" Christian groaned and rolled over, taking the cover with him.

They heard Susie cry out and then Christian sat up as well. Joel was the first to leap out of bed.

"Put something on," Christian yelled at him.

"Fuck that."

Joel flung open the door and rushed onto the landing. He stopped, listening. Christian came barreling up behind and crashed into his back.

"No, please don't," Susie gasped. "Please, don't."

Joel burst into her room. She thrashed around in the bed under the covers, but there was no one with her. Christian switched on the bedside light.

"Nightmare," Joel whispered in relief, and knelt at her side. "Susie, it's okay," he soothed. "Wake up, sweetheart."

Christian dropped a robe on his back and Joel pulled it on. She was whimpering, her eyes fluttering beneath the lids. Christian crouched next to him and pulled on his own robe. Susie was still asleep but crying. Joel could feel the tears on her face as he stroked her cheek.

"No," Susie gasped, and opened her eyes.

"Susie, you're okay," Joel said. "You're having a nightmare, angel."

He took hold of her hand on top of the duvet and Susie clutched at his fingers. Her eyes closed again. Soon her breathing eased.

"Jesus," Christian whispered. "That was a bit intense. Think she's okay now?"

"She's holding on like I'm the only anchor in a flood." Joel lifted their hands to show Christian.

"Ah."

"Christ, I was scared," Joel whispered. "I thought she was being attacked."

They watched her sleep for several minutes.

"Come back to bed," Christian said.

"I'm going to stay with her a while and make sure she's fast off."

"The amount she drank she should be."

"I want to watch her."

"Okay."

Joel knew from Christian's tone he wasn't okay, but he squeezed Joel's shoulder and left the room. Joel stared at Susie in the half-light. She looked younger, smaller somehow. Her lips were apart and he could hear her breathing. He moved closer and her sweet exhale hit his face. Joel wanted her so badly, he ached. His balls were hard, his cock even harder and Christian lay a room away waiting for him, trusting him.

It looked like Susie was naked. Joel could see no sign of bra straps or a nightdress. If he eased the blue-checked duvet down an inch or so, he could see if he was right. Her breasts had teased him all night, swaying loose under the vest she'd worn, her perky nipples begging to be tweaked. More than tweaked. Now he had a chance to see whether they were as beautiful as he imagined.

Only Joel couldn't do it. Susie's grip eased. He slipped his hand from hers, got to his feet and went back to the other bedroom. Christian lay facedown, snoring quietly. Joel stood there, looking and thinking then turned to cross over the landing.

Christian opened his eyes and watched Joel leave. He knew what was going to happen. Joel was tired of waiting for him to make a move so he was going to make it himself. Christian was torn between relief and disappointment. Disappointment won and a single tear rolled down his cheek and sank into the pillow.

Joel had no idea what he was doing. Was this crazy or the only way to make things happen? Christian would be drawing his pension before he ventured past holding Susie's hand or kissing her knee where he couldn't be seen. He'd never pluck up enough courage to suggest she join the two of them in bed. Only Joel wasn't sure he knew how to arrange that either. Different in a club or a bar when a woman's behavior might indicate she was up for it, but Susie wasn't like any woman he'd met before. That was the attraction and the problem.

He only knew for certain that he didn't want to leave her on her own. Joel shrugged off his robe and sat on the bed. Even if she wanted him, he couldn't make love to her. No rubbers. He and Christian had been tested regularly before they'd met. They hadn't bothered since. They were faithful, at least as far as male partners were concerned. Women were different. With women they always wore condoms.

Joel had fucked a few women when Christian had thought he was working late. He knew he should have been honest with Christian, that's what they'd agreed. But after Christian had told him that he loved him, Joel had been afraid of hurting Christian by telling him he still needed sex with someone else, even if that someone else was a woman. It would be like telling Christian his love wasn't enough. Shit, well, it wasn't but Joel couldn't be that cruel. He *did* love Christian but he wouldn't tell him. Couldn't tell him. If he did, he'd be handing Christian the power to hurt him just as Christian had handed that power to him.

It would have been so much easier if Joel didn't care for him. He sighed. Joel knew he was fucked up. His parents had done a real good job. And now Susie had come into his life and thrown everything upside down. Joel had imagined she'd keep Christian warm after he'd gone but Christian wasn't going to make a move to ensure that happened so Joel had to. If they managed a ménage before he went back to the States, then that was a bonus. But as Joel sat looking at Susie, he wasn't thinking of three of them now, he was thinking of two.

He reached out to stroke Susie's hair. She was so soft and cute, and she'd been hurt. Joel knew that was part of her attraction, at least as far as he was concerned. Damaged goods like him. Was he going to make that worse, pulling her into a relationship that was in no way conventional? Maybe he ought to leave her alone and get back in bed with Christian. But knowing what he should do and knowing what he wanted to do, were at war in his head. Joel wanted her for Christian, wanted her for both of them, but right at that moment he ached to hold her body against his. He wanted her—now. His cock twitched in agreement.

The bedside light still shone. Joel watched his hand reach out and pull the duvet back from Susie's shoulders. He drew it slowly down to her hip. She had her back toward him. No bra. No nightgown. He stopped breathing. Her back was so smooth, the sloping curve from her ribs up to her hip a gentle dip he longed to kiss. Before he could talk himself out of it, Joel lay next to her. He wanted to pull her into his arms and look after her, more than that, but for now it was enough to lie there. Joel could smell his soap on her skin and beneath that the delicate scent of Susie. Beneath that, the scent of sex.

She turned and her eyes were wide open. Joel started to say something, to apologize, and changed his mind. Susie's hand crept toward his chest. When she touched him, he made a pathetic, strangled noise in his throat. *Shit, can't I even manage a manly growl?* Her fingers feathered his collarbone, traced his abs, ran along his ribs and swept back to his nipples. Joel had definitely forgotten how to breathe. Her hand moved higher, up his sternum to his neck, over his chin to his lips. One finger slipped into his mouth and he sucked it greedily before she pulled free and put the same finger into her mouth, tasting him.

"Geez, Susie," he whispered. "You sure you're awake?"

She smiled and Joel could stand it no longer. His mouth zeroed in on its target, his lips touched hers and he sobbed in his throat for the softness, the sweetness of her. Her mouth opened and his tongue surged forward, exploring, pulsing, plundering because he couldn't get enough of her. But he didn't touch her. He wanted only their lips to be joined, wanted nothing to interfere with this moment. He nibbled her lip, soothed with his tongue, kissed in every way he knew and every second that passed wound him tighter. When they finally broke apart, they were both panting.

His fingers pulled at the remains of the duvet lying between them and he kicked it off the bed. *Ah God, she was so beautiful.* Joel wanted to tell her that and he couldn't speak. He reached to stroke her breast and changed his mind, wanted his lips to have the first touch. He still couldn't quite believe this was happening. Joel lowered his head and ran his wet tongue around her breast, circling toward the jewel at the center and when he reached it, he suckled gently, pulled a cry from her lips. Joel nudged her onto her back and leaned over, his mouth laving each breast in turn until that wasn't enough and he wrapped his hands around them, squeezed and teased while Susie writhed beneath him. Joel pressed his body alongside hers, rocked his aching cock against her hip and held her close while he brought himself back under control.

Hopeless quest. He had to have more. He was incandescent with lust for her and forgot all about the man he loved, lying alone in the next room.

Susie had watched Joel leave the first time and then felt him come back. When he'd pulled the duvet down, she'd known no matter what she'd wondered, what she'd seen him do with Christian, Joel wanted her. His kiss was electric, his touch sent lightning bolts of lust slamming through her. When he kissed her breasts, Susie's muscles clenched and a flood of cream soaked her thighs. The feel of his body lying against hers was almost too much for her overactive heart. It pounded so hard, Susie felt sure Joel could hear it.

Only what the hell was she doing? Christian lay a few feet away. She glanced toward the door.

"What is it?" Joel whispered.

"Is this okay with Christian? I mean I thought the two of you were..."

"Gay?"

She nodded.

"We're bi and yes, Christian's fine about this."

He pressed his face into the curve of her neck and Susie's heart lurched as her pussy muscles clenched. So this was full-blown, mind-altering, body-energizing lust? She needed to touch him.

Susie slid her hand between their sweaty bodies and tentatively reached his cock. A single stroke with her finger made him catch his breath. The knowledge that he felt the same as her made her brave. She wrapped her hand around his thick girth and squeezed. Joel blinked and moaned.

"You're hot," she said in surprise, and he chuckled.

Not just hot, he was really hard and big, yet the skin on his cock felt so soft, like satin. Susie had caught occasional glimpses of her brothers' dicks when they'd not locked doors they should have, but this was the closest she'd ever been to one, the first she'd ever touched. She ran her thumb up to the head and it was wet just like it said in the books.

"Can I look?" she asked.

"I thought you were."

"Close up."

He sighed. "Sure."

Susie scooted down the bed and lay on her side. His cock was beautiful, a rock-hard, thick-veined rod, rising out of a nest of wiry, black curls. She trailed one finger from the base of his balls to the crest. A gleaming pearl of moisture rested at the tip. A precious liquid jewel. Susie scooped it up and licked her finger. Salty. Joel's taste in her mouth. He groaned again, his fingers playing with her hair.

"Christ, Susie. Be careful."

She didn't want to be careful. She leaned forward and ran her tongue over the crown of his cock as if she were licking an ice-cream then put her mouth around him, gently settling her teeth behind the ridge below the top. Joel was groaning and gasping so he must like what she was doing, though Susie had no real idea of how to do this. She'd seen pictures of erections, and she'd read about blowjobs. How difficult could it be? She pushed down with her mouth.

"Susie, Susie. You're going to have to stop that." Joel tightened his grasp on her hair.

She moved her head away and looked up at him, a thread of saliva still attaching her to his dick.

"Do you want me to stop?"

"I'm going to come any moment," he said.

She smiled, turning from his flushed face, and took as much of him into her mouth as she could, letting him press into the back of her throat. She put her hands around what she couldn't get into her mouth, pumping and squeezing at the bottom of his shaft. Unsure what to do with her tongue, she licked, sucked and teased and felt him throbbing, heard him gasping.

Joel stiffened, his fingers slid to her shoulders and he spurted into the back of her throat. Susie swallowed the salty emission, gulped it down, loved it, wanted more, milked every last drop from him until he slumped back on the bed, his arm thrown across his face.

He didn't speak, he hardly moved and Susie had a moment of doubt. Maybe she'd done it wrong and freaked him out. Oh God, had she hurt him? Sucked too hard? Should have blown? It was blowjob, right? Maybe she ought to go home. Susie sat up and swung her feet off the bed. Joel's hand shot out and grabbed her arm.

"Where are you going?"

"Home."

He leaned up, his mouth open in astonishment. "What?"

"Did I do it wrong?" Susie whispered. "Did I hurt you? I'm sorry. I've never done it before."

"Christ." Joel pulled her into her arms, landing kisses all over her face. "Sweetheart, you didn't hurt me. It was fantastic. You've blown me away, literally."

"Is that why it's called a blowjob?"

Joel laughed. "Exactly why. You drove me crazy. Now I'm going to do the same to you."

With his head next to hers on the pillow, Joel ran one hand down Susie's neck and over her breast. Her nipples came to attention. His hand swept over her stomach and then slipped between her legs.

"God, Susie, you're soaking wet."

He stroked her swollen folds and slipped one long, thick finger inside her. Susie moaned. She was going to come as fast as a bullet.

"So soft and tight."

Two fingers. She gasped at the intrusion, groaned as he twisted his fingers. Joel pressed his face into her neck as his hand slid deeper into her body. Sparks turned to flames and they grew, spreading through every part of her. When he touched the hard nub of her clit, Susie fell apart. One slight touch enough to make her clench around his fingers, her muscles contracting in a dance of delight. She wanted more even as the pleasure faded.

"So quick, you little minx," he whispered in her ear. "And I thought I was fast."

He withdrew his fingers and slipped them first into his mouth and then hers. Susie caught hold of his wrist. Kissed his palm, nipped the side of his thumb with her teeth.

"Joel, make love to me."

He morphed into a statue. "I can't."

Susie tried to pull away but Joel kept her close.

"Hey, stop it. Listen to me. I didn't say I don't want to. I can't think of anything I'd rather do at this moment, but I can't. I don't have any condoms."

"Well, I'm on the Pill. To keep my periods regular. Does that make a difference?"

She felt him shudder against her.

"Oh Christ. My willpower just evaporated like a drop of water on a hotplate. You really are going to kill me."

Chapter Fifteen

ဢ

Joel wasn't sure whether he'd just heard the best news in his life or the worst. The rubbers weren't only about birth control. He'd made a promise to Christian of no sex with women without a condom. It was a rule that shouldn't be broken, except Joel had never wanted to break a rule more. He was amazed to find himself hard again. It had to be mind over matter. The thought of burying his cock in Susie's hot cunt enough to make him rigid.

It probably didn't matter that Susie was on the Pill because Joel doubted he had any little swimmers left. He'd already come with Christian then again in her mouth, so expecting his balls to produce another load so soon would be pushing it. Not that his dick cared. Joel thought about Christian lying across the landing and felt a pang of guilt. More than a pang. But if Christian was in here, he'd be doing the same thing. Joel wished the guy would walk in and join them but suspected there was a greater chance of Christian turning into a neat freak.

Joel held Susie in his arms and rocked her. He'd never fucked a woman without a condom. He wondered what it would feel like, the heat, the softness around his cock, the tight clasp. He shouldn't do it now. Everything told him not to, except for his dick that sent a stream of messages to his brain urging action...action...action.

He ran a line of slow, wet kisses from her lips, over her chin, down her throat, veering off to each breast for a long hard suck before he continued down. Susie's hands twisted in his hair and he could feel her dithering between pulling him back and pushing him on. Joel smiled against her bellybutton. She bucked her hips when he played in the little dip with his tongue. Her skin trembled and fluttered under his mouth and she made these little breathy moans. Oh God, he wanted to fuck her so much, make her come, make her scream his name.

Joel pushed her thighs apart and buried his head between her legs, lapping the cream from her delicate folds. He explored the soft lips of her sex, slid into the creases, ran his tongue in a circle around the most delicate part of her, the tight rosy bud of her clit and bit down gently. Susie writhed and moaned, clutching his hair, his back, any part of him she could reach. He flicked her tiny hard-on with the tip of his tongue and slid his hands up to her breasts, cupping each. As he fucked her with his mouth, making long and slow thrusts with his tongue, he drank in her honeyed essence and felt her come against his lips.

"Oh my God," Susie moaned.

Joel raised his head. "No, that was me," he teased.

He moved up the bed and stroked her as she came down, watching as she softened and melted like butter. He smiled at the rise and fall of her chest. Joel was desperate to get inside her, but he wouldn't rush this. If she said no, he'd walk away. A tiny bit of him wanted her to say no, wanted her to save him from himself, but she opened her eyes and looked at him and Joel fell straight into a deep hole with no way to climb out.

"I had no idea," she whispered. "Oh God, I feel like I'm falling apart."

"You are so sexy." He kissed her nose. "I love watching you unravel."

"Will you make love to me?" she asked. "Please."

What hope did he have of saying no? Joel positioned himself between her thighs and Susie slid her legs around him. He nudged at her opening with the tip of his penis and slid a little way inside. She was so warm and wet and soft. He groaned and edged a little deeper but could feel the resistance against his entry and heard her give a tiny mew of discomfort.

"Relax, angel. You're so tight. I don't want to hurt you."

"Joel?"

"What?"

He was sliding backward and forward gently. No more than his tip in and out, only it was driving him insane because he wanted to ram himself inside her. In a minute, that was what he was going to do. He didn't think anything could stop him.

"I haven't done this before."

Except that.

"Oh shit."

He tried to move off but Susie wrapped her legs tighter around him.

"No, don't stop. Please. I want you to."

Joel hesitated. "Are you sure? Christ, Susie. I—"

"Please."

"Let me go get some lube. I don't want to hurt you."

"Okay. But...promise to come back?"

"I promise."

He got to his feet and once he was on the landing, he looked at Christian's door and hesitated. A good guy would have gone and lay next to his partner. The bad guy turned and went to his room. Moments later Joel was back in bed with Susie.

Squeezing out a walnut-sized blob of gel, he rubbed it around his dick. It was still going to hurt her, but at least he'd done what he could. He lay on his back.

"Sit on top of me to start. You can control what's happening. Take things at your pace. Okay?"

Joel clutched her hips as she took hold of his cock.

"Are you sure you'll fit?" Susie whispered. "You're really big."

Joel groaned. "I can't do this slowly if you're going to make me laugh."

He had his eyes fixed on hers. As she made a tentative move up and down, Joel struggled to keep control, his face taut in concentration. Susie took a deep breath and pressed a little harder.

"Oh God," she moaned.

"Are you okay?"

"I can't do this myself."

Joel rolled them both over in one graceful movement and held himself up on his elbows.

"Ready?"

She nodded.

"It'll only hurt for a minute, angel. Then I'll make it good for you."

Joel knew he just had to do this, push inside her only he didn't want to hurt her. But she lay there looking up at him, wanting him and the barrier in his heart finally gave way. Joel pressed into her, kept pushing and surged into her sweet, wet heat with a groan. Susie gave a little gulp but then smiled.

"Okay?" Joel gasped.

"I've changed my mind."

He gaped at her and then laughed.

"Oh that feels nice when you laugh," she said. "You sort of jiggle."

"Susie, you are something else."

Joel started slow and gentle, but even as he tried to rein himself back, he knew he couldn't. He increased the speed and power of his thrust and began to surge into her, long, deep drives as if he were trying to reach her heart. The feeling of her clenching around his cock sheer magic, as if he were wrapped in wet satin. Her hands were all over him and each touch wound him tighter. Joel felt like he was racing his car down a mountain, going too fast, but the thrill of the ride overwhelming the need for caution. He'd crash and burn but he'd go happy.

150

As he slammed his whole length inside her, his hips clashing with hers, Susie gripped him tighter. It had hurt for a moment when he'd pushed in, but the pain lay enmeshed with acute pleasure and now all she felt was excitement. As he ground himself into her, the hair surrounding his cock rubbed at her clit, bringing her off again. She came just before he did, like a flame taking paper, an explosive burst of brightness. Susie felt Joel's warm spurts spray into her and sighed with pleasure as their bodies fused together.

Joel smothered her with kisses, the wet, silken glide of his tongue pulling a ragged groan from her throat before he collapsed at her side. Susie could feel his cum dripping down the inside of her thighs and all she could think was how she wished she hadn't waited so long to do this, how much she adored the feel of a man's body against hers, inside hers, how lucky she was to have this at all.

Joel nestled up to her, cuddling her in his arms.

"Are you okay?" he asked, brushing a damp tendril of hair from her cheek.

"Exhausted."

He laughed. Then leaned forward, cupped her face and kissed her gently on the lips.

"Thank you," he said.

"What for?"

"For that gift. It *is* my birthday today, but I don't celebrate it. I don't have very good memories of birthdays. The cake was as far as I'd go. But this was something special, Susie. I'll never forget it. You've worked a miracle because I'm going to think about my birthday in a different way now. I've never made love to a woman without wearing a rubber. I've never made love to a virgin before. I feel honored you wanted me. Making love with you was wonderful, like I was being wrapped in something soft and special. There was no risk to you, I swear."

He kissed her on the nose. "I'd die rather than hurt you or Christian."

Shit, Christian. Susie immediately felt guilty. "What about Christian?"

Joel tensed. "What about him?"

"Is he going to be upset?"

"I don't know."

"I know you're lovers," she said carefully.

"Yeah. You watched us."

Damn.

"So what did you think?" Joel asked, twining a strand of her hair in his fingers.

"That you both looked beautiful. It turned me on."

He smiled.

"Christian's got a lovely butt," Susie said. "All firm and muscly."

Joel laughed. "Yeah."

"Maybe you should go back to him," she said.

Joel exhaled noisily. "I don't want to leave you."

"You're going to keep me awake if you stay here. It's okay, Joel. I know you're a pair."

He hesitated as though he was going to tell her something then kissed her on the lips and swung his legs out of bed. He pulled the duvet back over her and tucked her in. Susie had to fight not to cry. The tenderness in that action brought a lump the size of an orange to her throat. Joel closed the door behind him and Susie took a gulp of air. Everything had changed.

Joel paused before going back to Christian, wondering if he was doing the right thing. His heart was torn. He wanted to stay the night with Susie but figured that would hurt Christian more. When he pushed open the bedroom door, he saw Christian lying curled up with his back to him. Joel went into the bathroom, cleaned up and then climbed into bed. He snuggled behind Christian, wrapping his arm around his chest and pulling himself tight to Christian's back.

"Did you fuck her?" Christian asked.

Joel froze.

"Yeah, I can smell you did."

"I love you," Joel said.

Christian recoiled as though Joel had stabbed him, shooting to the edge of the bed before he turned to face him. "*Now* you say that? Now that you've fucked her, you tell me you love me? I wait and I wait and now you tell me? You bastard."

"I'm sorry."

"Couldn't you have waited to say that to me? It's your fucking birthday. I thought... Couldn't you have waited?"

The truth was that no, Joel didn't think he could have waited but he knew he'd hurt Christian in a way he hadn't imagined.

"Did you use a condom?" Christian asked quietly.

Fuck. "No."

Christian groaned. "You fucking prick." He shot to his feet and began to pace.

"It's okay. She's on the Pill," Joel said.

"Fucking hell, Joel. It isn't fucking okay, you stupid wanker."

Joel was bewildered. He needed to make this right but he didn't know what to say.

"She's on the Pill to sort out her periods," he blurted. "She'd never slept with anyone before."

Oh Christ, well that would have been better kept quiet.

"She's not sleeping with anyone now, is she?" Christian snapped. "Fuck off back to her."

Joel sat up. "I want to be with you."

"I know you're fucking lying. You can't look me in the eye."

Joel's mouth tightened. How come he was the villain? "I'm not lying, Christian. I want to be with you."

"Well, right this moment I don't want to be with you."

"Go in there and fuck her yourself, then," Joel retorted. "That's what we were going to do. I just sped things up."

Christian paused in his stomping. "Don't you try and tell me you did that for me."

"You'd never have gotten around to it. We'd have spent weeks thinking about it being the three of us, about how we'd ask her but we never would have."

Joel didn't think he'd seen Christian this angry. He didn't know what to say to him.

"This isn't supposed to be about you fucking her and me fucking her," Christian said. "This is supposed to be the three of us."

"Christian, you're living in cuckoo land. What are the chances of her agreeing to that?"

"But you've not given her a chance. You stepped in and took her. Just fuck off to her room and leave me alone."

He turned his back on Joel.

"What are you so angry about, Christian? The fact that I fucked her or the fact that I fucked her first?"

Christian didn't answer.

Joel waited a moment and then got out of bed and went to his room. No change about birthdays being bad news. One of the best nights of his life had turned into the worst. He was furious with Christian for ruining everything and furious with himself for losing self-control around Susie. Joel sat with his head in his hands. He had no right to be pissed at Christian. There was only one villain here.

Chapter Sixteen

ဢ

When Christian woke, he reached automatically for Joel, felt an empty bed and remembered what had happened. He bit his lip as he thought about what he'd said. Christian had lashed out because he had a little green monster poking holes in his heart. Every time he looked at Joel, he still couldn't quite believe the guy wanted to be with him. Maybe he didn't anymore. Christian thought about going to Joel's room and apologizing, but then he didn't know that was where Joel would be. Maybe he'd done what Christian had shouted and returned to Susie.

Christian showered, dressed, and as he came out of the bedroom, he glanced at the closed door of the guest room. His heart felt heavy, as though it weighed twice as much as it should.

Downstairs, he smelled coffee brewing, and the kitchen table was laid for two. The Sunday paper had moved from the doormat to the table and four croissants waited under clingfilm. All traces of the previous night's dinner party had gone. The kitchen sparkled. A vase sat in the center of the table, holding two wilting yellow flowers. Dandelions. Christian smiled.

Then Joel walked in, dressed in his black jeans and a white T-shirt. They stood and looked at each other then at the table.

"I checked her room. She's gone," Joel said. "She must have done this before she left."

Christian had so wanted Joel to have set the table because that would have meant things were okay. He walked over to the coffee machine where a piece of paper lay.

"She's left a note. *I'm sorry. I don't want to come between you.* Shit."

Joel sat at the table and put his head in his hands. "I've fucked this up."

Christian knew Joel was giving him the chance to blame him so they could make up, but before he could move to Joel's side, Joel got to his feet and rushed out of the room. Christian stayed in the kitchen. After a couple of minutes, he heard the front door slam. Christian swept his hand across the table and sent everything flying.

* * * * *

Susie was a methodical worker. She peeled the potatoes and parsnips and set them on to boil for a few minutes before tipping them into the roasting dish. Pete and Mike hadn't yet made an appearance. Her father sat in the garden, reading the Sunday newspaper. They always wanted the same dinner, the one Susie's mum had cooked before she'd gone loopy. Roast beef, Yorkshire pudding, roast potatoes and parsnips, carrots and peas. And lashings of thick gravy.

Cooking helped Susie calm down. Her mind was awash, confused thoughts tumbling over and over. She'd left the guys' house early that morning because she couldn't face Christian. Guilt overwhelmed her because she'd let him down by sleeping with Joel. She'd wanted to speak to Joel but didn't feel she had the right. She'd probably messed up everything between them. Her heart ached at the thought of not seeing either of them again, but Susie couldn't stand the idea that she'd hurt anyone. She'd messed this up and the best thing to do was back off. She flinched when she heard a door slam upstairs. One of her brothers was up.

Mike slammed into the kitchen. He looked awful, his eyes bloodshot and his short, thick hair sticking up all over the place. Dragged through a hedge backward didn't come near it. Susie suspected he'd gone to bed in the clothes he was wearing.

"Do you want a cup of tea?" she asked.

"Please," he muttered. "Seen Pete?"

"No. He's not up yet."

"More like he's not back yet."

Susie stayed quiet. All three men in the house had terrible tempers. It didn't take much for them to verbally take it out on her. They'd never hit her. But even Mike, who she got on with the best, could be very touchy. She handed him a mug of tea.

"Thanks, Susie. Did you have a good night?"

She glanced at him in surprise. "Yes, it was great."

"Don't tell Dad how much they paid you. He ought not to be taking so much off you. It isn't fair."

"Well, I'm not sure I'm going back again."

Mike stared at her. "Why? What happened? Did they sack you?"

"Not exactly, but I really need to find a full-time job."

He continued to look at her for a moment and then nodded.

"What time's dinner?"

"One." It always was.

"I'm going to have a bath."

Susie had the meal on the table before she called her father and Mike. There was still no sign of Pete, which was unusual.

"Where's Pete?" she asked.

Her father Harry looked at Mike whose hands gripped his knife and fork as if he wanted to stab someone. Pete, Susie guessed, and wondered what her brother had done. They were halfway through the meal when the front door slammed and Pete strolled in, whistling. Mike rose to his feet.

"Mike!" Harry said in a sharp tone.

Mike sat down. Pete had a smirk on his face. He looked as though he'd won the lottery.

"Morning," he said, dropping onto a chair and reaching for the meat.

"Have a good night?" Mike snapped.

Susie felt her insides shrink a little. There was trouble brewing. She kept her head down and ate faster. Pete spooned roast potatoes onto his plate.

"Not bad." Pete grinned.

Like someone had lit the twisted paper at the top of a firework, Mike exploded and launched himself at Pete. As Pete's chair tipped, the table cloth went too and everything on the table slid to the floor. Mike hammered at Pete's face and Susie flinched as she heard the blows connecting. She looked toward her father, who'd lifted his plate to safety.

"Pack it in," Harry shouted.

They took no notice.

"Mike, for fuck's sake, get off," Pete yelled.

"Why did you do it? Why her?" Mike pinned him down and thumped him in his ribs.

"She asked for it."

That comment left Pete with a bloody nose. But Pete was smaller than Mike and getting hurt, and much as she liked Mike best, she didn't want this to go too far. She wrapped her arms around her oldest brother's back.

"Mike, don't."

"Susie, stay out of it," her father shouted.

Pete tried to wriggle free.

"You knew I wanted her," Mike roared. "But you just fucking couldn't leave her alone, could you? What is it with you? Trying to prove you're a better man?"

"I fucking am a better man," Pete yelled back.

Susie lurched forward on Mike's back as her brother launched a fist at Pete's face. The crunch made Susie shudder. She gave up trying to stop Mike and switched over to trying to protect Pete. She dropped from Mike's back and leaned between him and Pete, who was snuffling and wiping the blood from his face.

"Susie, get out of the fucking way." Mike grabbed her and yanked.

Susie caught her foot on Pete, fell against Mike and then everything became confused. The three of them struggled in a mess of food and broken chairs. Susie saw Pete's fist coming and even though she knew he didn't intend to hit her, his knuckles caught the side of the face. Her head flew back to the edge of the table and everything went black.

She came around to find herself lying on the couch with a damp cloth on her forehead. Pete's battered face was next to hers.

"Sorry, Susie," he said. "I didn't mean to hit you."

"I know."

She sat up, groaned and pulled away the cloth. A sharp spike of pain shot through her head.

"Dad made Mike clean up the mess since he started it."

Susie thought it had started long before the first punch. "What were you fighting about?"

"Shannon Nelson."

"Ah." Shannon had been out with Mike for several months before she'd dumped him. Mike's stories about housewives requiring personal plumbing services in addition to the work he actually did, having finally reached her ears. But Mike had convinced himself that he'd let "the one" slip away and still talked about Shannon as if she were Kate Moss. The last few weeks he'd been seeing her again. If Pete had made a move on her, he'd been asking to get thumped.

"What did you do?" Susie asked, looking at Pete's swollen nose and cut lip.

"Slept with Shannon."

"Oh Pete."

Her brother smiled and winced. "I didn't think he was going out with her anymore, so I didn't see a problem."

Susie stared at him.

"Okay, well I did. But she was there in the bar and we got talking. Mike was eyeing up some other bird, and when Shannon said she'd always fancied me in my uniform, I knew I was in."

"Yes, in trouble. So what are you going to do now?"

"I suppose I shouldn't see her again. I think Mike's cracked one of my fucking ribs, the bastard. God, he's welcome to her. She's not worth this sort of trouble. She was only a quick fuck after all."

Susie's heart felt as though Pete had reached through her ribs and squeezed it hard. Was that all she'd been to Joel?

"Maybe I'll just be more careful next time and not get caught." Pete winked at her.

Susie finished clearing up the mess in the dining room. Mike had only half done it before he'd gone to the gym. Probably to vent his temper on the punch bag. As she worked, she thought about what happened between her and Joel and what Pete had done to Mike. Susie wanted to believe she meant more to Joel than a quick fuck, but her heart told her it couldn't be more. He and Christian were together. They lived together. They were lovers and she'd interfered with that.

Even so, a little bit of her hoped that Joel would phone but he didn't. She'd blown everything, including her job.

By the time she went to bed that night, Susie knew who she needed to speak to. Christian. He was the one who'd been hurt. She wanted to tell him that she was sorry. Susie was horrified to think he and Joel might have gone at it like her brothers. She wasn't worth fighting over. Though deep down, in a tiny secret part of her heart, Susie didn't regret what had happened. Joel had loved her while she was in his arms, even if he hadn't afterward. She hadn't even thought about her scar while Joel held her. It had been as though it didn't exist.

Chapter Seventeen

ဢ

When Christian heard the knock at the door on Monday morning, he hoped Joel had come back to make up and forgotten his keys. They hadn't spoken on Sunday. The night had been spent in separate rooms and Joel had gone off to work this morning without waking him. Christian's life had imploded. All because he was too lazy to clean up after himself. If he'd kept the house straight, they'd never have needed a cleaner.

He flung open the door to find Susie on the doorstep. Her pale face looking even more wan because of the large bruise above her cheek. What the hell had happened?

"Joel's at work," Christian said. Christ, what had made him say that? Of course Joel was at work. She knew that.

"I didn't come to see Joel."

Christian's pulse leapt. She'd come to see him? "Why is your face bruised?" He hoped it was nothing Joel did.

Susie's hand rose to her cheek. "My brother hit me. An accident. Can I come in?"

Christian moved to one side. She wore a blue, flowered sundress and those sandals with yellow and white leather flowers across her toes. Christian thought of the great time they'd had in Greenwich and felt a tug of longing in his groin. *Pathetic, ever-hopeful cock.*

He walked through to the kitchen.

"Coffee?" he said.

"A glass of water would be nice, thank you."

He filled it from the fridge dispenser and sat at the table, gesturing for Susie to join him. She perched on the edge of the seat and fingered the glass, twisting it in her fingers.

"How come your brother hit you?"

"I got between him and my other brother. They were fighting about a woman. Mike was jealous of Pete."

Christian didn't miss her worried glance. "You think I'd hit Joel?"

She took a deep breath. "I'm sorry, Christian."

"Why should you be sorry?"

"I upset the balance."

He nodded and let a few seconds pass before he spoke again, pushing the words past the lump in his throat. "Why did you pick Joel?"

"I-I didn't. It just happened. He wanted me and I..." Her voice trailed away.

"Didn't you want me?" Christian asked quietly.

Susie raised her eyes to his. "What?"

"I thought you liked me. We got on well, I thought—"

"I do like you," Susie said.

Christian could feel his heart hammering in his chest. If he didn't say something now, he'd always regret a missed opportunity.

"I want you too."

He waited to see what she'd say. When she stood, he thought she was going to walk out but she didn't. She came to the other side of the table and sat on his lap. Her arms moved around his neck and she snuggled against his chest.

Christian laid his hand across her back, pulling her closer. His other hand slid onto her knee and moved under her dress. Susie's head came up and his lips came down. He kissed her gently at first with a languid sensuality, whisper touches along her mouth until he allowed his tongue to brush her lips.

Christian explored tentatively, afraid she might change her mind and bolt.

He loved the hot, damp taste of her. She was so warm and soft in his arms. No hard muscles, only rounded curves. Christian found himself growing increasingly hot and hard. His hand slid farther up her thigh, and when he reached the line of her panties, he released a trembling breath into her mouth. As he ran his finger along the edge of the material, she groaned. One fingertip slipped underneath, touched damp curls and he kissed her harder. *Oh God, is this really happening?*

As her legs moved apart, Christian's fingers moved inside her panties. She gasped into his mouth and tensed as he eased one finger between her soft folds. Susie made a tiny sound and melted into him. She was already soaking, her clit a little rounded button, waiting to be pressed. As Christian rubbed his finger over it, she jerked in his arms and he felt the contractions surge against his hand. If he'd been in any doubt over whether she wanted this, he wasn't now.

"Susie." He pulled away from her lips and breathed her name into her beautiful hair.

Susie tingled all over. That felt so good, his firm finger playing with her. She'd come so fast, only what would he think of her? She'd sat on his lap and let him put his hand in her pants. That hadn't been quite what she'd intended as an apology. Only maybe it had worked. Christian held her as though he'd never let her go. She'd been brave and now she had to be even braver. Christian was shy, that's why he'd held back, why Joel had stepped in.

She reached to stroke the stubble on Christian's cheeks.

"I haven't shaved," he said.

"Can I do it?" Susie ran her fingers over the creases in his forehead.

"It's not an electric razor."

"I'll be careful. You can trust me."

Susie eased off his lap and held out her hand. Christian took it and she pulled him to his feet, led him upstairs and through his bedroom into the bathroom. Susie tried not to look at the hard-on he sported, outlined behind the material of his pants. She'd felt it pressing into her as she sat on his lap.

This hadn't been what she'd intended either, but maybe it would make things right between them. If they'd both slept with her, one wasn't more to blame than the other. There would be no room for hard feelings between them. But Susie wasn't doing it just for that. She wanted Christian. Joel had awakened something inside her, the knowledge that she could be attractive, the belief she was desirable. He'd given her the taste for sex.

"Sit on the edge of the bath," she said.

Susie had seen her brothers do this often enough. It was a matter of being careful. She squirted a dollop of shaving foam onto her hand and rubbed her palms together before smoothing them over Christian's face. With the tips of her fingers, she caressed his skin, moving over his cheeks, under his nose, across his square chin and down his neck. Christian's hands stayed fixed to the side of the bath, his knuckles white.

Susie put a tiny spot of white foam on the end of his nose and smiled.

She drew the razor over his cheek, slowly following each line and contour until she reached the limit of the bristles on his neck. His Adam's apple moved up and down and Susie smiled. She rinsed off the razor and started another path over his face.

"How does that feel?" she asked.

"Am I bleeding?"

"No," she said indignantly.

"Then it feels lovely."

As she leaned forward to make sure she captured every tiny bristle, Christian's hands slid under the back of her dress onto her bottom. She shivered as his fingers swept over the rounded cheeks of her ass.

"This feels even lovelier," he whispered.

"You're putting me off," Susie said.

She pulled away and went back to the wash basin, picking up a flannel and soaking it. When she turned, Christian still sat there, watching. But the top button of his trousers was undone and the zip pulled down a couple of inches. He looked so sexy, the breath caught in her throat.

Susie wiped the warm flannel over his face and Christian closed his eyes and sighed in pleasure. She removed every trace of foam and then bent to inspect her work. It looked like a pretty good shave.

"Okay, you can open your eyes now," she said.

Christian blinked and pouted. "I thought you were going to be naked."

He stood and went over to the mirror, running his hand over his jaw.

"Good job. I think it's only fair I should reciprocate."

"Hey, I already did my legs. The advert says they should be like silk. Want to check?"

"Yes, but I wasn't thinking of your legs."

Susie gulped. "Not my head?"

Christian shook his head, laughed and then narrowed his eyes. "Will you let me?"

Susie saw the longing in his face and heard herself say "All right" when she'd been trying to say no.

"Lie on the floor."

Susie let him press down on her shoulders until she lay on the tiled floor. He rolled a towel and put it under her head and then pushed up her knees. Her dress fell back to the top of her thighs and Christian slid it farther so it lay across her waist. He released a shaky breath as his fingers wrapped around the top of her blue cotton panties and peeled them down. Susie lifted her bottom off the floor so he could take them off.

"My God, Susie. You are so pretty. Look at these cute folds and your—"

"Don't you dare tell me my ass is pretty."

"It is. Like a little rosebud."

Christian squeezed the foam onto his hand and then smoothed it over her. Susie watched his face. He seemed a little bewildered as though he wasn't sure what was happening. Well, that made two of them. She jolted when a finger slid inside her but it didn't linger.

"Sorry, I slipped."

"You don't look sorry," she said.

Christian smiled. He picked up the razor and bent down. Susie could no longer see his face, only feel the pull of the smooth metal against her skin. Christian was slow, gentle and careful. He rinsed off the blade several times and worked his way down the triangle of curls to the crack of her butt. Susie could feel his fingers rubbing her, then the sweep of warm, hard metal, then soft, firm fingers again. As he touched her swollen lips she tensed, but he shushed her and she relaxed again, trusting him.

The warm cloth jolted her. The sweep of dry fabric over her clit dragged a gulp from her throat.

"You like that?" Christian whispered. "The rub of the towel on your pussy?"

Susie nodded.

He made one slow drag between her legs and she began to squirm. Christian laughed.

"Don't tease me," she gasped.

"I'm going to spend all day teasing you."

Susie was torn between closing her eyes, and watching Christian's face. In the end, watching his face won. He looked as excited as she felt, the intent in his green eyes mesmerizing.

"Harder," Susie gasped, and Christian obliged.

She arched her hips off the floor as the contractions seized her pussy. Her eyes closed as her body was caught in a maelstrom of muscles twisting and clamping, legs jerking, heart stuttering, hands trembling. Christian pulled her into his arms and held her as she came down.

He breathed her name into her ear, over and over. "Susie, Susie, Susie."

She collapsed like a falling ribbon, boneless in his embrace. He was kissing her face, her neck, kissing her back to earth. Susie clutched his waist as he pulled her upright. Her gaze settled on the damp circle on his pants.

"I'm leaking," he said. "I don't think I've ever been this desperate."

Susie reached for the hem of her dress and he caught her hand.

"I want to see what you've done to me," she said.

"Wait."

He guided her back into the bedroom and stood behind her as he positioned her in front of the mirror. Christian lifted her dress to her waist.

"You look so sexy," he whispered. "I could come just looking at you."

"That would be a waste," Susie said, and he laughed.

Christian released the dress and his hands slid up her sides and onto her breasts, cupping them through the material, twisting her nipples gently between his finger and thumb. He kissed her neck and pressed his cock against her back.

"I fell in love with you the moment I saw you," he whispered. "Standing on our doorstep with your knees all scraped and bloody, looking like a naughty angel."

Oh my God. He loved her? Susie turned to face him. Christian smiled at her. She pulled the zip the rest of the way down on his jeans and tugged them over his hips along with his boxers.

"You were so shy," he muttered.

"Was. So were you."

"Was," he said.

They laughed. Christian kicked off his pants and pulled off his T-shirt. No longer constrained, his cock reared up to his stomach, a rock-hard monument to his desire. He looked magnificent and Susie reached for him.

Christian stepped back. "If you touch me, I've had it. One touch and I'm gone, I swear it."

He lifted the dress over her head and it fell from his fingers. Apart from her sandals, she was naked.

"God, Susie, you are so pretty. I've spent so long thinking about this, about us standing here naked in my room, about touching you."

He put his hands around her waist and ran them up her body, his thumbs grazing her skin until they reached her nipples. Christian bent his head and kissed her. This time the kiss was deep and hard and Susie's hands swept across his back, pulling him against her.

They tumbled to the bed, arms and legs entwined, mouths sharing oxygen. She could feel herself winding again, a twister building up momentum, turning her body inside out in slow motion. Christian edged her onto her back and pushed her legs against her chest.

"Oh God," he muttered, and clamped his hand around the base of his dick.

The look he gave her was one of despair and Susie knew she wasn't the only one of the verge of explosion. Christian pressed his cock against the entrance to her body, the blunt head nestling on her wet, receptive folds.

"I want to make this good but—"

"Get inside me," Susie said. "Now."

A long, slow lunge and she felt every thick, luxurious inch.

"Don't move," he gasped. "Please."

He took a couple of deep breaths and then began to thrust into her. Susie groaned with every withdrawal, wanting him back inside her. Christian's hands swarmed over her body as he drove into her then settled on her breasts as he gave one final, violent surge. For a moment he hung suspended, not breathing, not moving and then Susie felt the warm jets of his cum spewing from his cock, coating her pussy. Her orgasm grabbed her by the throat and she spasmed around him.

"Christ, Susie. Oh God."

As her vision cleared and the room reconfigured, Susie gave a deep sigh of contentment. She was addicted to sex. *Fuck.*

Christian pulled out of her, moved her legs down, then took her in his arms.

"Too fast. I'm sorry," he whispered.

"Not as fast as Joel, but don't tell him I said that."

She felt him freeze for a moment and then his body shuddered as he laughed. "God, he'd kill you for that."

"And if I tell him how hard you laughed, he'd kill *you.*"

Chapter Eighteen

ဢ

Christian lay with Susie cradled in his arms. He'd missed the softness of a woman. The gentle curves and sweet smell. He loved holding Susie, wrapped tight in his embrace, protecting her. No matter how much he might at times wish it otherwise, Joel was the protector, the one in charge, but sometimes Christian wanted to be the strong one. After what happened on Saturday night, he could scarcely believe he had Susie in his bed, in his arms, in his heart. Christian hadn't thought he'd see her again. He'd brooded about getting in touch with her, but hadn't wanted to make things worse with Joel. *God, Joel.* Now Christian had to make things right.

As Susie slept, Christian thought about Joel and whether this changed things. *Of course this fucking changed things.* But for better or worse? Susie knew now that he and Joel were bisexual, that they both wanted her but she didn't realize they'd like to have her lying between them. Did Joel still want that? Christian wasn't certain Joel even wanted him. The pain of that stopped the breath in his throat.

Why had Susie come here this morning? Had she let him fuck her so he didn't feel left out? Christian began to grind his teeth. This was a mercy fuck. She didn't want him to feel bad, to feel jealous.

"Stop it," Susie said.

"Stop what?" Damn, that came out sharper than he'd intended.

"Stop thinking and worrying. Just accept what is."

It wasn't that easy. "Why did it have to be Joel who fucked you first?"

Oh God, he wished he hadn't asked her that, though he did want the answer.

"You should have kissed me harder when you walked me home."

"What?" A snail could have outpaced Christian's brain.

Susie rolled over to look at him. "I wasn't sure whether it was an 'I've had a nice day, thanks very much' kiss, or 'I'll just try a little peck and see what happens' kiss."

"Fuck."

"You were nervous and I was timid. I didn't think anyone would want me."

Her hand went up to her face and Christian caught her wrist. "I know you worry about your scar but I don't even notice it. I see you. I see Susie. What happened to you was terrible. Even worse if you'd not survived but you did. You're still Susie."

She smiled and he trailed a finger over her lips.

"Are you cross with Joel?" she asked.

"Jealous."

She smiled. "But where is Joel now and where are you?"

Christian beamed. "Want to go out in the backyard and lie in the sun? I'll make us some lunch."

"Okay."

She sat up and as her nipple skimmed his mouth, Christian's tongue shot out and snatched a lick. "You taste so sweet."

"Not as filling as a sandwich." Susie climbed off the bed and reached for her dress.

Christian jumped to yank it out of her grasp. "You don't need that. The backyard is secluded. No one can see us."

"Are you sure?"

"Positive. I don't want you to wear anything but a smile."

He took hold of her hand, pulled her out of the room and down the stairs. Christian lifted a large blanket from the cupboard next to the dining room and opened the back door. He urged her on.

"Really, it's okay. No one can hear us. Both neighbors are at work."

He led her to a place halfway down the lawn where evergreen bushes created a small semi-circular glade. Christian opened the blanket and flapped it in the air before spreading it flat on the grass.

"I'll be back in a minute," he said.

When he returned, Susie lay facedown in the sun. Christian was torn between biting her little white backside and rolling the cold bottle of wine down her back.

The devil in him won. His reward was a shriek and a view of her front as she spun over.

"Sorry," he said.

"You're such a liar."

"I'll go and get the food." Christian handed her the glasses. "Don't drink it all while I'm gone."

Susie watched as he walked backward up the lawn to the house, a broad grin on his face. He was tanned all over. No lines. He really did have a lovely toned body. His chest was smooth and his legs hairy, his cock ringed by brown curls. Susie wished she'd thought to offer to shave his groin. She smiled to herself. The moment Christian moved out of sight, she slipped back to the house.

By the time she returned to the blanket, Christian had laid out their lunch. Bread, cheese and fruit.

"What have you got there?" he asked as Susie put a plastic bag under one of the shrubs.

"A surprise."

Christian raised his eyebrows. He handed Susie a glass of wine. She hadn't missed the fact that he was hard again. They didn't take their eyes off each other as they ate. Susie wasn't hungry but managed to force down a chunk of French baguette and a slice of soft cheese. Christian leaned on his side, watching her.

"You look sexy when you eat," he murmured.

"Thew — thin — tho?" Susie spat out crumbs as she spoke and he chuckled.

She loved making him laugh. He had the most fantastic eyes she'd ever seen, as green as holly. His eyelashes curled long and thick and his lips were full and sensuous. Christian was prettier than Joel who was an archetypal movie-star hunk. They made a perfect couple. Susie took a gulp of wine. They were a pair and she was — she didn't know what she was. A bit of fun? Was there anything wrong in that? She was enjoying herself. *Just accept what is.* That's what she'd told Christian and what she believed herself. She was happy and it wasn't a feeling she was used to.

Susie scanned his chest. Christian's nipples stood out, brown rings with a dark copper core. She loved how hard they went. She licked her lips and heard him groan.

"Stop looking at me."

She laughed and her gaze sank lower. Lying on his side made his hip bones look even more angular. She couldn't ignore the furry ball sac and the long, thick length of his cock, marveling how all that had been inside her. Then her gaze dropped to his firm, muscular legs stretched out in the sun. She needed them wrapped around her, holding her tight. Bur first there was something she wanted to do.

"Lie on your back and close your eyes," Susie said.

"What are you up to?" The suspicion in his voice was quite clear and Susie tried to look innocent. "Susie, that expression doesn't work. I know you're planning trouble."

"Not trouble. It's something good. You have to keep your eyes closed, hands by your sides and trust me."

Christian gave her a long stare and then dropped onto his back.

At first, her hands confined themselves to exploring the contours of his chest and stroking his nipples, which was sexy enough, but then her fingers slid between his legs and he stiffened. Well, part of him was already stiff but his body tensed. When Christian felt her smoothing something over his groin, he groaned.

"Tell me that's not honey and you don't have an army of ants marching toward me."

"No, it's your shaving foam."

Christian's eyes sprang open and he scissored upright. "What?"

She knelt with his razor in her hand.

"No," he said firmly.

"Yes," Susie said just as firmly, and pushed him down again.

"It'll itch."

"Oh, so it's okay for you to do it to me but not the other way around?"

Christian mumbled to himself. "Okay, but just watch what you're doing."

"Ooh, spoil my fun, why don't you. I'd planned to keep my eyes closed."

He glared.

It felt strange as she shaved him, the combination of the razor scraping over his skin and Susie's delicate fingers on his cock and balls. He liked the sensation of the cold shaving cream and the way she rubbed it in. His cock seemed unperturbed by the risk of bloodshed and grew thicker with every pass of the razor. She'd even brought out a wet cloth to wipe him down.

"All done."

Christian leaned up to stare at his groin and sighed.

"It's draughty," he said, and she laughed.

"Lie back again. Now you get a reward for being good."

She planted moist, open-mouthed kisses down his chest, pausing at his nipples to bite gently. Christian gasped when he felt her fingers on his dick. He was already leaking pre-cum, glistening drops had spilled onto his belly. A groan bubbled from his throat as she rubbed his juice around the head of his shaft with her palm.

The next moment Christian's back arched off the blanket. Susie had wrapped her lips around him but it wasn't that. It was the gulp of wine she'd taken before she did it. She held the liquid in her mouth as she pressed her lips against his dick. The wine was cold, but she was warm. *Jesus.* Christian felt himself throbbing as she sucked and swallowed what hadn't dribbled down his legs. Speech was beyond him.

"Didn't you like it?" she asked in a small voice.

Christian tried to fashion incoherent mumbling into sense. He lifted his fist and sprinkled grass over her. He'd ripped up the lawn as he'd tensed.

"Not sure," he said. "Try again. In fact, I might need you to repeat it over and over so I can make up my mind."

By the third time, Christian thought he would explode in joy. Soft fingers played gently with his sac while her other hand teased the base of his shaft. His balls had transformed into volcanic rocks, hard as glass and just as brittle. The lack of hair had made them ultrasensitive. He wondered if Joel—no. His cock strained at the leash like an impatient puppy desperate to fling itself into the game. He twitched inside Susie's mouth and she coughed wine all over his crotch. Christian laughed and sat up to pat her on the back.

"Well, you get a choice now," he said.

"What's that?"

"You either finish what you've started or I fuck you senseless."

"Umm, let me think."

"Don't take too long."

"I think I'll go for being fucked senseless."

He slid his fingers down her stomach, over the smooth, shaved mound and straight inside her.

"You are so wet. God, I have to taste you."

He pushed her back, dropped his head between her legs and rubbed his face along her inner thighs, licking her gently then not so gently until he was outright eating her.

Susie squirmed on the blanket. "Ooh, Christian."

He blew a puff of warm air over her clit and her hips bucked.

Christian lifted his head. "Don't you dare come yet. I want to be inside you."

He shuffled up the blanket and positioned the blunt head of his cock over her entrance.

"Now," Susie urged him. "God, Christian, fuck me, please."

One long, hard drive into her wet heat and her pussy clenched around the base of his dick. She squeezed him so tight he almost came on the first thrust. Christian's legs trembled. It was like being held by a firm, slick fist. With a supreme effort, he pushed back his impending climax and began to pulse into her, slow and steady, core-deep surges that had her gasping with every thrust.

She curled her legs around him and massaged his backside with her toes. Christian slanted his hips to change the angle and moved up a couple of gears into the rapid-pounding action Joel loved so much. Susie too. She gasped, quivered and panted beneath him, wrapping her arms around him as he drove into her. He brought her off in moments and she cried out beneath him, her face twisted in pleasure.

"Christian! Christian!"

Hearing his name on her lips kick-started Christian's response. His lungs were tight and constricted. He gasped for air. Pressure seized the back of his head and electricity jolted his spine. When he felt a second set of contractions clamp around his cock, Christian ground himself against her. His stomach coiled, his balls tightened and he exploded with a muffled cry, pumping his essence into her. The sensation was exquisite, the release of the tension with each wrenching spasm and the subsequent slide into bliss, an unbeatable ecstasy. For a moment, Christian thought that if he died now, he'd go happy.

Only he wanted to do it again.

He slumped on top of her, as though every bone he possessed had been surgically removed. When Christian heard her groan, he managed to slide to one side, but they were both soaked with hot sweat, sticking together, joined irretrievably in more ways than one. His cock remained inside her. He was still half hard. Neither of them spoke. Breathing was enough of a challenge. Christian reached for Susie's hand and wrapped his fingers around hers.

When his lungs resumed their normal rhythm, he kissed her, a slow sweep of his lips across hers.

"Did I fuck you senseless?" he asked.

"Who am I? Where am I? Who are you?"

Christian chuckled. "Now I need to make love to you."

Susie groaned. "Then what was that?"

"Fucking you senseless."

"What's the difference?"

Christian smiled. "That's what I'm going to show you."

He rolled her onto her stomach and began at her shoulders, trailing his fingers over her skin, licking down her spine, savoring the salty tang and finally kissing her backside. He wanted to play in the secret, tempting valley between the cheeks of her bottom, but he was afraid of freaking her out, so he slid farther and teased the backs of her knees, tickling her with a blade of grass until she squealed for him to stop.

Christian rolled her over and paid as much attention to the front of her body, covering every inch of her with tiny butterfly kisses. When he knelt at her side, Susie sat up and squirmed round until she could lick his cock. Christian sighed. He was rock solid again, but he didn't know how, considering he'd only just come. He thought his cock must be in denial. Christian slid around on the blanket so Susie's face pressed against his groin and he could lick her pussy.

Holding her hips, Christian kissed her newly shaved mons and then slid his tongue over the nub of her clit. He felt her squirm and then Christian squirmed as Susie ran her tongue around the head of his cock and took him in her hot mouth. Christian gave a husky purr of contentment. Could there be anything better than this? Out in the open air, mouths on each other? One moment she was giving him light, teasing sucks and the next deep heavy ones. He'd died and gone to heaven. There could be no other explanation. He liked doing this with Joel but it was different with Susie. Her mouth was softer and smaller. The tighter fit made him quiver with excitement.

He loved sucking her off, loved the taste of her honey, loved the way she clenched her mouth around his cock when he found an ultrasensitive spot. Christian put his hands on her backside, pressed his fingers into the crease of her butt and pulled her down onto his face. They were both slick with sweat as they moaned, slurped and writhed on the blanket. Christian was desperate to come at the same time as her. When he felt her orgasm hit and the ripples of contractions flutter against his mouth, he pushed past the ring of muscle at the back of her throat and the tighter sensation triggered his release. After the first spurt, Christian pulled back, afraid he'd choke her but she wrapped her lips around him and teased every drop of cum from his dick as he lapped silky cream from her pussy.

Christian's heart pounded and his pulse raced. He still thought he was dreaming, that none of this could be happening. He was lost inside one of his erotic novels. Actually, that wasn't a bad idea for a plot, a writer caught up in his own creation. He could write himself to ecstasy. Susie crawled around and nestled in his arms, snuggling up against him.

Not a dream, just one of the best days of his life. They fell asleep with the sun beating down.

Chapter Nineteen

ഇ

Joel found them when he came back from work. Christian hadn't answered his call, so Joel looked out of the kitchen window and saw four legs on a striped blanket. His heart skipped more than one beat when he realized one pair of legs wasn't male. He went into the dining room so he could get a better view. Susie lay sleeping in Christian's arms. They were stark naked and Joel grinned.

He ran upstairs, tore off his clothes, flung them on the bed and jumped in the shower. Clothes could lie in a heap but Joel had to wash away office grime and London transport dirt before he leapt into the fray. He already had an erection. The moment he'd seen the pair of them, he'd gone straight to diamond on the hardness scale. He'd thought about the weekend all day, his head full of what he had done, should have done and didn't do. Though he'd billed sufficient hours at the office, Joel was aware it hadn't been his finest day's work. He'd come home ready to make up with Christian and take him out for a meal, but now he had a much better option.

It occurred to Joel as he padded naked across the grass, that he still had no idea whether Susie would be up for this. Joel assumed she'd now had sex with Christian too and Christian wasn't just lying there, underneath her, being a martyr, though that didn't mean she wanted both of them at the same time. Well, only one way to find out. When Joel reached the foot of the blanket, Christian opened his eyes. Joel put his hand to his mouth, licked his fingers, winked and crouched down. He knew Christian understood the message.

Susie awoke as Christian kissed her, his cock a hard ridge between their bodies.

"You're very warm, Susie. I think we've spent too long in the sun. I brought some lotion out, but forgot to use it."

He ran his hands over her back and along her backside, trailed his finger down the cleft of her bottom.

"Like to lick my lollipop?" Christian asked, and gave her a little grin.

"Shall I get that chocolate syrup from the fridge?"

He held her hips. "Not this time."

When Susie moved down his body, Christian raised his knees and spread his legs, bringing his feet round to tickle her thighs. Susie knelt with her butt in the air and kissed the triangle of skin beneath his balls, intoxicated by the musky scent of his body. As she trailed her tongue over him, Christian's breath hissed from his mouth. She could see his asshole, a tempting dark pucker but she wasn't that brave. Not yet. She wrapped her lips around his balls, separating them with her tongue and then sucking gently.

Christian's hands stroked her hair then her shoulders as he groaned beneath her. Susie liked the way the different textures of his cock and balls felt under her tongue and lips. She pulled her mouth over the wrinkles, smoothed them out and then trailed the tip of her tongue along the prominent vein on the underside of his cock to the head.

"Oh God, I hope this happens in heaven," Christian whispered. "All the time. Perpetual bliss. I love the way your hair drifts across my skin. I love the way your lips can kiss in a million different ways. Jesus, Susie. I could forget anything when you're doing this."

Susie clasped the base of his cock and took the head in her mouth, pressing it into the inside of her cheek then pulling it back to tease with her tongue. She sucked slow and deep then fast and shallow. Christian's whimpers made her chuckle around him which made him whimper again. She loved doing this. Adored that Christian loved it. Within moments Susie was in thrall, lost in a dance of licking, teasing and flicking with her tongue. Christian's fingers roved through her hair and then gripped the strands as his hips thrust up to match her movements.

"Oh God, that is so good, Susie. Don't stop."

She felt his hands run over her shoulders, trickle down her sides then swoop back to her breasts. Stroking, kneading, caressing, so many ways of touching, driving her wild. His legs gripped her. His fingers teased her nipples. His hands swept over her backside.

On her bum *and* her breasts?

Too many hands.

Susie stopped sucking Christian and lifted her head. He gave a deep groan.

She thought she knew what she'd see when she turned. She was right. Joel, buck naked, on his knees. He grinned at her. She turned back to Christian. He looked apprehensive. Susie looked back at Joel. The grin had gone.

"What the fuck happened to your face?" Joel asked.

"My brother. An accident."

"He hit you?"

"No, he pushed me and I fell against the table."

Susie could see the rage rising in Joel, a ball of lightning ready to burst. His eyes darkened, his mouth tightened.

"Joel, don't," she said. "It's okay, really. It was just an accident."

The tension seeped away and his face relaxed. Joel reached out, touched the bruise and winced. "Good job I asked first and didn't thump Christian for hitting you."

"I—" Christian began.

"I know," Joel said. "Sorry. Have I wrecked the moment?"

The three of them were frozen in a tableau, no one willing or daring to make the next move. Susie couldn't. Christian hadn't blinked since she'd lifted her head. She looked at Joel.

He sighed. "What's it going to be, angel? The three of us together, or am I heading for an arctic shower?"

Susie's heart was already sprinting in her chest, now it hurdled into her throat ready for the long jump into her mouth. Was it wrong to want them both? She'd already been fucked by the pair of them. The idea of them both touching her at the same time was enough to make her come without them lifting a finger. Her pussy clenched and released a flood of cream. They waited, watching her. It was her choice and she loved them for that.

She smiled and tried to sound braver than she felt. "Hey, aren't we the three amigos?"

Susie dropped her mouth back to Christian's cock. Joel spread her legs apart then her backside and his tongue swept from her anus to her clit and then back again. Susie's legs quivered. *Oh Christ, is that his tongue at my ass?* As Joel played with her, she lapped at Christian's cock, running her tongue in a ring around the top, delving into the slit, pulsing in short jabs and then sucking out the salty pre-cum. The rasp of Joel's stubble against her delicate mons was driving her crazy. She groaned onto Christian's cock and he gasped, cantering his hips. Susie sped up on Christian, reaching for his balls. As her hand caressed them, his hips shot off the blanket and he spurted into her mouth, long jets of creamy cum.

Now Susie gave herself up to Joel's persistent caress, his tongue driving into her, fucking her, his face pressed tight against her. A moment later, Susie's vision went white. Every muscle spasmed and she stopped breathing. As the world exploded, she went with it and they caught her in their arms.

The three of them lay in a tangled heap and for a while no one spoke. Joel broke the silence. "You both shaved?"

"You want me to do you too?" Susie asked.

"No way."

"Could you hold him down while I get the razor?" Susie said to Christian.

Joel growled. "Don't you dare even try."

Susie slid her hand between their bodies, and when she reached Joel's rigid cock, she found Christian's hand there.

"I ache," Joel said in a little boy voice.

Christian pushed him onto his back and kissed him on the lips.

"Have we neglected you?" Christian dropped his mouth to Joel's corded neck.

Susie only hesitated a moment. She planted kisses on Joel's shoulder and met Christian's lips on Joel's chest. They kissed each other and kissed Joel all the way down to his purple-headed cock, the glistening drops of his pre-cum something to fight over. Their hungry mouths moved between each other and Joel's iron-hard erection, licking, sucking, nipping. They shared nicely for a while and then began to fight for control. Joel had his hands in their hair and gasped as if he were running out of oxygen. Susie ceded to Christian and slid lower to take Joel's velvety sac in her mouth.

"Oh fuck. I...I can't...Jesus...you..." Joel muttered incoherently.

"Get on your hands and knees," Christian said.

As Joel rolled over and pushed himself up, Christian and Susie positioned themselves beneath him. Joel struggled to keep his head up as he panted and groaned.

"Shh," Christian hissed.

Susie heard voices in the garden next door and suppressed the urge to giggle. When it became clear that Joel couldn't be quiet, she crawled up the blanket and slid her head under his, holding his cheeks, pressing her lips against his, letting his tongue wrap around hers. Susie jolted when she felt Christian's fingers in her pussy. He was sandwiched between them, working them both. Joel nipped her tongue as he came in a violent burst, one that sent a racking shudder through his body and hers. Susie clenched around Christian's fingers and moaned her release into Joel's mouth.

It took a moment for them to untangle and get their heads back in a line. Susie lay on her back in the middle. She grabbed their hands and pulled them onto her stomach. Joel wiped his fingers over his face and then turned to look at them.

"That was fucking sensational," he whispered.

Joel kissed her, a long, passionate, toe-curling connection that made a pulse charge through Susie's body. Then he leaned over her and kissed Christian but slid his hand to her breast and squeezed at the same time. Joel fell back at Susie's side and gave a low whistle.

"He's been going on about that since I met him," Christian said. "Wanting me and a woman to go down on him. That's it now, Joel. Nothing left to look forward to, mate. You might as well kill yourself."

"Oh, I can think of a lot more things to look forward to," Joel said. "For a start, Susie didn't stay down there with you."

"Someone had to shut you up," she said.

Joel laughed.

Christian ran his hand across Susie's stomach and his fingers stopped on her scar. "How did you get that?"

"I had my spleen taken out."

Joel sat up to look. "Wow, what happened? Were you in an accident?"

He leaned forward and kissed the white line. Christian's fingers brushed his lips.

"Was it a long time ago?" Christian asked.

"Oh God, what time is it?" Susie gasped. Forget changing the subject, it had to be late.

"About seven thirty," Joel said.

"Oh Christ. He'll kill me." Susie scrambled to her feet and fled to the house.

"What's the problem?" Joel asked when they came into the bathroom.

"My dad. I'm supposed to make him dinner every night." Susie slipped on her dress and checked her mobile. "Three missed calls."

"I'll run you back," Joel said.

"I came on my bike."

"Leave it here. The car's quicker."

"Thanks." Susie put on her shoes. "Do I look okay?"

Christian untangled a lock of hair. "You look like you've spent all day having rampant sex in the garden."

Susie swallowed hard.

"Ignore him," Joel said. "Come on."

"Wait." Christian pulled her into his arms. "One kiss."

Joel recognized the look in Christian's eyes, the intense affection he knew Christian felt for him and he was filled with joy that Christian was so happy.

"Okay, so where do you live?" Joel asked as they set off.

"Milborough Crescent. Up the road to the top and then turn left."

"Your father won't do anything to you, will he, for being late?"

"No. He'll just be cross."

"Has he ever hit you?" Joel asked.

"No. He just stops speaking to me for a while."

Joel sighed. "My mother used to do that too."

"Really?"

"Yeah. How long can your dad keep it up?"

"A few weeks. He used to leave notes everywhere."

"Christ, I think our parents must have read the same crap parenting book. Is it worth calling him?"

"Not now. Second street on the right. We're nearly there. Pull up in front of that red car. That's fine. Thank you, Joel."

She turned and smiled. He caught hold of her face and pressed his lips against hers.

"Bye, beautiful," he said.

"Bye."

"So when are you coming round again?"

"Wednesday, I guess."

"I don't think I can wait that long. Anyway, you've gone by the time I get back from work. Oh God, I'm tempted to have the day off tomorrow. If I wasn't in the middle of a deal, I would. Can you come tomorrow night? After you've fed the ogre?"

"I don't know."

Joel cupped her face and kissed her. "Try." He kissed her again. "Try hard."

There was a sudden banging on the passenger window. Susie spun round.

"Shit. It's Pete. I have to go."

Joel watched as she leapt from the car and slammed the door. She pushed the man away, muttered something to him and then the pair of them walked down to a blue door. The guy turned and looked at Joel before he disappeared inside the house.

Chapter Twenty

℘

"Where the hell have you been?"

"I'm sorry." Susie flinched at her father's tone. "My clients threw a garden party this afternoon and it took time to get everything sorted and cleaned up."

"I can't see why it took so long."

"The dishwasher broke and flooded the kitchen." *Oh God, that was a lie too far.*

"I called you."

"My bag and phone were in the hallway and we had music playing. I didn't hear it. I'm really sorry, Dad. I lost track of time."

Susie stood there while he ranted about her selfishness. They'd been working hard all day and expected a meal waiting. Her first duty was to them and not the guys she worked for. She had to get her priorities right. Blah, blah, blah. Susie stayed silent and let it wash over her. Pete sat with his legs hooked over the arm of the couch and a smirk on his face. Susie had asked him not to say anything about how she'd gotten home, but she could see him waiting to blab.

"We had to have pizza," her father said as Susie tuned back in.

As if that were a hardship, she thought.

"Is he married?" Pete asked.

Two heads swung to look at him.

"Who?" Harry demanded. "What the hell are you talking about?"

"K...I...S...S...I...N...G," Pete sang. "Our Susie smooched the guy who gave her a lift back."

"Married?" her father asked.

"No, he's not married."

"So you lied about the dishwasher?" Harry said. "You were with a guy."

"No, I didn't lie. There was water everywhere."

"You should have called Mike," Pete said.

Bastard. "The cleanup was the problem. I think they're going to get a new machine."

Oh God, more lies. Susie knew she'd get caught out sooner or later.

"As soon as I realized the time, I came home. I left my bike. Joel gave me a lift, that's all. I'm really sorry I missed getting your dinner. It's never happened before and I won't do it again...without warning."

"Is this the same guy who kissed you before?" Harry asked.

Shit. "Yes."

"It's not very fair encouraging a relationship, is it? Given your condition," her father said.

The knife went through her heart and out her back. Why was it wrong to want to be happy?

"But I'm better now," she said in a quiet voice.

"No—you're in remission."

As if the scar across her stomach wasn't enough of a reminder, her father never let her forget she lived on borrowed time. And she *was* better.

"The doctor said..." She let her voice trail away when she saw the look on her father's face.

Susie had been ill for a long while, always tired, no appetite, struggling with flu-like symptoms, losing weight and sharp pains in her chest. It was put down to stress after her mother had attacked her. It wasn't.

"You know how sick you were," Harry said.

"That was then," Susie muttered a quiet protest.

Tubes had been put down her throat, whole armfuls of blood taken and finally they'd told her she had to have her spleen out so they could make the diagnosis. She'd wanted to ask—what diagnosis?—but she'd known before they'd sat her down and quietly told her. She had cancer.

"You have to be upfront with people," her father said. "You'd want to know, wouldn't you, Pete, if you were interested in a woman who'd had cancer?"

Susie sank her teeth into the inside of her cheeks. "We're not getting married, Dad. It's only a few kisses."

"Make us a cup of tea," Pete asked.

Susie escaped to the kitchen. She'd suffered eight months of chemotherapy followed by radiotherapy. Two months later came more bad news. The cancer was back. She needed a stem-cell transplant from Pete, who was the closest match, and now she was in remission. The doctor had told her to go out and live her life. Her father kept reminding her the cancer could return at any time. Maybe it could, but Susie didn't waste energy thinking like that.

She carried two mugs of tea through to the lounge where Pete and her dad were now riveted to the TV.

"Shall I put them on the table?" she asked.

"Yeah, I'll call you when I want it lifted to my lips," Pete said from the couch.

He was only half joking. Pete thought she owed him. He never let her forget all the injections he endured before he could donate the cells. From the way he spoke, it was worse than the cancer. Mike wanted to do it but wasn't a match. Susie went upstairs and locked herself in the bathroom. She'd eaten nothing since the cheese and bread at lunchtime but she wasn't hungry. Just tired.

She started water running in the bath and stripped off. She glowed from lying in the sun, her skin tingled. She radiated from the whole experience of being with two men at the same time. *Two, oh Christ!* She knew people would think it was wrong, but really, what was wrong about it? They hadn't hurt anyone. It wasn't perverted or degrading. Three consenting adults having fun. It had been her choice and she was glad she'd made it.

It wouldn't be the way her father or her brothers saw it. Her dad thought homosexuals were the scum of the earth. She didn't think his opinion of bisexuals would be much different. In fact, it would probably be worse. Susie wasn't bi. She had no interest in women, just two guys, so what did that make her? As far as her father was concerned—a slut. He'd go ballistic if he found out, so Susie had to ensure he never did. She wasn't going to let him spoil this. She, above all people, knew that life could be too short not to seize the moment, not to do what her heart told her was right.

Susie lowered herself into the warm water and lay back. The best day of her life. She'd gone to the house, afraid of what Christian would say, and ended up lying between two guys who drove her so wild with desire she thought there was something wrong with her. She wished she was with them now, wished they were touching her. It wasn't just sex. They cared about her. Didn't they?

* * * * *

Christian was waiting for Joel when he got back from taking Susie home. He had water boiling for pasta and had thrown together a mix of onions, peppers, mushrooms and pesto. No longer naked, he'd showered and slipped on a pair of sleep pants, but his chest and feet were bare.

"Well," Joel said as he walked into the kitchen, a broad grin on his face. "How the fuck did you manage that?"

"She just turned up and sat on my lap."

"That would work." Joel laughed.

Christian tipped the pasta into the water. Joel took a corkscrew from the drawer and opened a bottle of wine.

"So how are we going to persuade her to move in?" Joel asked.

Christian glanced at him.

"Well, you want her to, don't you?" Joel cocked his head on one side.

"Yes, but I'll never get any work done if she does. I've had her in my arms all day. I couldn't stop fucking her."

Joel smiled. "How about we pay for her to go to college?"

"As a reward for fucking us? Sounds like we'd be buying her. And how do you know she wants to go to college?"

"I asked her."

Christian's shoulders slumped. How come he hadn't found that out?

"She wants to study English. That would mean she'd be out in the daytime and back at night while we were both here."

Christian perked up. "She could do the cooking and cleaning and we could pay for her classes, plus money for clothes and books."

"We have to be careful. Don't push too fast."

"Okay."

"I asked her to come around tomorrow night," Joel said.

Christian laughed. "That's not fast, then. Do you think she knows what she's letting herself in for?"

"She had a taste of it today. She didn't act unhappy."

"No, but this is a bigger thing for her than it is for us. We already know what it's like to be different." Christian spooned the pasta mixture onto two plates and sat at the table. "We have each other, Joel. It's easier for us."

"She's an adult. She can make up her own mind. I know what I want."

"What?" Christian asked.

"For as long as I can have it, you and her."

And if you had to choose between us, Christian thought, *would it still be me? And if I had to choose, would it be Joel?*

* * * * *

When Joel came home early from work the following night, Christian didn't make the comment that he'd rarely made it back early when Christian had asked him to. They didn't even know if Susie would come. Joel was certain she would, Christian wasn't sure. They ate and then sat in the lounge with something on the TV, Christian had no idea what. His mind was wandering.

Joel put his arm around him and hugged him. "What would you like to do when she comes?"

"You really think she will?" Christian asked.

"Yep. I'm certain."

Christian piggybacked on Joel's confidence. "Have a long, slow bath together."

"I'm not sure the tub's big enough for three."

"We ought to have bought a paddling pool."

"Hey, that's not a bad idea," Joel said with a smile.

They both jumped when the bell rang.

"You go," Christian said.

Joel pulled him to his feet. "We both go."

Susie wasn't sure what she was doing there. No, that was a lie. She knew exactly why she'd come. She was already wet thinking about the pair of them, imagining what they could do. Joel opened the door and flashed his big, white, wolfish smile. Christian stood, looking nervous at his side. The moment the door closed, Joel pulled her into his arms and kissed her. A long, slow smooching kiss that made Susie tingle from her toes to her nose. She could feel Joel was already rigid as he pressed himself against her.

"Christ, you make me hard," Joel whispered.

"You make me wet."

He laughed and bent his head to her ear. "I want to eat you."

Susie's knees buckled. Joel chuckled and pushed her toward Christian. As they kissed, Susie felt Joel's hands sliding up her legs, under her skirt and she groaned into Christian's mouth. They ended up in a tangle on the hall floor with Susie being tickled into uncontrolled giggles.

"We'd never have been able to do this before," Joel said. "The hall was knee-deep in Christian's shoes."

He swung her into his arms, carried her into the lounge and dropped her on the couch. Christian sat on one side and Joel the other.

"As far as your father's concerned, where are you?" Joel asked.

"Cinema."

"Will you get quizzed on the film?"

"Seen it before," Susie said. "I go to the cinema a lot."

Joel slid his hand over her knee. "Good."

Susie released a shaky sigh.

"Okay?" Joel asked.

"I feel safe when I'm with you," she whispered.

"We'd never hurt you," Christian said.

"Not unless you wanted us too," Joel added.

Susie's eyes opened wide.

"Don't worry. I'm not into pain. I was thinking about a gentle spanking," Joel said, and ran his tongue over his upper lip.

Susie's pussy quivered.

"You ever get spanked?" she asked Christian.

"My dad walloped me for something I did at school. I got caught sitting on the cellar steps in the playground looking up girls' skirts."

"Then you deserved it," Joel said.

"What about you?" Susie asked Joel.

"I'm never naughty."

Susie noted the look in his dark eyes and smiled. "Follow my lead," she whispered, and tugged Christian to the other side of the lounge. "We have to go and see Mr. Cooper, Christian. Do you think he'll be mad at us?" she asked in a childish tone, swinging Christian's hand in hers.

Christian fell straight into role. "Not with you, but he will with me. I'm always in trouble."

"But it's my fault. I sort of wanted you to look," Susie muttered, running her hand up Christian's T-shirt.

Joel slid back on the couch and watched.

"I wanted you to touch," Susie whispered. She felt a shiver of excitement as she took hold of Christian's hand and pushed it under her skirt. "Feel me, Christian. I go all wet when you touch me, all creamy and slippery."

"Christian Harris! Susie Hood! Get in here at once," Joel barked, and Christian's hand fell away.

Joel tried to look stern and failed. Christian tried to look scared and failed. Excitement was the emotion she saw their eyes.

"I've been told what you two were doing on the cellar steps," Joel snapped.

"What was that, Mr. Cooper?" Susie asked in a singsong voice.

"Lifting your skirt to let Christian look at your underwear. Have you no shame, girl?"

"Yes, sir. No, sir. I wasn't, sir," Susie said.

"Are you calling Mrs. Hatchet a liar? You're sixteen years old. You should be setting an example to the younger children."

"I'd never let them look up my skirt, sir."

Christian snorted. Joel started to laugh and then glared.

"Insolent boy. You think this is funny? Take down your trousers."

"In front of her, sir?"

"Yes. Teach you some shame. Trousers down and bend over the arm of that chair."

Christian stepped over to the chair and slowly unbuttoned his chinos. He let them fall to his ankles.

"Underpants too," Joel demanded.

Christian pushed them down. His boxers were covered in apples. Susie had noticed Christian had a thing about fruit on his underwear. But what was under them was far more riveting. His cock glistened with pre-cum, pumped with blood it reared up his stomach, a hard swollen stalk of belligerence. Christian pulled his T-shirt down to cover it.

"You're not hiding. T-shirt off," Joel snapped.

Christian pulled it over his head and tossed it aside. Then he wrapped his hands protectively over his groin.

"You think you can be shy now? Bend over the edge of the seat and spread your legs, boy."

Susie was mesmerized. She might have started this off but the game was no longer hers to command. Joel got to his feet and slammed his hand over Christian's backside. The first smack wasn't very hard, but the second made Christian jerk forward and groan. He took his hands off his dick and clutched the couch. Susie felt a tightening between her thighs as she watched Joel slap him. There was a red tinge growing on Christian's ass. Joel beckoned her.

"Miss Hood. Over here. Three strikes from you."

"No, sir, please, sir."

"Do as you're told, girl."

Susie was torn between kissing Christian's rosy bum and smacking him. Kissing won.

"I can't hurt him, sir," she said, dropping down on her knees and licking up from his balls. Christian moaned. This was a game, Susie thought. She could be daring. She pressed her face deeper, burrowed her tongue into his cleft and licked. She touched the puckered rosebud and heard Christian cry out. Joel jerked her head back.

"I see you need to be taught a lesson too," he said. "Bend over my knee, Susie Hood. Christian Harris, you stay exactly where you are."

Joel sat on the couch and pulled her across his lap. Christian's hand slid to his cock the moment she bent over Joel's knee. He lifted her dress and she heard the intake of breath from both men. Susie had been shopping in Greenwich market. She wore a narrow silver G-string. It seemed the less you wore, the more expensive the underwear but she'd not been able to resist.

The first blow made her gasp, but it also sent a warm tingle through her body. She wiggled on Joel's lap and felt his erection rub against her stomach. The second slap made her cry out and Christian reared up.

"Stay where you are, Harris," Joel said. "And get your hand off your dick, young man."

Another stinging slap landed on Susie's backside and her pussy clenched. Just as she braced herself for another blow, Joel stood her up.

"You can't keep your hand off your dick, can you?" he said to Christian.

"I'm sorry, Mr. Cooper. I'm so excited. I want you to smack me again. Harder. I want Susie to smack me as well."

"You two are little perverts. I shall have to tell your parents."

Both Christian and Susie dropped to their knees in front of Joel.

"No, please. You can't," Susie begged. "My dad will kill me."

"Please don't say anything," Christian said.

"We'll do anything you want if you won't tell," Susie said.

"Anything," Christian echoed.

Joel smiled.

"I think I fancy a sandwich," he said.

"I can make one, sir. Cheese or ham?" Susie asked.

"Not that sort," Christian whispered.

Susie blushed. She'd missed the meaning there.

"Take off my clothes," Joel ordered.

Christian stepped out of his bunched-up pants and boxers and helped Susie strip Joel. She loved looking at the pair of them when they were naked. They had such great bodies.

"Seems there's an odd one out," Joel commented, staring at Susie.

"You sure you won't tell my dad?" she asked.

"Not if you do exactly as I say."

She lifted the dress over her head and dropped it on the floor.

"Wow," Christian muttered.

The tiny silver G-string was matched by an equally tiny, push-up, silver bra that her breasts were struggling to escape. Susie reached around and unfastened the clasp, letting the bra fall from her fingers. She slid her hands into the G-string and pushed it down her thighs until she could step out of it.

Both Christian and Joel had their hands on their cocks. Susie dropped to her knees and locking her arms behind their thighs, first she licked Christian's turgid shaft and then Joel's. Once she knew they'd stand together, she released their legs and used her hands to bring the tips of both men into her mouth.

"I don't think this is in the National Curriculum." Christian groaned.

"I'm introducing it," Joel gasped. "And it's compulsory."

Susie glanced up. Christian pressed his lips against Joel's, beginning to explore his mouth. As she licked and sucked at their cocks, she pumped with her hands, giving each man in turn, a deep-throated caress. Joel was the one who pulled away.

"Susie, lie down," he said.

She lay on the floor and Joel leaned over her, pressing his lips against hers, plundering her mouth. She ran her hands over his warm, solid shoulders, up through his hair. She could feel the wet tip of his cock stroking her stomach. His hands were on either side of her head so she knew the fingers inside her were Christian's.

Joel pulled back and smiled. Susie watched Christian guide Joel's cock inside her. She felt full and warm, and squeezed her muscles around the steel-hard length of him. Christian's hair brushed the inside of her thighs and then his tongue licked her ass. From the way Joel gasped she guessed Christian was licking him too. Joel held himself up so that he didn't crush her but he wasn't moving and Susie wanted him to move. She flexed her hips and Joel groaned.

Cold lube splashed her backside and Joel pushed hard into her pussy with a gasp. Susie realized Christian had slid into Joel.

"Oh Christ," Joel muttered. "Fucking hell."

Joel was gulping and panting, pleasure written in the curve of his mouth, his widened eyes, the way he arched his head. She could hear the slap of Christian's balls against Joel's backside as he pounded into him and by default into her too. Susie raised her head and kissed Joel's face, stole his breath for a moment. He felt so good, each slamming thrust driving her closer to heaven as pleasure ripped over her nerve endings. Susie had her legs wrapped around both of them, her thighs against Joel's hips, her feet rubbing against the backs of Christian's legs.

Christian came suddenly, one heavy thrust that drove Joel balls-deep inside her. Christian yelled out and Joel stopped moving for a moment, his face screwed up in the pleasure of the moment. Then he began to move again and the tempo of Joel's pistoning hips increased until Susie was wound so tight, so racked with desire, she hardly knew what was happening.

"Come now," Joel commanded, and moments later Susie let the rippling orgasm take her, a lightning flash of heat with thunder rumbling through her limbs.

Joel gave a bellowing cry and tipped himself over the brink. His muscles contracted with hers as their climaxes ran out like ripples on a lake. They collapsed in a sweaty heap. Susie lay still for a moment, getting her ragged breathing back under control and then spoke.

"So was that a steak sandwich or cheese?"

Chapter Twenty-One

ॐ

"Want to go upstairs and run us a bath?" Joel asked.

Christian grinned and raced out of the room.

"Is it like having a puppy?" Susie whispered.

Joel laughed. "Worse. I can't get him house-trained."

"That's why you need me."

He curled his finger under her hair and lifted it from her face. "That's why *we* need you." Joel pushed himself up, pulled Susie to her feet and wrapped his arms around her. "You're perfect."

He brushed his lips across hers, catching her bottom lip and tugging gently before he eased his tongue into her mouth. Her hands slid over his backside, pulled him close and Joel groaned into her. He wanted nothing to spoil this, no one to take her away from them. He had to make it work.

"How long do we have you?" he whispered.

"I have to be back by eleven. I know it sounds like I'm on a curfew or something but Dad gets worried and I can't come up with a reason to stay out all night."

"You could try the truth."

Joel tugged her toward the stairs.

"What? That I'm starring in my own sexual fantasy?"

He turned to look at her. "Is it?"

Joel loved the way she blushed. Even her ears went red.

"Oh yes," Susie said.

They reached the bathroom door, and Christian yelled, "Wait a minute."

Joel dropped his hand between Susie's legs and wiped up a finger of his cum and her cream. His gaze fixed on her, he slipped his finger into his mouth and sucked.

"You taste divine," he said.

"Most of that was you."

Joel smirked. "Well, I taste divine too." He cupped her chin and stroked her cheek with his thumb. "This isn't just sex, Susie. You do know that? I've never seen Christian so excited."

Christian flung open the door. "Ta-da."

The tub was full of foam, slabs of it sticking up like icebergs in a frozen sea.

"Do you think there's any chance we'll all fit?" Susie asked.

"Oh yeah," said Christian.

He swept her into his arms and she squealed as he carried her over to the water. Susie sank beneath the foam for a moment before she emerged covered with bubbles.

"Very cute. Christian, you get the tap end." Joel slid into the tub, lifted a leg either side and pulled Susie face forward onto his chest.

Christian draped a towel over the taps and climbed in. He laid his legs over Joel's and pulled Susie's legs over his chest. Foam overflowed to the floor.

"See, we fit just fine," Joel said. "Just don't try to move."

Susie blew a mouthful of foam at his face.

"I think we need you turned over." Christian twisted her legs and Joel lifted so she lay on her back, her head resting against Joel's shoulder.

"We can't see anything in this foam." Joel blew a mound off Susie's stomach.

"It'll go once we use soap," Christian said.

Joel grabbed the dispenser, squirted a dollop of coconut soap onto his palm and tossed the bottle to Christian. Joel began at her fingers and worked the creamy lotion over each digit before continuing to her elbow and shoulder in smooth, sweeping strokes. Susie groaned and closed her eyes.

"Comfortable?" Joel asked.

"No, there's something hard poking into my back." Susie wriggled against him and Joel bit back a gasp.

Christian started on her foot, rubbing her arch, working on each toe before he moved to her ankle and up her calf. He dropped his feet into the water and tucked them either side of Joel's hips. Joel cupped Susie's breasts, teasing her nipples into a state of readiness, pert little peaks asking to be nibbled only he couldn't get at them. He shifted to edge his cock into a more comfortable position and raised Susie's butt out of the water. Christian looked across at him and smiled.

One of Joel's hands swept lower, the other stayed on her breast. A slide over her belly and shaved mons to her folds and then Joel trailed the flat of his nail backward and forward over her swollen lips. Susie gripped the side of the tub, her knuckles white.

"So pretty," Christian whispered. "All soft and wet and hot."

Joel's fingers touched Christian's, rubbed them as well as Susie. Joel's cock throbbed as they teased her together, Christian's finger sliding out of her cunt as Joel's slid in. She wriggled on his chest, her breathing ragged.

"Oh God, God."

"It's okay, sweetheart. Let us play," Joel said.

Joel's finger touched her puckered asshole and Susie gave a shuddering groan. He looked at Christian. He didn't need Christian's permission but he wanted to know he was all right about this. Christian's eyes were glazed, but he mouthed, "Please." Joel pulled his finger back and sank it into Susie's cunt, his thumb flicking her clit. He could wait for his turn there. Joel could tell exactly what Christian was doing from the way Susie tried to squirm back up his body. He laughed and clamped his arm across her chest.

"Hold still, Susie. Let Christian touch you."

"I can't."

"Yeah, you can. Press down, angel. It'll slide in, no problem," Joel said.

Susie jerked, then slumped and gave a deep groan. Joel felt the press of Christian's finger through the thin membrane that separated Susie's channels and the breath caught in his throat. Joel looked at Christian and they smiled.

"You okay, Susie?" Christian asked.

"Oohagaawd."

"I think that was alien-speak for I'm fine, thank you," Joel said.

Susie made a choked sound that was half laugh, half groan, all pleasure. Joel pressed his finger in as Christian pulled back.

"So sweet," Joel whispered.

He turned one finger into two and twisted as he pushed and Susie began to wail. She tipped her head back, locked her hands behind Joel's neck and kissed him. As her body arched into their combined touch, she pressed her tongue deeper into Joel's mouth.

His cock objected to being crushed but there was nothing Joel could do. He finger-fucked her and plundered with his tongue as he took control of the kiss. He felt the little ripples against his finger, the clenching that increased in intensity as Susie's body wound to a peak. Joel moved his fingers faster and on each thrust caught her clit with his thumb and she shattered, screaming into his mouth.

Joel kept his hand where it was, let the contractions play out and then withdrew at the same time as Christian. Joel pulled back from the kiss and Christian tugged Susie across into his arms. He stroked her hair and soothed her, kissing her face, wiping foam from her nose. Joel's cock was so relieved to have room to grow that it seemed to swell before his eyes, stretching up toward his navel. He eased his legs off the side of the bath and stood.

"Tomorrow, order a bigger tub," he said.

Susie wasn't sure if she could ever move again. She lay on Christian's chest, listening to his heart pounding beneath her ear. She was only too aware that both guys had hard-ons that could drill for oil, but wasn't sure if she could cope with either of them in her backside.

"I didn't hurt you, did I?" Christian asked.

"No."

Joel lifted her from the tub and wrapped a towel around her.

"We'll be gentle. We'd never hurt you," Joel said. "Trust us?"

Susie nodded. She did trust them and it made her feel warm and wonderful that they wanted to look after her. She could look after them, after the house and they'd take care of her.

Christian climbed from the tub and Joel carried her to the bedroom.

"I don't—" she began.

Joel put his finger over her lips. "Neither of us will do anything you don't want."

Christian settled at her side, a streak of foam making a Mohawk on his head. Joel laughed and brushed it off. He lay down on Susie's other side.

"Let us take care of you, angel. Anything we do you don't like, tell us to stop. We will," Joel said.

"Okay."

"Feel like riding a cowboy?" Joel asked.

Susie straddled his body and knelt with the lips of her pussy pressed against his cock. She rubbed herself up and down his velvety length as his hands settled on her hips.

"Your dick looks angry." Susie wiped her finger over the dark purple, plum-shaped head.

"No, just desperate." Joel lifted her hips. "I'm all yours, darlin'."

Christian slid his hand between Susie's legs and pulled Joel's cock back so it nudged her folds. Susie wiggled her hips against the press of the blunt head and then sank down, one long, slow press that had Joel biting his bottom lip. Joel slid his hands onto her back and pulled her down so he could kiss her. The guy could work magic with his mouth. Susie loved being kissed, loved the way his tongue found so many places to tease her.

She tensed when Christian's fingers slid into the crease of her butt, except Joel kept kissing her, kept his arms wrapped tight around her. Cold lube hit her asshole and Susie yelped into Joel's mouth. She tried not to clench as Christian's finger circled her anus. He didn't push in, just pressed around it. When she felt the wet touch of his tongue, she reared up from Joel's mouth. He caught hold of her head.

"Enjoy it," he whispered.

"But—"

"Only your butt," Joel said with a laugh. "It's bad and it's fun."

Susie laid her head across Joel's shoulder and relaxed into Christian's caress. It felt wrong, it felt right. The sensitive nerve endings in her ass rippled and Susie groaned. Then his finger replaced his tongue, pushing through the burn until she felt comfortably full and Susie clenched around it. Clenched Joel at the same time.

"Fuck us both, Susie," Joel said.

She pulled up off Joel's cock and Christian's finger withdrew a little. When she pushed back down, his finger pressed back. If she felt full now, how the hell could she cope with two cocks? But she would. It was what she wanted. Christian moved his head onto her back but his hand stayed where it was. His finger slid in and out of her ass, slow and gentle. Susie started to breathe faster.

"Is that good?" Christian whispered.

Susie could only nod. She felt Christian's knuckle and then gasped as something larger thrust inside her.

"What...?" she groaned.

"Two fingers, sweetheart. I have to stretch you a bit. You're so tight. You have such a cute backside."

Susie could hardly think about what she was doing to Joel as Christian continued his assault, pressing and stretching her channel, scissoring his fingers apart. She wriggled and groaned at the conflicting sensations and emotions. It felt good, but different. It felt perfect but wicked to have Joel's length in her cunt and Christian's fingers in her ass. She wished it was Christian's cock, but she was afraid between them they'd split her apart.

As Joel moved her up and down on his engorged dick, Christian kept a matching rhythm. For a while, his fingers surged in as Joel pressed into her, then they changed and as Joel pulled back, Christian pushed forward. Susie could only cope for a short time before the pulsing sensations became too much to resist. She cried out as the orgasm swept over her, carrying her on a tidal wave of pleasure that rushed from her groin to every part of her body then left her quivering on Joel's chest like a stranded jellyfish.

Christian shifted and when Joel's hips lifted, Susie realized that Christian was pressing his cock into Joel's ass. Joel pushed her up and both of them had their hands on her breasts, stroking her nipples, tracing shapes with their fingers. Susie felt the familiar coils of pleasure begin to stir back to life. Joel cantered his hips into her, plunging into her wet sheath. He kept his eyes on hers as he thrust up, his breath exploding from his lungs in short, loud bursts. Joel tensed and gave a deep guttural groan. He clutched her tightly as he spurted long wrenching blasts of cum straight toward her heart.

Susie had Christian pressed against her back. He'd lifted Joel's legs and he pushed them toward his body as he drove into him. Susie felt every jamming thrust of Christian into Joel echoed in her pussy. As Christian growled his release, she came again, her muscles clamping around Joel's softening cock. Just for a moment, Susie wished she wasn't on the Pill. She imagined Joel's seed rushing toward a receptive egg, assuming the cancer treatment hadn't made her infertile.

She curled up with her guys in a tangled mess, let them hold her safe in their arms. Being loved like this was more than she'd ever hoped for.

Chapter Twenty-Two

❧

Christian's life had never been better. Work poured in and Bella was negotiating a deal with a major publisher. Best of all, Joel came home from work as early as he could on Tuesdays and Thursdays so they had a few hours to play with Susie. Saturdays were perfect because they had the entire day and night with her. Susie had worked on every inch of the house, transforming it into the home Christian remembered as a boy. Everything sparkled. Vases overflowed with flowers. The air always smelled sweet with the aroma of freshly baked cookies or bread. Susie washed their clothes, tackled the ironing mountain, cooked their meals and drove them crazy with lust. When Christian wasn't working on one of his magazine assignments, he added chapters to his erotic fantasy, knowing no one would believe it and yet so much was true.

Not only did Susie transform the house, she transformed them. Although Joel was still the household's alpha male, he was more thoughtful and kinder. Susie had softened his edges. Sometimes Joel stared at Christian as though there was something he wanted to tell him. Christian could wait for as long as it took. The change in Susie had been her gain in confidence. She no longer tried to cover her scar. She looked happy. Sometimes she fucking bounced.

He couldn't stop smiling. Life was perfect. Almost perfect. Just one word missing. Not the feeling, not the link they had between them because it was there but not spoken. Only the word. Love. Christian wanted to tell Susie he loved her but he held the words back, waiting for Joel.

Christian lingered by the kitchen door. "Can I come in yet?"

Joel had been messing around in the kitchen for the last hour getting a picnic ready.

"Okay."

Joel was struggling to fasten the clips on a large hamper.

"Think I bought too much," Joel said. "Is Susie here?"

They lifted their heads when they heard the front door open and smiled. Giving Susie a key was a step toward asking her to move in. Joel had wanted to do it a week ago. Christian didn't want to rush her. They'd settled on taking her out for a meal tonight and popping the question.

"Hey, beautiful." Joel stepped forward to give her a kiss.

Christian loved watching them kiss. He knew it was something most people wouldn't understand, but sharing Susie enhanced his love for her. He adored seeing Joel this happy and the pair looked so damn sexy. Susie was precious, a special woman, and Christian would do anything for her. He wanted to make her the happiest person in the world.

As she turned from Joel, Christian tugged her into his embrace, pressed his lips against hers and tasted Joel. His cock purred in his pants.

"You look lovely," Christian said.

Susie glanced down. She wore jeans, her red, hooded top and trainers. "You always say that no matter what I'm wearing."

"That's because you always look lovely."

"Right, we're off," Joel said. "I want Christian as shotgun so I'm not distracted."

Christian groaned. "You just want to stop me having fun in the backseat."

Joel grinned. "I need a navigator."

"I could do that," Susie said.

"Right hand up now," Christian barked.

Susie flung up her left hand. She looked at it and sighed.

Christian high-fived Joel and Susie stuck her knee into the back of Christian's leg as she walked past. His knee buckled and Joel laughed.

"So where are we going?" Susie asked.

"Bisham Woods," Joel said. "Via the M25."

Susie and Christian groaned in unison. "We'll never get there."

But the traffic was lighter than Christian expected, the sun came out and Joel stopped singing after they both howled, so Christian thought the day would continue to be great.

By the time they'd trekked for miles into the woods, Christian wasn't so sure. Every time he thought they'd come across the perfect place for a picnic, Joel decided it wasn't quite right. Too shady. Too open. Too near the path. Poison ivy. Christian opened his mouth to point out there was no such thing in England but saw the determined glint in Joel's eyes and kept quiet. He had a feeling he knew what Joel was up to, but Susie looked too tired to walk much further. They were all hot. Susie had taken off her red top and tied it around her waist. Joel had his shirt unbuttoned and Christian had removed his T-shirt despite the teasing that he'd scare the local fauna.

"That's it," Christian said. "Here's fine, Joel."

They were in a shaded glen where the trees were less dense. Sunlight trickled through the canopy, trailing ribbons of light to the forest floor. Christian shook out the blanket and Susie collapsed on it.

"Hey, we need to put out the food," Joel said.

"I'm weighing it down in case the wind blows it away." Susie closed her eyes.

"What wind?" Joel asked.

Christian picked up two corners and motioned for Joel to do the same. The next moment Susie was shrieking as they tossed her in the air.

"Put me down," she yelled.

A couple more tosses and they obliged. Susie scooted off the blanket.

"Well done. I think you've frightened off all wildlife in the vicinity that weren't already freaked by the sight of Christian's bare chest," Joel said. "We shouldn't be bothered by bears or wild boar now."

"Why is it I think I'm already in danger from the local wildlife?" Susie said.

Christian laughed. Joel opened the picnic hamper and started to take everything out. Christian had carried two bottles of champagne in polystyrene tubes in his backpack along with glasses covered in bubble wrap. He'd wanted to bring plastic cups but Joel had insisted on the real thing. He could see how much trouble Joel had gone to. White linen napkins, plates and cutlery. The hamper must have weighed a ton. Christian felt guilty he hadn't offered to help carry it.

"Joel, this is lovely," Susie said. "How many people are joining us?"

There was a lot of food, Christian thought, but after all that walking he could eat a horse — and Susie.

The food looked great but Susie didn't feel very hungry. She tried to look as though she were eating a lot but wasn't sure that she fooled Christian. The champagne rushed around her bloodstream and she lay back, watching the trees circling above her head.

"Oh God, I'm drunk," she said with a groan, and turned to glare at Joel. "It's your fault. You're driving so you've given me your share."

"Who, me?"

Susie threw a strawberry at him and Joel caught it in his mouth. Susie loved the angular jut of his chin, loved—she knew she'd fallen in love with them. How could she not? They were kind and considerate and they made her laugh. Christian was soft, sweet and easy to talk to. Joel was dominant and very physical but funny. She liked the rougher edge to Joel and cherished the gentle touch of Christian. Susie could never choose between them. Together they were a perfect balance. Though Joel was the controller, the strong one, and without him there would be no three.

She pushed herself up on her elbows. Christian had packed everything back into the hamper and Joel lay on his side, watching her.

"Want to play a game, Red Riding Hood," Joel asked.

"What sort of game?"

"Hide and seek."

Susie looked from Joel to Christian. "And you two are the wolves?"

Christian dropped on all fours and growled.

"What a cute puppy," Susie said, and patted his behind.

"Answer me before I show you what big teeth I have," Joel said.

Susie narrowed her eyes. "What are you really chasing?"

Joel sighed. "First one to catch you gets your asshole tonight."

She glanced at Christian. He shrugged and gave a timid smile.

"It seems the only fair way," Joel said.

"You could let me choose," Susie pointed out.

Joel sat up. Susie was pleased to see he looked shocked at the idea. Not that she'd be choosing. Susie knew Joel wanted her ass, he'd told her often enough. She knew that Christian would accept he had to come second, but she didn't see why she should make life easy.

"Where's the incentive for me?" she asked.

"What would you like?" Joel grinned.

"If I get back to the blanket without you catching me, you have to be my slaves for the day."

"Ah, Susie. What have we done? We've created a monster," Joel said.

She stood and put her hands on her hips. "Well?"

"Okay," Christian said.

She knew Christian would agree. Joel looked at her, sighed and then nodded.

"Facedown on the blanket, hands over ears, eyes shut. Count to two hundred," she said, and ran.

Joel dropped to press his nose into the blanket and chuckled.

"Christ, Joel, how did you come up with that?" Christian turned to face him.

"I'm trying to be fair."

Christian raised his eyebrows. Joel and fair were not words that went together.

"Okay, I fucked her first but we both know that if we'd waited for you to make a move, we'd still be waiting. Am I right?"

Christian nodded.

"This way we get an even chance. I brought a butt plug with me. She needs stretching. She can take our fingers but you've got a thick cock, pal."

"So when are we going to ask her to move in?"

"Tonight. You going to do it?"

"Okay."

Joel smiled. "Right, we've lain here long enough. May the best man win."

"You don't think Susie will?"

"Not a chance in hell."

Joel jumped to his feet and bolted. Christian rolled onto his back and tucked his hands behind his head. He wasn't running anywhere.

Susie soon realized that hiding in woodland wasn't easy. She could stand behind one of the thicker tree trunks but she wanted somewhere more secure. She didn't fancy crawling into a low lying thicket to share space with creepy crawlies. Anything with more than four legs freaked her out. Could she climb a tree? Yes, if the branches hung at convenient levels, but they didn't. In the end the decision was taken for her because she heard someone crashing through the foliage to her right. Susie nipped behind the nearest large tree and didn't move.

"Little Red Riding Hood," Joel called.

Susie didn't think he could see her, though he could probably hear her heart the way it pounded.

"Come and see the surprise Grandma's got for you."

Ha, Susie wasn't falling for that.

"Did I ever tell you that I'm an expert tracker?"

She'd probably left a trail of trampled undergrowth a child could follow.

"I can smell you, Susie."

A flood of cream wet her panties. He was nearer.

"You know what I'm going to do when I catch you?"

She pressed her lips together to capture the whimper of excitement.

"Run now and I'll give you ten seconds start."

She wasn't falling for that either. Joel wandered around, still on her right. She risked a glance. *Shit.* He was looking straight at her. Adrenaline surged and she raced off, weaving her way around the trees and jumping fallen branches. She could hear Joel behind her. The bastard was laughing. Susie knew she'd lost this. She wasn't even sure of the way back to the picnic spot but she kept running. Smack into a solid chest. How the hell had he managed to get in front of her?

Arms wrapped around her. "Mine," Joel said.

Susie began to struggle but one brush of his lips against hers and she melted. Susie's arms crept around his neck and Joel's tongue plunged into her mouth. His hands slid to her waist and pulled her tight to his body, his cock, a rigid length between them. This guy could kiss, Susie thought. If there were Olympics for kissing, he'd be a cert for the gold. Joel somehow knew when to pull back, when to be strong. It felt as though he were sucking out her soul, only in a good way.

They broke apart with a gasp.

"Oh, what big eyes you have," Susie said.

Joel grinned. "All the better to see you with, Miss Hood. What long legs you have."

"All the better to wrap around your waist. What big ears you have."

"All the better to hear you with, Miss Hood." He flicked out his tongue. "What sweet lips you have."

"All the better to kiss you with." Susie squeezed his biceps. "What big arms you have."

Joel ran his arms down her sides. "All the better to hug you with, my dear."

Susie put her hand on his cock and stroked. "Ooh—"

"Yeah," Joel said with a laugh. "I think we can miss that one."

"What big teeth you have," Susie whispered.

His eyes darkened. "All the better to eat you up, Miss Hood."

He slid one hand onto her left breast.

Susie took a chance. "What a big heart you have."

"All the better to love you with," Joel whispered.

His hands fell to his sides. Susie sensed he wanted to say more and waited but the expression on his face changed and his lip curled. He pointed left. "The blanket's that way. I don't think Christian moved. Ten seconds start and if you get there first, I'll be your slave."

The thrill of the chase made every one of Joel's nerve endings sizzle. He felt like a wolf, strong and in control of his pack. He loved the way Susie had grown since he'd met her. He loved it when she resisted because it allowed him to be dominant. He didn't want someone who did everything he said, hung on his every word, someone who loved him unconditionally because he didn't deserve it. The more she defied him, the crazier she drove him. It was different with Christian. Their relationship was complex. Not a simple top and bottom, Joel relied on Christian to keep him level.

Joel bounded after Susie, saw her racing ahead of him. Of course, she was going the wrong way. There was no chance of her getting back to the blanket before him. As she slowed and he gained on her, Joel thought about what he'd said. He'd sort of told her he loved her. He didn't regret saying it but he was glad he hadn't said more. Joel tightened his mouth. How the fuck did he know if he loved her?

Susie stopped. She turned to face him, her chest heaving.

"You...are such...a sod," she panted. "It's not this way...is it?"

"Climb on."

Joel turned so she could jump on his back. Susie leapt up and wrapped her arms around him. She laid her head on his shoulder.

"Home, slave," she said, and Joel laughed.

Chapter Twenty-Three

Christian sat up when he heard Susie laughing. She slithered off Joel's back a few yards from the blanket and made a run for it. When Joel tried to grab her, Christian launched himself at his legs, knocking him sideways. Susie threw herself onto the blanket.

"I won," she shouted.

"Cheats never prosper," Joel said, and ground his fist into Christian's ribs.

"Slaves certainly don't," Susie snapped back.

Christian was relieved when Joel let him go and laughed. "Okay. Slaves for the day. But I choose when."

"No, no," Susie said. "Slave, not slaves. I only beat Joel back."

Joel opened his mouth and then closed it again. Christian had to snap his own jaw shut. How far would Joel let Susie go?

Susie grabbed a bottle of water, took a drink and threw it to Joel. He drank half, tossed it to Christian and sat down on the blanket.

"Why didn't you try to find me?" Susie asked Christian.

"I had a plan but it didn't work. I should have known better than attempt to outfox a lawyer."

"Or a wolf," Susie said.

She looked at Joel and Christian saw his eyes darken.

"You won one race but I won the other. Take your clothes off," Joel said.

"Here?" she whispered.

Joel raised his eyebrows. "There's no one around."

"But someone might come. There could be a whole trail of happy ramblers heading this way."

"Have you seen or heard anyone other than us?" Joel asked.

Susie shook her head.

"Take your clothes off," Joel said again.

Christian's heart jumped around in his chest. He'd seen Joel in these moods before, pushing and goading until he got his way.

"I don't think I want to," Susie said.

Christian wanted to tell her it wasn't worth arguing but kept his mouth shut.

Joel lay on his side, supporting his weight on his elbow. "Yeah, you do. I'm not going to fuck you in the ass out here, don't worry. But I've got a present for you, only it's something to wear so strip."

She didn't move.

"What's the matter, Susie?" Joel asked.

"It's...against the law."

Joel laughed. "But that's why it's fun, that's why you're creaming in your panties at the thought of getting fucked in the woods. Doing what's forbidden is far more exciting than doing what's allowed." He reached over and trailed a finger along her jawline. "How far can you go, Susie? Don't you want to see?"

She gave a shaky sigh. "Say please."

Joel tipped his head. "Please."

Her fingers moved to the top button of her shirt and Christian's breath caught in his throat.

"Stand up," Joel said.

Susie stood. Joel unzipped his pants and adjusted his cock. Christian knew how arousing Joel found this kind of power play. Joel had once persuaded him to jack off while they sat in a restaurant. Thank Christ for paper napkins.

Susie glanced around as she unfastened the buttons on her shirt but she pulled it off and let it fall.

"Jeans." Joel stared up at her with his dangerous eyes.

Christian licked his lips when Susie bent, taking off her tennis shoes and socks. She wasn't trying to look sexy and somehow that made her more so. She stood there, in white cotton pants and matching bra, wiggling her toes on the blanket, her hands brushing her hips as she clenched and unclenched her fists. Christian swallowed. He could have come at the mere sight of her.

"Strip Christian."

Christian's cock did a whoop of joy. He couldn't take his eyes off Susie. Every curve was a delight. She even had a hint of color in her skin after the day in the garden, and gleamed in the sunshine. With her shining, silver blonde hair and soulful eyes she looked like an angel. Christian scrambled to his feet. Not much left to take off, his shoes had gone, his loose-fitting pants spilled over his feet. Her fingers fumbled with his button, his cock tried to help with brute force and Christian took over. Susie tugged pants and cherry-covered boxers down together and Christian stepped out of them.

"Suck his cock," Joel said.

Susie dropped to her knees, licked the end of Christian's dick and then wrapped her lips over the tip and gave gentle suck. Christian curled his toes into the blanket and threaded his fingers in her hair. Tremors of arousal shuddered through his body.

"Take off her bra, Christian."

He reached down, unclipped it and when Susie shrugged, it fell to the blanket.

"Lie down, Susie. Christian, panties off."

Joel had his cock out of his pants, stroking it gently. Christian wondered if he was going to join in or not. A smile crossed his lips when he pulled off Susie's pants. They were soaked. She was as excited as him. When no more instructions came from Joel, they both looked at him.

Joel had to squeeze the base of his cock hard to stop himself coming. Ordering Christian around was never very successful, but now Susie was playing too, Christian had become more biddable. Joel wondered how far he could make them go.

"I want you to fuck, but when I say stop, you have to obey," he said.

As Christian began to kiss Susie's breasts, Joel retrieved a plastic bag from the bottom of Christian's backpack. In it were lube and two butt plugs, one larger than the other. Christian slid his mouth down Susie's body and she writhed on the blanket. Joel was tempted to rip off his clothes and join them but he needed to keep himself away from Susie for a while. That confession she'd teased out when they'd played around with the words of that fairy tale had thrown him. He couldn't fall in love with her. He had to get himself back under control.

Christian draped Susie's legs over his shoulders and eased his cock into her. Their faces were flushed with lust, their breathing ragged. Watching the pair of them in that intimate act dragged a large drop of pre-cum from Joel's dick. He wiped it with his thumb and caught Susie watching him. Joel leaned, daggling his hand over her face and let her lick the smear away. She sucked long and hard and Joel felt as though she were dragging part of him into her. Christian had begun to pant, his spine arched into a taut bow as he thrust between her legs.

Joel lubed up the larger butt plug and pressed it against Christian's ass. Christian froze.

"Did I tell you to stop," Joel snapped.

A second's hesitation and Christian resumed his rhythm. He groaned as Joel pressed harder, but the plug slid in, popping past the ring of restrictive muscle and lodging snug inside Christian's butt. Joel couldn't resist tormenting Christian for a while and pulled the plug in and out as he thrust into Susie.

"Oh fuck," Christian gasped.

"Stop moving," Joel said.

Susie was the one who wailed and tried to buck her hips. Christian trembled with the effort of keeping still.

"Susie, I told you to stop moving," Joel said.

He pushed Christian's thighs apart so he could see Susie's butt. The sight of Christian's thick cock buried in her cunt dragged another spurt of pre-cum from Joel's cock. He squirted a ring of lube onto the purple rubber plug and pressed it against Susie's tight puckered rosebud.

"What are you doing?" she gasped.

"It's okay, Susie. Push down," Christian said.

"Christian, pull out as I push," Joel ordered.

Joel moved so that he could see her face as he worked the plug into her butt. Pain and pleasure side by side. He knew it would burn as he pressed it deeper. She yelped and then the rubber was sucked inside. Joel shuddered at the thought of pushing his cock inside that forbidden passage, knowing how tight and hot it would be.

"Joel," Christian gasped.

"Now you can fuck her."

Christian eased his way back into Susie, the space for his cock now restricted by the plug. Breath sawed in and out of her mouth. Her fingers pressed deep into Christian's arms as he thrust his hips into her. Joel lay at their side, twisting their plugs, fucking them both at the same time. Imagining what they were feeling brought him a different sort of joy. They looked good together, staring into each other's eyes, and it was exactly what he wanted, what he'd planned, so why did he have this ache in his chest?

Susie had lost count of how many times she'd come. She had to remind herself to take a breath. One orgasm blurred into another, fire and ice rained inside her pussy and ass. The feeling of fullness as Christian had fucked her while Joel twisted the damn plug, too much to stand. Her head swam on sensory overload. When Christian burst inside her, the flood of his cum went on forever. When Christian withdrew, it was Joel who straightened her legs, stroked her head.

"You're so beautiful," he said. "When you come you look like an angel, your hair spread out around your head like a golden halo. I can hardly wait to be where that butt plug is right now. You have to keep it in until we get home. It'll stretch you, get you ready for my cock."

Christian rolled to her side, wrapped an arm over her chest and snuggled into her neck.

"Babes in the wood," Joel said, and gave a little laugh.

Susie was aware that something had changed with Joel, as though he'd deliberately put himself on the outside of them emotionally. She had a feeling she knew why and she wouldn't let him get away with it.

"I need you inside me," Susie said.

"Want to wrap your hot little mouth around me?" Joel asked.

"No, I want your cock inside me, your cum filling me. I want you, Joel."

She saw his nostrils flare.

"Why haven't you taken off your clothes?" she asked.

"Someone might come."

Susie laughed and then she narrowed her eyes. "Christian, let's strip him."

Joel didn't put up much resistance but the three of them tussled on the blanket for a while before Christian managed to drag off the last item of Joel's clothing. Christian pulled back then lay on his side and watched. Susie sat astride Joel, her pussy pressed against the base of his cock, but she knew any second he'd roll her over.

He surprised her. Joel turned her so the hard flat muscles of his stomach pressed against her back. Joel lifted her leg over his thigh and nudged the blunt, wet head of his cock against her folds, soaked by her cream and Christian's cum. Air washing over her shaved pussy added another sensation to those swarming her mind. Joel didn't push in, just held her tight and rubbed against her until Susie tried to squirm her way onto him.

"Please, Joel," she begged.

His breath hit her neck in little bursts as he panted.

"Please."

Joel shifted her leg higher over his thigh and slid inside her. Susie gave a long moaning cry.

"Jesus, so tight," Joel gasped. "God, you feel good."

His hands roamed her breasts, teasing her nipples as he began to pulse into her, long gentle thrusts and a slow withdrawal.

"Damn it, Joel. Fuck me hard," Susie said.

She felt the change in him, the wolf unleashed and he began to thrust, pulling his hips farther back to drive himself forward. Christian's hands moved to his cock as he watched and his tongue slipped between his lips.

"Joel," Susie wailed.

The growing tightness was bliss, was hell. The butt plug felt enormous but every withdrawal, she wanted his cock back, each pounding drive sent waves of sweet heat tumbling through her and each thrust wound Susie a little more. She knew Joel was close, could tell from the change in his breathing. She kept having to remind herself to draw air then gulped as if it were the last breath she'd take.

"Joel," she cried again.

His mouth slipped to her neck and he nipped her. The bite bordered on painful and sent Susie spiraling into the void, rivers of bliss pouring through her body. Joel was kissing her now, melting her pain, flooding her with his cum. Her muscles dragged every drop from him but it wasn't just his cum that Susie wanted. She was after his heart.

* * * * *

She slept all the way back, a satiated heap sprawled over the backseat, the safety belt an awkward restraint around her middle. Christian had his hand on Joel's thigh, stroking gently with his fingers. They didn't talk. They didn't need to. Christian didn't remember ever being so happy. They worked together as a three. He wasn't jealous of Joel. He loved him. He loved watching him make love to Susie because that's what it was. Not fucking.

"Are you happy?" Christian asked.

Joel glanced at him. "Yeah."

Only why didn't Christian think Joel was telling the truth?

Christian carried Susie into the house and laid her on the couch. She was still asleep.

"We wore her out," Christian said.

"And the day's not over." Joel gave Christian a tender kiss. "You let me win."

"You're faster than me."

Joel chuckled. "I hope you mean at running."

Christian opened his eyes wide. "What else?"

"Make something to eat and then we'll wake Sleeping Beauty."

Christian chaos-defrosted a bolognaise sauce Susie had prepared for them and put water on to boil. Joel set the table, opened a bottle of red wine and unpacked the hamper.

226

"Susie didn't seem to eat much at lunch," Joel said.

Christian had noticed. "She drank plenty though."

Joel laughed. "That's probably why she couldn't eat."

Christian grated a dish of parmesan cheese and put it on the table.

"Pasta ready?" Joel asked.

"I'm not throwing it against the wall now that Susie's cleaned." Christian pulled out a strand with a fork and bit it. "It's fine. Want to wake her?"

"I am awake," Susie said from the doorway. "I wondered why the walls in the kitchen were sticky."

Her hair was wet and she wore one of Joel's blue shirts. Joel pulled out a chair for her to sit between them.

"Do you still have the—" he began.

"No, I took it out. You're not supposed to keep them in for hours and hours."

"How do you know that?" Joel poured her a glass of wine.

"I read it."

"Where?" Joel asked.

"In a book."

"What book?"

"*Harry Potter and the Chamber of Secrets.*"

Joel laughed so hard it made him cough.

Christian put the plates on the table. He could guess what book but he didn't want Joel to tell Susie he was Raphael Strange.

"Alternatively?" Joel asked.

"It was a book I read called *The Club*," Susie said.

"Good book?" Joel asked, turning his fork in the spaghetti.

Christian tensed. He did not want to hear that she thought it was crap. Joel glanced in his direction.

"I enjoyed it," Susie said.

Joel watched her. "Would you like to go to a club like that?"

"You mean they exist?" Susie said with gasp. "I thought it was made-up."

"Poor naive Susie. I suppose you believe in the tooth fairy and Santa Claus," Joel said.

"You're breaking my heart." Susie made her chin wobble.

Joel ran a finger along her lip, wiped up a smear of sauce and put the finger in his own mouth. "There are clubs where you can do whatever you like, you just have to know where to find them. But how far would you go?"

"I'm not brave," Susie said.

Joel smiled. "I think you are. I think you're braver than most women."

"I'd never do this with anyone else," Susie said. "Only us three, no more people, only with you. I trust you not to hurt me, not to break my heart."

The breath caught in Christian's throat. He laid his hand over hers. He had a million things to say and couldn't get them out of his mouth.

Susie gave a little grin. "Of course, if you do hurt me, my brother Mike will kill you."

Chapter Twenty-Four

Susie had no appetite. Nervous about what was to come, her body humming in anticipation, she played with her food while the guys cleared their plates as if they hadn't eaten all day. When she rose to stack the dishwasher, Christian pulled her down and Joel cleared the table. Christian didn't let go of her hand. He ran his thumb around her palm and stared into her eyes.

"You can say no at any time," he whispered. "No one's going to force you to do anything."

Susie glanced at Joel's back.

"No one will force you," Christian repeated.

Joel closed the door of the dishwasher, turned and leaned back against the counter, his dark eyes glittering. "Ready to fuck?"

His words sent goose bumps skittering down Susie's spine. Joel held out his arms and Susie went to him, let him hug her.

"No pressure, angel," he whispered. "Christian's right."

They led her upstairs to Christian's bedroom. Joel let go of her hand and went to draw the curtains while Christian switched on the bedside lamps. Her guys were so gorgeous. Similar yet so different. Open-hearted Christian with every emotion written on his face. Joel, the controller, who held part of himself back.

Susie stood her ground as they advanced. Christian stepped behind, and through his pants she felt the whisper touch of his rigid cock as it brushed enticingly against her backside. Joel undid the buttons of her shirt, bottom to top, and Christian reached to pull it over her shoulders and down her arms. The collective intake of male breath froze her own. After her shower, all she'd put on was Joel's shirt.

"Damn, you're beautiful," Joel said.

"Pretty good from back here too." Christian slid his hands over her bottom.

Joel unfastened his shirt and tossed it to the floor. He never took his eyes off her. Susie could feel Christian stripping too, the draught of his clothes falling behind her. She dropped her gaze to the smattering of dark hair that ran down the center of Joel's body, the central darker arrow that ran to his groin, pointing to a surprise. Susie's eyes widened. His cock rose long and thick from a bed of black curls, its wide, flared head already dark with blood and shining with pre-cum. But it was the slender, black ring that encircled his cock and balls that held Susie's attention. She turned to look at Christian and he wore the same.

"Don't I get one?" Susie asked.

Christian laughed but Joel tweaked her nipples. "You could wear rings here."

The pinch sent a tremor racing to her pussy. "Wouldn't it hurt?"

"A little. That's the idea. Pain and pleasure side by side. You like the idea of something tight on your nipples, angel?" Joel nipped her again then dropped his head and soothed the place he'd hurt with his slick tongue.

Susie caught her breath as Christian's fingers slid between her legs.

Joel laughed. "I think you do. You're wet thinking about it."

Christian spun her around and his hungry mouth locked on hers, his tongue sliding through her lips and beginning the dance. His hands cupped her cheeks, tilting her head so the kiss could deepen. At the same time Christian pushed her into Joel's hard muscular body and Susie felt the solid ridge of

Joel's erection lying along the crease of her bottom. Christian's cock pressed against her belly as she stood sandwiched between them. Their heat made her burn, sent fire racing through her body, propelling her heart into a pumping frenzy. She was so wet between her legs, her cream ran down her thighs.

Susie moaned as Christian nibbled her lip, teasing her before diving back into her mouth. Joel's hands drew patterns on her hips. One swipe with his fingers over her swollen folds and he painted lazy circles on her hips with her juice.

A heart?

Christian turned her and they pressed her tight between them again. Joel kissed her so hard it almost hurt then pulled back and kissed her better. It was the way Joel always played, hard and soft as though he didn't trust himself to only be gentle.

She twisted between them, wiggled and squirmed against their cocks, knowing it would drive them crazy. She drove herself mad at the same time, her tender nipples rubbing against the hair on Joel's chest, her bare pussy against his wiry curls while Christian's cock edged deeper into the crease of her bottom.

Joel lifted his mouth, panting into her face. "Little Red Riding Hood, I think the wolves caught you."

"If you two move, I'll fall over," Susie said.

Joel winked at Christian and she wondered what was coming. Susie squealed as the two men threw them and her sideways. They landed on the bed in a tangle of arms and legs. Christian tugged the duvet from beneath them and tipped Susie onto her knees. Joel smacked her backside. She rolled over and smacked his. Moments later the three of them were tussling, laughing as they tried to pin each other down.

Susie had a feeling that when she found herself astride Christian it was more by their design than hers. Joel positioned himself behind her, straddling Christian's thighs. He pulled her against his chest, his hands holding her breasts. Susie reached back to wrap her arms around Joel's neck and dropped her head back onto his shoulder. When Joel's mouth trailed up her taut neck, Susie gave a deep groan.

Christian's hand played at her pussy as it sat over the length of his cock, his fingers rubbing her cream over them both. He brushed her clit and Susie moaned, digging her fingers into the hair at the back of Joel's neck. One circular caress of her eager nub by Christian's finger and Susie came, lightning clamping her muscles, rumbling pleasure enveloping her body as she dropped over a cliff into the abyss.

Joel's mouth slid over her neck, kissing her, laving her, his strong arms holding her up while Christian sank his finger inside her.

"Susie, you're on fire," Christian whispered.

Arms lifted her and Christian's hard cock nudged at her wet folds. One tilt of her hips and Christian slid through her swollen lips, kept going and going until he was buried deep inside her.

"Oh God," she groaned.

Joel pushed, Christian pulled and she collapsed on his chest.

"Okay, sweetheart?" Christian whispered.

"I want you both inside me."

At that moment Susie didn't think there was anything in the world she wanted more. Her guys loving her at the same time, filling her with their cocks, their cum, their hearts. Joel's hands ran up the back of her thighs and spread open the cheeks of her butt. Susie trembled and Christian wrapped his arms around her waist. The warm, wet tease of Joel's tongue sliding up and down the crease of her bottom made her cry out. Christian groaned and Susie knew Joel was licking him too, could feel his caress at the point Christian's cock entered her body.

Joel licked and teased until Susie could think of nothing but the sensation his touch was bringing. Cold lube replaced his warm tongue and then Joel's finger eased its way inside her. He moved up the bed to lie with his head near hers, watching her face as he finger-fucked her ass. Two fingers and the burn was greater but the pleasure greater still.

"You still want this, Susie?" Joel whispered at her ear. "Like my cock in your ass?"

"Yes," she gasped.

"Tell me what you want."

"I want...I want you to fuck my ass while Christian fucks my cunt. I want both of you at the same time and I want you now."

Joel moved back and Susie tensed.

"Relax, sweetheart," Christian said. "All you have to do is push down against Joel."

More lube and then Susie felt the thick head of Joel's shaft pressing against her asshole. *Oh God, could she do this?* Her anus twitched at the pressure then opened and a tiny part of him moved forward. The burn in the ultrasensitive channel was intense but Joel didn't stop. Susie felt the fire inside her as the nerve-rich tissue responded to the intrusion, blistering bites of sensation spreading through her pelvis to her spine and he still pushed on.

"Oh God." Susie's fingers scrabbled at the sheet and Joel's hands settled over hers, holding her still.

"It's okay...nearly there...you feel so good," Joel gasped.

A bead of sweat rolled down the side of Christian's face. Susie wanted to lick it and then the sensation of being filled by Joel's rock-hard cock stole Susie's ability to think. Her pussy began to spasm as she clenched down on Christian's shaft and at that moment, Joel's shaft slipped through the ring of restrictive muscle and surged into her tight passage.

"Fuck, fuck, fuck," Joel grunted. "Jesus. Ah, Susie, you're so hot and tight. What the hell are you doing to me?"

Joel gulped for air at her back, Christian panted at her front. She could feel both cocks throbbing as she contracted around them. Other than that, no one moved. Susie was awash in a kaleidoscope of sensation, colors swirling, senses flying as she struggled to keep control.

"Do something," she groaned.

Christian laughed. His hips flexed and he drew back his cock, allowing Joel to move. They settled into a rhythm, a smooth entry and withdrawal so she only had one of them fully inside her at time. Each forward thrust sent a flash of electricity tearing through her, clamping her gut, dragging a gasp from her lungs.

"Oh Christ, Susie," Christian moaned. "I can feel Joel moving inside you. It's fucking fantastic."

Their thrusts grew stronger, more powerful drives into her cunt and ass, one after the other, speeding to a point that she forgot to breathe.

"Now, Susie," Joel ordered. "Let go."

Let go of what? She wasn't holding on. Her body didn't belong to her but to them. She needed to breathe. The world faded at the edges, her vision blurred. Why couldn't she breathe? Joel sank his teeth into her shoulder and Susie broke like a piece of glass. She screamed as she was wrenched apart, wild convulsions wringing her body, tossing her in a perfect storm of pleasure that went on and on.

Christian cried out her name and lost his rhythm, driving into her as Joel did the same. Susie's muscles tightened on Joel's cock as her pussy relaxed. She felt the hot spurts of Christian's release, liquid fire shooting into her womb. Joel's body locked tight as his cock throbbed in her tight channel and his explosion sent further ribbons of fire blazing to her core.

Susie had never felt so good and so deliciously wicked in her life.

They collapsed in an exhausted pile of shaking limbs, hoarse breathing the only sound. Susie had never had a climax like that, maybe never would again. Her lungs hurt. She could hardly feel her body. Nothing worked when she told it to.

"Susie, Joel, I love you," Christian whispered.

The reaction of Joel at her back was slight but Susie didn't miss him tensing. Her face toward Christian, she smiled at him, mouthed "I love you" and hoped he knew why she'd not spoken out loud.

"Susie, how would you like to live here with us," Christian asked.

"You mean, move in?"

Christian nodded. "You can have your own room only we'd sort of like it if you shared our bed. I'm going to order a new one, a bigger one."

"And a tub," Susie said.

Christian laughed. "And a tub. We were thinking you could go to college. I've been checking and there are lots of places you could apply even though you don't have formal qualifications."

Her heart was sprinting. "But I wouldn't be earning any money, I—"

"You could still do things for us, the cooking and cleaning and we'd pay you."

At her back, Joel had said nothing but Susie felt his arm creep over her shoulder.

"Say yes, Susie," he whispered.

"Yes. Just let me have a few days to talk to my dad about it."

Christian gave her a fierce look. "Don't let him change your mind."

"He won't. I promise."

Chapter Twenty-Five

ഇ

Christian was working in his study when he heard Susie arrive. The door slammed. Adrenaline surged and he smiled. He didn't remember ever being this happy. When the three of them had made love it had been the best feeling in the world. First time for him and Susie, though he wasn't sure about Joel. Still, it was the first time for the three of them and that's what counted. His cock hardened at the thought of having Susie between them. Well, maybe he didn't need Joel right that moment.

Where was she? Christian had expected her to call him and run upstairs.

He shouted, "Hello, gorgeous."

No answer. As he padded downstairs he heard her throwing up in the bathroom. Christian stood by the door, wondering what to do.

"Susie, are you okay?" he asked. *Yeah, she's fine, stupid.*

The toilet flushed and a couple of minutes later, she emerged looking white and shaky.

"Come and sit down." Christian guided her into the kitchen and sat her on a chair.

He poured a glass of water and put it in her hands. Susie sipped it slowly. The question moved from Christian's head to his lips but he kept it there, not wanting to ask because if he was right, the consequences would be far-reaching for all of them. Oh God, he hoped she was pregnant, but what the hell would they do? Whose child would it be?

He slid his hand across the table and took hold of Susie's fingers.

"Are you sure you're okay?" he asked. "I noticed you were throwing up."

Susie let out a shuddery breath.

Christian swallowed hard. "Are you pregnant?"

"No."

She sounded so certain, he found himself disappointed. "Are you sure?"

"Yes, I'm sure."

"What is it then?"

"I must have eaten something that's upset me. I don't feel well."

"Go up to bed and have a sleep."

She was pale to the point of transparency. And something told Christian Susie was lying. She *was* having a baby, had no idea which one of them was the father and didn't know what to do.

"I think I'd better go home," Susie muttered.

"I'll drive you."

She kept so still and quiet and un-Susie-like, Christian's anxiety level rocketed. Susie sat with her eyes closed. Her hands trembled on her lap. When he pulled up on her street, Christian reached for her fingers.

"Sweetheart, what is it? Whatever's the matter, you can tell me. We can sort it out. There's nothing that can't be fixed."

"I'm okay."

"Is it your father? Do you want to move in with us now? I'll come into the house with you and get your stuff and you don't need to come back here again."

"I'm fine, Christian. Or I will be when I shake this off. I better not come round for a little while until I'm feeling better. Wouldn't want to give you and Joel a nasty bug."

Christian watched her until the door of the house closed and then drove home with an ache in his gut.

Alone in the house, Susie slid down the wall in the hall. This wasn't fair. Hadn't she been through enough? She shivered as though she was cold, but she was burning up. Part of her wanted to crawl into bed, pull the covers over her face and pretend everything was fine. The other part of her knew exactly what was wrong. Tired, no appetite and now sick—it could only be one thing. Tears ran down her cheeks and for a moment Susie didn't make a sound. Then, as her mind railed at the unfairness of life, she was overwhelmed with racking sobs. She'd found happiness at last and now it was going to be snatched away, just as she'd begun to believe she might have a future.

The key rattled in the lock, the door opened and Susie gulped, pressing her lips together.

"Hey, Suze, what you doing on the floor ? What's the matter?" Mike asked.

"I don't...feel...well," she hiccupped.

He dropped to her side and pulled her into his arms. "You think...?"

Susie nodded.

"You don't know for certain, Susie. You need to see the doctor. Where's his number?"

After the tears subsided and she had herself back under control, Susie made the call. "Could I speak to Mr. McMillan, please?" She'd either get him or an answer machine. She got him. "Hi, Mr. McMillan. It's Susie Hood. You remember—"

"Hello, Susie. Of course I remember you. What can I do for you?"

"I need to come and see you."

"Are you due for a check up?"

"No, but there's something wrong. I..." She broke off, gulping for air.

"Tomorrow, ten thirty," he said.

"Thank you."

"Well?" asked Mike as she put the phone down.

"Tomorrow morning."

He winced. "Sorry, Susie. I can't come with you. I told Shannon I'll take her to an interview in Maidstone."

"It's okay, Mike. I can go on my own."

"Why don't you get—what was his name? Joel?—to take you."

She nodded, not missing the fact that he didn't bother suggesting their dad or Pete.

"Go up and lie down. I'll make you a cup of tea before I head out again."

Mike gave her a hug and nudged her toward the stairs.

Susie crawled under the covers in her clothes. It was worrying that the doctor wanted to see her the next day. Susie curled up tighter. How could she talk to her dad about moving out now? She couldn't go and live with the guys. They wanted a healthy, fun Susie, not a sick, miserable one.

* * * * *

"I'm home," Joel called from the hall.

The moment he saw Christian, Joel knew something bad had happened.

"What is it?" he asked.

"There's something wrong with Susie."

"What sort of wrong?"

"When she got here this morning, she started throwing up."

Joel's gut clenched. "Is—"

"I asked her that."

"What did she say?"

"That she wasn't."

"Where is she?"

"I took her home."

Christian winced under Joel's glare.

"I know, but she wanted to go."

Joel exhaled noisily. "It could be a stomach bug."

"She said she was going to have a couple of days off."

"Right. So should we send her some flowers or something?"

Christian smiled. "That's a good idea."

Joel followed him through to the kitchen. Christian had made a chicken Caesar salad.

Both of them picked at the food.

Finally, Joel tossed down his fork. "She's pregnant," he said in a flat voice.

Christian sighed. "I think so."

"Fuck. She said she was on the Pill."

"She *is* on the Pill. I've seen the packet in the bathroom."

So had Joel.

"You don't think she'd do anything stupid, do you? Like get rid of it?" Christian asked.

"I don't know." Joel looked up from his plate. "Would that be stupid?" Christ, Christian looked so determined and Joel felt confused and bewildered. But then Christian had been thinking about this all day.

"Why didn't you call me?" Joel asked.

"What could you do? Look, if there is a baby, I don't want her to get rid of it. I don't care whose it is. I mean, I'd like it to be yours."

Joel felt a stab of guilt so sharp it trapped the air in his lungs. It had been announced at work today that he'd be leaving in a month. He'd come home to break the news to Christian and Susie and now he couldn't say anything.

Christian said. "Will you call her?"

Joel opened his mouth to ask why him and then closed it again. He took out his mobile.

"Hey, Susie."

"Hi, Joel."

"I'm here and you're not. That won't do."

"Sorry."

She sounded different. Too sick to joke? "Christian said you weren't feeling well this morning. How are you now?"

"Not so good. I've been throwing up all day."

Was morning sickness an all-day thing? Joel wondered. "Can I come over and give you a hug?"

"Better not in case it's catching."

The amount of time they'd spent together, they'd already have it.

"You don't think it's something you've eaten?" Joel asked.

"I don't know."

"Well, get better soon, sweetheart. We miss you."

"Bye, Joel."

"How did she sound?" Christian asked as Joel put the phone down.

"Not like Susie. Tired, maybe. I don't suppose you had chance to ask her when she was going to move in."

Christian shook his head and smiled. "I hope she *is* pregnant. We'd be a proper family. I'd love a boy with your beautiful face and Susie's sweet nature."

"You saying I don't have a sweet nature?"

"Only when you get your own way."

Joel grinned. "Don't I always get my own way?"

"I let you think you do."

Christian waited for a response but Joel kept quiet.

241

"Are you okay?" Christian asked.

"You really want a baby with Susie?" Joel asked.

Christian hesitated and Joel knew it was only because he wasn't sure of the right thing to say.

"Yeah, I do but you don't," Christian said, stiffening. "Why not?"

"I didn't say that. I just don't want to get excited about something that might not happen."

"Think about it, Joel. It would be so great. I'd love kids, love to give them everything I didn't have. Christ, our kids would have two dads. How great is that?"

Joel pulled Christian into his arms and held him tight. Everything was falling apart. How could he tell Christian now that he was leaving? It wasn't that he wanted to go, but he couldn't stay in London forever. A tiny bit of Joel wanted this child, if there was one, to be his because that would be his link to Christian and Susie, one he'd have forever.

Chapter Twenty-Six

ഔ

Susie went through a battery of tests and was told to return at four to speak to her consultant. No one had come with her. Pete was working—not that she wanted his company. Her father had offered to have the day off but Susie didn't want him there either. But she did want a hug.

Joel's office wasn't that far away. She'd looked up Horton and Standish in the telephone directory. Less than a mile from the hospital.

It felt like ten miles by the time she got there. Susie didn't think she needed to go back for the test results. The cancer was back. Only she couldn't tell Joel. She didn't want them to feel sorry for her and feel they had to look after her. She just wanted a hug.

Susie gave her name at the desk and was asked to wait in a spotless leather and chrome reception area. She'd just sat down when Rachel, who'd been at the party, walked past.

"Hi, Susie, what are you doing here? Come to see Joel?"

Susie pushed herself to her feet. "Hi, Rachel. Yes, if he's free."

"I expect he can spare a minute, though he's always rushed off his feet. We're going to be sorry to lose him."

What? "Me too." Susie smiled. *Oh God, Joel is leaving.* "Does he know yet how long?"

Shit, did that even make sense? She mustn't give herself away. Susie clamped her teeth into her cheek.

Rachel looked puzzled. "A month, isn't it?"

"Well, he was hovering over one or two months. I wasn't sure what he decided."

243

Go, Susie urged. *Leave now.* She needed Rachel to disappear before Joel came. "Well, have a good day," Susie said, wondering how inane she could sound. But Rachel left and Susie slumped back onto the chair.

Joel was leaving? Going back to the States. Her world was collapsing. Susie wondered how long he'd known. Since she'd first started to work for them? Did Christian know?

"Susie? What are you doing here?"

She looked up to see Joel smiling down at her.

"Just…passing," she gulped.

Joel sat next to her. "How are you feeling? You look pale. Still throwing up? You should let Christian take care of you. He'd enjoy it."

"What? Watching me throw up?"

Joel smiled. "It won't go on for months, will it?"

A trickle of icy water ran down Susie's spine. Joel thought she was pregnant. He stared at her and Susie knew he was waiting for her to say something.

"I can look after myself," she whispered.

He put his mouth against her ear. "I know you can, sweetheart, but please let Christian look after you. He can be there for you when I can't."

Susie stood up on shaky legs. "I better go. Sorry to have disturbed you."

Joel got to his feet and ran his hand down her arm. "You never do that. Well, never in a way I don't like but unfortunately I *am* really busy."

"Lots to do and little time to do it?"

"Exactly. I'll see you later, okay?"

Susie watched him stride away, watched until he'd turned the corner and was lost to her sight and when he'd gone, the pain in her chest sent her tumbling back onto the chair. Why hadn't Joel told her he was leaving? Had they planned to tell her together? Did Christian even know? She somehow didn't think so. Christian was open and Joel closed. Susie had the uncomfortable feeling Joel had been trying to manipulate her. *Stay with Christian and let him look after you.* Presumably while Joel swanned off back to the States. Oh God, and he thought she was pregnant. He didn't even care if the baby was his. Not that there was a baby.

Once Susie knew her legs would support her, she got to her feet and walked out. Was she supposed to be Christian's compensation for Joel leaving? Did Joel think Christian wouldn't mind as much if she was with him? He wouldn't have wanted Christian to be with another man but Susie could hardly be seen as a rival. Only she wouldn't be in anyone's arms. This had to end now. Joel didn't care about it. Susie had no intention of being second best for Christian.

It was an even longer walk back to the hospital while she went over every possible scenario. The worst being that Christian knew and they were going to leave her. She sat for hours in a waiting room, pretending to read magazines while her mind whirled. By the time her consultant called her in, Susie had steeled herself for bad news. A tiny part of her wanted it to be bad but the tests proved inconclusive. She was to be admitted immediately for further investigation. A waste of time. Susie knew the cancer was back.

* * * * *

"Any word?" Joel asked as he walked through the door.

Christian shook his head. Joel had called to tell him Susie had been to his office and after he'd repeated the conversation they'd had, Christian had been worried. They'd spent the afternoon calling Susie's mobile and each other, wondering where the hell she was. Christian had tried not to feel upset that Susie had sought out Joel and not him and failed.

"Shit," Joel hissed.

"I've been 'round to her house three times but there's no one in," Christian said.

Joel slumped onto a kitchen chair. "Did we do something wrong? Move too fast? Freak her out? Would she be afraid to tell us she was pregnant?"

"I don't think so."

Christian kneaded the tight muscles at the back of Joel's neck. Joel reached back, caught hold of one of Christian's hands and pulled him round to face him.

"Sit down," Joel said.

Why was something telling Christian that was the last thing he should do? His backside hit the chair but only because his legs gave way.

"This is shit timing," Joel said, holding on to both of Christian's hands.

This is not about Susie, Christian thought. This is Joel. Leaving. *Leaving me. Leaving us.*

"If it wasn't the fact that it's been announced at work, I would have waited."

"You're leaving," Christian said.

Joel nodded.

"How long?" *Oh God, that came out as a squeak.*

"A month."

A shudder ran through Christian. "Why…so…soon?"

"A senior partner had a heart attack and they need me to fill the void."

Christian stared straight at Joel. "I don't want you to go."

A muscle ticced in Joel's cheek. "I don't want to but I have to."

Ask me to come with you.

"We knew this wasn't going to be forever," Joel said. "You understood from the start."

Christian couldn't speak. Had he got this all wrong? He'd thought—well, it didn't matter what he'd thought. Everything was ruined.

"At least you'll have Susie," Joel said.

Christian wrenched his hands out of Joel's. "What? Is she your going-away present? You think it'll be okay because I'll have her when you're not around?" He jumped to his feet. "Well your plan's fucked up, mate. Susie's not here, in case you hadn't noticed. She came to see you today. Had she come to tell you she didn't want me, that she wanted you? Maybe you're taking her with you and leaving me behind."

"Christian, no, you've got that all wrong. I don't know what Susie wanted. She said she'd just called to see me."

"Any chance she heard you were leaving?"

Christian watched Joel think about that. The fact that he had to think about it told Christian it was a possibility. Though it didn't explain what Susie was doing in the city visiting Joel when she was supposed to be sick.

"Maybe she'd come to thank me for the flowers," Joel said.

"So why didn't she say that? Why hasn't she responded to our calls?"

Joel jumped to his feet. "I'm going to her house."

Christian got up and followed. There was a lot more he wanted to say to Joel but it could wait.

When they got there, Joel stormed from the car and strode to Susie's front door. Christian had wanted to speak to Susie on his own but he was too pissed off with Joel to argue. He stayed in the car. The front door opened and Joel started speaking. Then the door closed and he walked back to the car. No Susie then. But Joel didn't make it. He staggered, clutching hold of the gate post. *What the…?* Christian leapt from the car and rushed to Joel's side.

"What's wrong?"

"Susie's in hospital."

"What...an accident?" Christian's mouth had lost all moisture. "Is she badly hurt? What happened?"

Joel looked straight into his eyes. "She has cancer."

Christian heard the word but didn't take it in, not for a long moment. "Cancer?"

"Her brother said the doctor thinks the cancer's come back. That scar on her stomach. Her spleen. Christ, why didn't she tell us?"

Christian shrank under the weight of the sky, his shoulders dropping, his heart falling. "Where is she?"

"St. Thomas' hospital. They've admitted her for tests."

They got back in the car.

"Let's go and see her," Christian said.

"We can't tonight. It's too late. They won't let us in. Tomorrow. I won't go in to work." Joel started the engine. "Put your seat belt on, Christian."

They returned home in silence. Christian thought of his joy at the chance she might be pregnant because he'd had this image of holding a little boy in his arms with Susie's smile and Joel's hair. Only there wasn't any baby. There might not be any Susie. Losing Joel suddenly came into perspective. Joel might be the other side of an ocean but he'd be alive.

Joel pulled onto the drive and dashed into the house, leaving Christian to sort out the gate. When Christian went inside, he found Joel on the couch, his elbows on his knees and his head in his hands. His shoulders were shaking and juddering breaths jerked from his mouth. Christian sat by his side and pulled him into his arms. He'd never seen Joel cry before.

"Joel, we don't know—"

Joel raised his head. "I don't want to talk or think. I want to forget. I want to fuck."

Christian wiped the salt trails from Joel's face with his thumbs. "Don't—"

"I mean it, "Joel said. "I don't want to talk. I just want you."

He reached for Christian's shirt, ripped off two buttons in his haste to remove it.

"Upstairs," Christian said.

Joel looked bewildered. Christian grabbed his hand and pulled him up to their room. When he turned from drawing the curtains, Joel was already naked and moving toward him, his thick cock dark with blood. Christian felt a tremor ripple through him. He shucked off his pants and boxers and waited.

"I need you," Joel said.

He spun Christian belly first on the bed, fell on top of him and buried his face in the place where Christian's neck connected with his shoulder. Joel bit down and Christian cried out, bucking his ass into Joel's hips. Christian slid his hands under the pillow, curled his fingers over the edge of the mattress and clung on. He knew Joel was marking him and knew why. Then his teeth were gone and Christian heard the pop as the lube bottle opened and a wet squelch as Joel squirted out the thick liquid. Slick fingers pressed into the crack of Christian's backside, seeking his asshole. Christian tried to relax but his body was tense, his mind galloping.

As Joel massaged his way inside Christian, he landed stuttering gasps of air in the middle of Christian's back. A knuckle breached his muscle barrier, and as Joel's finger burned a route inside him, Christian groaned into the pillow. One finger withdrew and two returned, surging down the tight passage. Joel pumped them a few times and then pulled out and the wet crest of his cock touched Christian's anus. No words of kindness, the perfunctory foreplay over, Joel shoved down and forced himself inside Christian in one long thrust. Then froze.

Christian wished he could see Joel's face but knew that was why he'd been pushed facedown on the bed. Joel didn't want to look at him. Christian's heart ached with

249

disappointment. Joel began to move, driving his cock into Christian's body in long, deep slides that increased in speed and force. Christian whimpered into the pillow as Joel pounded his hips down, time after time until all Christian could think about was the burn in his ass, the ache in his balls and Joel above him. He guessed this was what Joel needed, fast and furious fucking so he wiped everything from his mind but physical pleasure.

It wasn't the answer to the mess they were in but Christian didn't have a better one. They were hurting and Christian wasn't sure things could ever be right again. He loved Joel. He loved him more than he'd ever thought he could love anyone and it was that love that made him take this, Joel's cock driving into his ass in a loveless fuck. Words moved from Christian's head to his mouth, but he pressed his lips together and trapped them there.

With every drive Joel made into him, Christian's cock rubbed against the sheet, the sweet friction building the need to come. Joel slammed down, over and over, riding Christian faster, pulling out and banging down harder. Despite everything, even thinking Joel didn't care who he was fucking, only that he needed to fuck someone, Christian loved taking every hard thrust of his lover's cock, every thick inch, every wet slap of his balls. Christian clenched down on Joel's dick and felt him come, roaring his release into the air, spurting deep inside him.

It wasn't a surprise to Christian when Joel pulled out at once and disappeared into the bathroom. He eased his aching limbs off the bed and stood. His rigid cock was weeping pre-cum but Christian didn't think he was going to get any help from Joel. He heard the shower start and wondered if Joel would object if he joined him.

Christian found him sitting on shower floor, leaning back against the tiles, his face upturned into the flow. One long minute thinking and Christian went to sit by his side.

"My mother walked out when I was seven," Joel said. "I came home from school to find her gone. She'd packed her things and taken my sister but not me."

Christian's heart sped up. He blinked the water out of his eyes and stared at Joel.

"My dad used to beat my mom. He was always accusing her of things she hadn't done, looking at other men, flirting. If she tried to make herself look pretty, he said she was a whore. If she didn't bother, he called her an ugly bitch. When I tried to stop him hitting her, I got locked in the cellar. He broke my leg once, throwing me down there. He used to leave my mother bleeding and crying but when he hurt me, he was real upset. Took me to the hospital, bought me a toy. He told me women have to be kept in their place. Their role was to look after their husbands and do as they were told. When he started beating on my sister, my mother upped and left."

Joel turned to look at him. "I thought for a long while, she'd send for me, that she was finding a house, someplace safe and she'd come get me. Didn't happen. She didn't want me." Joel gave a short laugh and leaned back against the tiles with his eyes closed. "Seven years old and she'd had enough of me."

Christian wanted to hug him but didn't dare touch him.

"We never moved, my dad and I, so you'd have thought she could have sent me a birthday card at least. She never did."

So that was why Joel didn't like celebrating his birthday.

"The sad, awful thing was with my mother gone, my life improved. No more screaming, hitting, meals thrown around. I brought myself up. Came home from school and put a frozen dinner in the microwave. That was all I ate for years."

Christian put his hand over his and Joel turned to look at him.

"When I reached my teens I convinced myself that my mother and sister were dead. I thought Dad had killed them and buried them somewhere on the property. I started digging holes. I told him I was looking for gold." Joel gave a short laugh. "He made me fill them all in again. I tried to look for them on the internet but there were over half a million hits for Jenny Cooper and I didn't even know if she'd changed her name. Once I was earning, I could have paid people to look, but why bother? I didn't need her any more. She could have found me if she'd wanted to."

"So you keep your heart locked up tight," Christian said. "No entry or exit allowed."

Joel cast him a glance.

Christian tightened his grip on Joel's hand. "You're in a job where you use your head and not your heart. You never let people get close. You like sex with guys because you can be strong and in control. Same-sex relationships allow you to be passionate without needing to show it. Relationships with women you keep short because you know they need more. They want to own you but you don't trust them not to reject you. You do it first."

Christian struggled to keep his voice steady. "The one person who should have loved you more than her life, let you down. That doesn't mean it's going to happen again. Are you leaving because you have to, or because you need to reject me before I reject you? You brought Susie into this and I thought it was because you saw a future for us. You didn't, did you? She was your get-out clause. Christian won't be so upset at me leaving if he has Susie. But I love *you*. I don't want you to leave. If you have to go, then ask me to go with you. Take a risk, Joel."

When Joel's head dropped and he stayed silent, Christian got out of the shower and went to the other bathroom.

Chapter Twenty-Seven

❧

Susie looked up. Joel and Christian stood at the door of the three-bedded side room. She was in the middle bed, the other two were unoccupied. Joel held a bouquet of yellow flowers. Christian carried a large soft toy, a wrinkled Sharpei puppy.

"You're late for work," Joel said. He dropped the flowers on the end of the bed, leaned over to kiss her gently on the cheek and took hold of her hand.

Christian moved to the other side and bent his head to hers, fluttering his lips from her mouth to her ear. "I love you," he whispered, and grabbed her other hand.

Susie gave a choked sigh. Christian bounced the puppy up the bed and onto her chest.

"He's called Botox," he said.

Susie smiled. "He's gorgeous, thank you."

"How are you feeling, angel?" Joel asked.

"I'm okay. How'd you know where I was?"

"Mike told me."

"Are you supposed to be in here?"

"Joel flirted with the senior nurse." Christian flashed him a mock glare.

"Hey, she was cute." Joel turned to Susie. "But not as cute as you."

"I don't feel very cute. I need a shower."

Christian stroked her fingers. "Why didn't you tell us?"

"Tell you what?" But Susie looked at their faces and knew. "I hoped I'd never have to tell anyone. My consultant doesn't seem to think there's anything to worry about."

"Then why are you lying in a hospital bed?" Joel asked. "Do you need a second opinion? I'll pay —"

"No, it's all right, Joel. He's a really good doctor."

"When you get out of here, come and stay with us," Christian said.

Joel's grip tightened on her hand as if he was frightened she'd pull away. Christian held her fingers gently as though he was afraid she'd break. Their other hands were entwined lying on her stomach.

"What the hell is this?" Harry Hood demanded.

Susie flinched at her father's harsh tone. He stood in the doorway, Pete lurking behind him, glaring at the three of them. Christian and Joel let go of each other but kept hold of Susie.

"Dad, these are the guys I work for, Christian and Joel."

"You're the two she cleans for?"

"Much more than clean. Susie takes care of our home." Joel stood and held out his hand. "Hello, sir."

Harry eyed the hand so recently resting on his daughter's stomach and then looked at Susie. "What are they doing here?"

"We came to see Susie," Christian said.

Her father looked between the three of them.

"You were the one I saw kissing her," he said to Christian.

"No, it was him." Pete pointed to Joel.

Susie felt like a piece of glass that had cracked, waiting to shatter. No one spoke. Her father stared at her and she sensed his rage coming to the boil.

"You sleeping with both of them, Susie?" he asked.

She was afraid to admit it but wouldn't deny it.

"You stupid little slut," he hissed.

He moved toward her and clenched his fists. Joel stepped in front of him.

"Sir, please don't speak to her like that." Joel's voice was icy cool.

"She's my daughter. I'll speak to her how I like. How dare you do this to her? She's just a kid."

"I'm twenty-four," Susie said. "I'm not a child. I know what I want."

"No you don't. You've got no idea what you want. You've got no experience with men. You didn't have the chance to go out with boys when you were a teenager. You don't have that foundation to understand what men want. They're using you, Susie. "

"That's not true. I'm happy. They make me happy. They care about me."

"Only to get you into bed."

"Don't, Dad. Don't spoil this for me."

He glared at her. "I'm not going to stand by and let you throw your life away."

"But it's my life. It's up to me what I do with it." Susie could hardly believe she was standing up for herself like this and judging by the look on her father's and brother's faces, neither could they.

"Well, looks like you've got what you deserve. A sick mind inside a sick body. I want you out of the house."

Susie jolted. "Dad, please."

"Come on, Pete. They're all fucking perverts." Harry stormed out.

Pete winced. "Sorry, Suze. I didn't think."

No, you never do, Susie thought.

"Three of you?" Pete said. "Christ, Susie, why couldn't you get one boyfriend like normal people."

"Ever had a fantasy about being in bed with two women?" Joel asked.

Pete gave a short laugh. "What guy hasn't?"

"Then Susie's kind of lucky, wouldn't you say? She has two guys who care for her, who want to make her happy in every way they can. Just because it's unconventional doesn't mean it's wrong or it can't work. In fact, if you think about it, you could say it was Christian and I who were getting short-changed because we have to share her."

Pete bristled. "I don't want her to get hurt."

"We'd never do anything to hurt Susie," Joel said. "Never."

There was silence for a moment and then Pete bent to give her a kiss.

"I'll talk to Dad," he said, and walked out as Susie's consultant came in.

"Hello, Susie. If your visitors would like to leave for a moment?"

"We'll be right outside, angel." Joel flashed her an anxious smile.

Susie steeled herself for bad news. Her life was dropping down a deep chute at a rate of a million knots. It could only be moments before she lay in a crumpled heap at the bottom. She tightened her fingers around the plush toy.

"It's not the lymphoma," the doctor said.

Susie's brain whirled. Was there a negative in there? Not cancer? "Not? You mean the cancer hasn't come back?"

"No. That's the good news. The bad news—"

"Do you have to tell me anything else?"

Her consultant smiled. "It really is good news, Susie. But—"

"No," she wailed. "No buts."

He pulled her hands away from her ears. "Your white cell count was way down. You're very anemic and because you have a weak immune system, it's knocked you back more than it would most people."

Susie gradually took it in.

"So I'm okay?"

"You will be, if you rest. Stop doing so much for your father and your brothers. You work too hard. More rest, less stress and eat iron-rich foods."

Susie knew that although her consultant had managed to persuade Pete to donate stem cells after he and Mike had been tested, he hadn't been impressed by Pete's whiny objections that it might hurt. Though Pete had gone through with it in the end, Susie thought that was what counted.

"Can I go home?"

"You need antibiotics from the hospital pharmacy and then you can leave."

The moment the doctor left, Christian and Joel rushed back into the room.

Susie got out of bed. "It's not cancer."

Christian grabbed her and Joel closed his eyes before stepping forward and pulling both of them into his arms.

"Thank God," Joel whispered.

They stood together for a moment, holding each other, feeling each other's hearts beating. Susie kissed first Christian then Joel on the lips.

"Take me home."

Joel held her in his arms all the way back. He rocked and soothed her with soft kisses and gentle caresses, pressing his face into her hair while he wrestled with his emotions. Susie lay still with her eyes closed but Joel knew she was awake from the tense way she laid against him despite his touches.

He had things to put right. He'd felt like killing Susie's father for speaking to her like that but he wished Susie had stood up for herself. He saw now what Susie was hiding from, not the scar on her face but a father who had no respect for her, one who could call her a slut. She was sick and it wasn't fair to expect her to do it now, but Joel wanted her to go and see him and stand up to him.

When Christian pulled up on the drive, Joel tapped him on the shoulder.

"Would you—"

"I'll nip to the supermarket and get us something for dinner. Is there anything you'd like, Susie?" Christian asked.

"Homemade sushi."

Christian groaned. "Alternatively?"

"Spaghetti bolognaise."

"That, I can manage. I'll be about an hour."

Joel's heart ached. Christian had known he wanted to be alone with Susie before he'd even asked. Christian didn't look at him before he pulled back onto the road.

"Can I get you anything? A cup of tea?" Joel asked.

Susie shook her head.

He took her hand, tugged her into the living room and pulled her down on the couch next to him.

Joel took a deep breath. "Why did you come to my office? What did you want to tell me that you didn't want Christian to hear?"

Susie's eyes opened wide. "Nothing. I didn't want to tell you anything. I just needed a hug before I got the test results. Your office was so close, I thought…"

The pain of not being there for her, hit like a dagger in Joel's chest. "Is it too late to give you one now?"

"It's never too late," Susie said.

Joel wrapped his arms around her, swung his legs onto the couch and draped Susie over him.

"Why didn't you wait?" he asked.

"Rachel came by. She said…they were going to be sorry to lose you."

Joel winced. "Ah shit."

"Does Christian know?"

"Yes."

Susie pushed herself up so she could look at him. "I don't want you to go. Christian doesn't want you to go. So why are you leaving?"

"They need me at head office. They said eighteen months but it was always understood it might not be as long as that."

"Why are you leaving?" Susie repeated.

"I just said—"

"What are you frightened of?"

Joel sighed. "I—"

"You're a coward, Joel. Afraid of being too happy in case it all gets taken away. You think it's better to back out while things are good? Are you running away from us?"

"You and Christian—"

"No. Without you, there is no me and Christian. He'd blame me for driving you away. Every time I looked at him, I'd remember you. Even if you don't want me, you must want Christian."

Pain lurched from Joel's chest, stopped the air in his lungs and paralyzed his limbs.

"Don't throw happiness away when you find it. Look at what happened to me. One day I was well, thinking about my future, the next day I had no future. You need to enjoy life while you can. *Carpe diem* and all that. Don't waste Christian's love. Don't waste my love."

"Oh God, Susie." He shuddered.

She stroked his arm. "I know it's there in your heart."

"I-I can't s-say it," Joel gasped.

"Yes, you can." She touched his cheek.

Joel struggled to breathe. He closed his eyes.

"Come and show me," Susie said, and got to her feet.

Joel let her lead him out of the room and up the stairs. His heart stuttered, trying to get back to a stable beat. He'd expected her to shout at him, throw things, cry, scream—not want him to make love to her. Joel stumbled on the top step. That's what he wanted to do—make love to Susie. Not fuck her.

She tugged him to the room she'd slept in the night of the party and somehow to Joel it all made sense. He closed the door and turned to face her. Susie slipped her dress over her head and kicked off her shoes. She stood in front of him in her plain white bra and little cotton panties. The inside of her arm was dark with bruises where blood had been taken and Joel gave a choked sigh. Nothing lacy or fancy and she still looked sexy as hell. Her slim, toned body with its nipped-in waist and swelling breasts sent a surge of heat to his struggling cock.

"Susie, Susie." He breathed her name.

She stepped toward him and unfastened his shirt, her delicate fingers working at each button. He could hear his heart thundering, feel blood rushing to his groin.

Joel stared into Susie's soft eyes as she tugged off the shirt. She slid her hands around him, her breasts brushed his chest and he pulled her into his arms. His balls ached with need, his cock begged for more room.

Susie's fingers struggled with the button on his pants, popped it free and eased down his zipper. Joel held his breath as she pushed his chinos over his hips. Her breasts brushed his cock as it tried to tunnel out of his boxers and Joel groaned. He toed off his shoes and stepped out of his pants. When he opened his mouth, Susie put a finger to his lips and shook her head. She stepped forward and slid her hands up his chest, over his nipples. He loved her touching them. The feel of her soft fingers drove him crazy. When she rocked her hips against his impatient cock, a spurt of pre-cum wet his boxers.

Joel nudged her backward, smiling at her expression when she hit the cold wall. He pressed his knee between her legs, edging his muscular thigh between hers. Joel felt the dampness of her panties and knew she wanted him as much as he wanted her. She was so hot, she made him burn. He touched her face, gentle caresses with his fingers on her cheeks, and then brought his hands down the side of her neck, the curve of her body, down to her hips. Joel rubbed his thumbs over the cotton panties then swept his hands to her butt, clutched the cheeks of her ass and dragged her tight against him.

"Susie."

He whispered her name into her ear as he massaged her backside, pressing her into the length of his swollen cock. His hands drifted up her silky back, unclipped her bra and let it fall. Joel stroked her breasts, cupped them, squeezed gently, watched the nipples darken and harden to tighter buds. She was so beautiful. Joel thought he could never tire of looking at her.

Susie's hand slipped under the waistband of his boxers and she wrapped her fingers around his cock. Joel shuddered as her palm rolled over the sensitive head and spread silky fluid down his length. One long, slow caress made the blood simmer in his veins, and Joel moved her hand. This was about her, not him. He tugged his boxers down and stepped out of them, put his hand on her white panties and froze. Oh God, she was so sweet—and so wet. While he hesitated, Susie stripped away her last item of clothing. Joel touched the scar on her belly, his chest tightened and he released a trembling sigh. Susie grabbed his hand and put it on her heart.

"Still beating, Joel."

He got the message. He stared into her eyes. He wanted to savor the moment because a little voice told him this could be the end, that he had to walk away for everyone's sake, so this might be the last time he touched her. Only the pain of that was too much. Joel lowered his head and covered her warm, moist lips with his. Susie's eyes slid shut and she moaned into his mouth as he rode his hips into hers, nestling his cock against her belly. Her soft little tongue slipped between his teeth, found its partner and began to play, gliding, teasing, flicking until Joel couldn't help but take charge. He nibbled her upper lip, licked the velvety inner surface of her swollen lower lip, pressed the two together then forced them apart. He was as gentle as if he touched a butterfly then forceful enough to make her gasp into his mouth. They shared air and traded kisses. Her hands were all over him, his hands all over her. They rubbed and petted, panted and moaned, their chests heaving, hearts hammering, limbs shaking.

Joel used one hand to cup her face, tilt her head so he could deepen the kiss and his other hand set off down her body, a tour around her breast and a climb to the gently rounded peak for a light pinch that had her grunting into his mouth. Then on down her ribs, over her shaved mons to her wet folds. Her hips jerked as he slid his fingers through her cream, teasing her asshole and returning to slither through her swollen lips to the little treasure inside.

His cock surged into a tightening spiral of desire. Joel found the rough place inside her that made her breathing quicken, her hold on him tighten and he pressed and rubbed until she cried her release into his mouth. Joel swallowed it, fed on it, felt his heart almost burst with it. Her pussy rippled around his fingers and he wished he had his face there, wished she'd come against his mouth. He wanted all of her before Christian came back, wanted this to be just for him and Susie, something to remember forever.

When he felt her hands move to his dick, Joel pulled away and dropped to his knees but Susie tugged on his shoulders. "No. I want you. Please."

Joel let her pull him up and press him against the wall. He jerked when she took his nipple between her teeth. Christ, he was hanging on to his control by the thinnest thread. He stroked her hair as she licked the place she'd bitten, soothing it with her silky tongue. Another bite and Joel's cock spurted pre-cum against her belly. The pain excited him, but he pulled himself back from the brink. When she trailed her tongue down his chest, licking his skin on the way to his cock, Joel stopped breathing.

Susie wrapped the fingers of both hands around his cock and Joel clenched his teeth, forcing back the need to come. He stroked her hair as she brought the head of his cock to her lips, pressed it against them while they were closed, let him force his way in and Joel felt his control begin to crumble like a dry sandcastle. Looking down at her sweet face as she looked up at him almost undid him. Her hot little tongue lapped a drop of pre-cum from his crown. She spread it over his silky helmet and then wrapped her lips around him. Joel let out a series of groans as arrows of pleasure shot up his spine and pierced his brain.

Her mouth sucked at the swollen head of his cock, teeth just touching the ridge below and it felt so good Joel's knees began to shake. She drew him deeper, sucking and licking and even though Joel knew he couldn't stand it for long, he let her take him. The muscles of his stomach contracted as she sucked, sending fresh bolts of excitement to his brain as electric pulses shot along nerves, sparking in fiery bursts of pleasure. Susie made a humming sound and the vibration coaxed a long hiss from his lips. The need to thrust inside her was almost too much to withstand. Joel drew back, his cock glistening from the moisture in her mouth—her saliva, his pre-cum.

"I want to be inside you," he whispered. "The bed."

Susie stood. "No, here."

She lifted her leg to his thigh and Joel felt her wet pussy slide along his cock. He spun around and pressed her against the wall, lifted her other leg and she wrapped her thighs around his waist. Joel tilted her hips and slid straight into her, his desperate cock tunneling into her honeyed depths as far as it could go. She was tight and hot and wet and Joel's hips began to thrust even before he gave the command, sinking his erection into her as he held her pressed against the wall.

Susie clenched around his cock and as Joel pulled back against her grip, the pleasure of the sensation pulled a cry of delight from them both. Susie's head thrashed as he surged in and out, perspiration glistening on her skin, her fingers digging into his back.

"Joel. Joel. Joel."

Every gasp of his name sent him plunging deeper. He could feel her creaming around him, his cock coated with her sweet essence. Joel planted his hands under her ass and pulled her onto him as he drove up into her. *Not fucking. Not fucking.* Each ripple along his cock sent a burst of joy to his brain. He could sense her coming, feel her ecstasy climbing alongside his. Each sweet pull of her pussy dragged him closer. Each plunge of his cock drove her wilder.

"Susie, look at me," he gasped.

He saw the effort to open her lids, but she stared straight at him, her eyes glazed with lust, with love.

"I…love you," Joel said.

They came together, stiffened in each other's arms, fingers sinking into flesh, foreheads welded as he pumped into her, jet after endless jet of cum. Joel thought he'd never stop as her pussy contracted around him, milking his seed into her depths.

They came down together. Their heartbeats slowed, breathing eased and Joel slid her legs from his waist but kept hold of her. Now he just had to find a way of keep her forever.

Chapter Twenty-Eight

ဆာ

Susie rolled over and opened her eyes to find Joel's face inches from hers.

"I'm off to work, sweetheart. Stay in bed. No doing anything in the house. I want you to rest. Christian's already gone. He made the mistake of claiming he was an expert at paintballing, so before he can write the article, he's had to book himself a couple of sessions. He'll be out all day. You sure you'll be okay?"

"I'll be fine."

Joel kissed her, a long minty slurp, and grinned. "I love you."

"I love you too."

As soon as Joel had gone, Susie got up. She felt fine. No way would she lie in bed all day, not without Christian and Joel. Susie smiled. Joel hadn't said that he wasn't going back to the States but Susie sensed he'd try to find a way to stay. He'd said he loved her. He wouldn't want to leave them.

After a long soak in the tub, Susie put on the only clothes she had. At some point, she'd have to go home and get her things. Face her father. Well, maybe not if she timed it right.

Susie was eating breakfast when the bell rang. She answered the door with a piece of toast in her hand. Bella swept past her into the house.

"Hey, Christian," Bella shouted at the bottom of the stairs.

"Not here," Susie said. "He'll be out all day."

"Damn." She looked at the toast in Susie's hand. "They feed you as well?" Bella's eyes dropped to Susie's bare feet. "Not cleaning?"

"No."

Bella made her way to the kitchen. "I'll leave a note. On second thought, you can just tell him." She turned to Susie and beamed. "The book is fabulous. I stayed up all night reading it. Hot, hot, hot."

"Christian's written a book?"

Bella laughed. "You didn't know Christian's an author? He writes under the name Raphael Strange."

Susie's backside hit the chair. "Christian writes erotic books?"

"Aha," Bella said with a laugh. "You've read them. We came up with Raphael Strange between us. Christian's very good. I'm about to finalize a deal with a big publisher. This last one is his best yet. A ménage. Jack, Xan and Josie."

Shit. A ménage? What the hell had Christian done?

"I can't help wondering what the book's based on." Bella winked. "I'm beginning to suspect Christian's bisexual. You wouldn't know anything about that, would you?"

An instinct for self-preservation beefed up Susie's defenses. "As you pointed out, I'm only the cleaner."

"Did they tell you what happened to the last one?"

"I found her head in the attic."

Bella laughed. "Joel made Christian sack her. Christian told me she wouldn't leave him alone but the woman hated Joel. I guess they were looking for someone to accommodate both of them, no strings attached." She gave Susie a knowing look. "All this time I've been working on Christian, flirting like crazy and I should have been working on Joel. You're smarter than I thought."

The toast tasted of cardboard but Susie chewed and swallowed.

Bella bent over and tweaked Susie's cheek. "You're also a naughty girl. Who'd have guessed you had it in you."

Susie didn't move until Bella walked out and she heard the door slam. Jack, Xan and Josie. Joel, Christian and Susie. Had Christian really written about them?

Her willpower lay in tatters after ten minutes. She ran up to Christian's study. His computer was off. Not for long. Susie sat on his chair and waited.

There was no problem getting into his documents. No password. Christian might be untidy with his material possessions but his work was highly organized. Files for his magazine articles, files for his novels. All dated. The last was called *Training Josie*. Susie winced at the title, clicked it open and began to read.

Had the guys met like that? She'd never asked them. The bit about them knocking her off her bike hadn't happened but she could see Christian had created his own truth within the actual truth. Xan was tall with brown hair and green eyes. A fireman not a writer. Jack was a dark-haired American. A music producer, not a lawyer. The Josie in the story had a scar on her face and shoulder-length blonde hair. She wasn't very bright and hadn't been to college. But she was beautiful and willing. Susie began to chew her nail.

The story told how the men had come up with the idea of advertising for a cleaner and picked the one they thought would be easiest to train, the one most likely to accept being double fucked. The first one they picked wouldn't play the game. Then they found Josie. The scar made her perfect—who else would want her? They arranged a dinner party to get her to stay over, plied her with alcohol and tossed a coin for who'd fuck her first. The American won. *Oh God.*

Susie become more distressed the more she read. It was all her. Her story. The walk in Greenwich market. The chase in the woods and the game for who could have her ass cherry. Susie clicked "Page Down" faster and faster, wanting to know how the story ended.

She read the last few pages without taking a breath and finally gave a quiet moan. Xan and Jack went off to America and passed Josie on to two friends. Their housekeeper was okay about it. They'd trained her into acceptance. This housekeeper felt tears trickling down her cheeks, splashing onto the keyboard. She'd thought they loved her but this was a game. She'd trusted them and they'd betrayed her. Susie imagined them laughing together, thinking she was a gullible slut. She was. Stupid too and deeply humiliated. Susie knew what guys were like, her brothers treated the enticement of women into bed as a competitive challenge. She should have known.

Her first thought was to leave before Christian or Joel came back, only she didn't want to go home. Best-case scenario, she'd get yelled at and humiliated, but her father would let her back into the house. The worst, the door would be slammed in her face. The agony of betrayal by the two people in the world she thought loved her sent Susie tumbling to her knees. She crouched on the floor of Christian's study, the pain in her heart so bad she had to gasp for breath.

* * * * *

For one desperate moment when Christian heard the door slam, he thought it was Susie but it was Joel who shouted, "Hi there."

"I'm in the kitchen," Christian called.

Joel walked in and stopped short. "You look like you're about to throw up. Did you manage to avoid a single paintball? Need something kissed better?"

Christian opened his mouth and nothing came out. He was bruised all over but that wasn't the problem.

Joel's face fell. "Is it Susie?" He pushed Christian onto a chair and sat next to him. "Take a deep breath, buddy, and tell me what's happened."

"Gone."

Christian could almost see Joel's heart catapult out of his chest to join his on the floor.

"Gone where?"

"Don't know," Christian gulped.

"What did you do?"

No point being indignant at Joel's presumption. It *was* his fault. "She read the story."

"What story?"

"*Training Josie.*"

"What's so bad about that? When you showed it to me, the three of us were having fun."

"Go read it again."

Christian paced across the kitchen floor, growing increasingly anxious. He'd fucked everything up. Joel was going to be so pissed with him. When he heard him coming down, Christian stopped moving. Joel stood in the doorway.

"I'm sorry," Christian said.

"She thinks we're fucking off to New York and leaving her here?" Joel's mouth was tight with annoyance.

Christian sagged. "I left the computer off. When I got back, I moved the mouse and *Training Josie* was on the screen."

"Fuck it, Christian. You're an idiot."

"I know."

"Where would she go?" Joel asked.

"I don't know."

* * * * *

She wasn't at her father's.

They sat in the car down the road from the house. Joel put his hand up to his jaw and felt it gingerly with his fingers. Pete packed a mean punch. But then so did Joel and he'd drawn blood, he thought with a grim smile.

"I'm sorry," Christian said.

"For fuck's sake, Christian. Stop saying you're sorry. It isn't helping," Joel snapped.

"Do you think he's lying and she's in there?"

Pete had said not, listened to what Joel had to say and then launched a fist at his face.

"I don't know," Joel admitted.

"How long are we going to sit here?"

"Just fucking drive home," Joel said, more sharp than he'd intended.

He felt Christian cringe. Joel was furious. This would have been so easy to avoid. Now Susie had entirely the wrong end of the stick. She'd grabbed the pointed, jagged thing and stabbed herself in the heart. Joel knew she'd think they didn't care about her. The notion of the pair of them going off to the States and leaving her behind for others to use had appalled Joel. He could barely bring himself to speak to Christian.

Christian pulled onto the drive and switched off the engine. There were no lights on in the house. Susie hadn't come back. Joel sighed and got out of the car. Christian followed him into the kitchen.

"You know it's just a story," Christian said.

The plaintive note in his voice annoyed Joel. "Of course I know that."

"I hadn't thought of going off to the States with you and leaving Susie."

Joel turned to look at him. "Would you come if I asked you?"

Christian didn't answer for a moment. "Are you asking?"

Joel's jaw twitched.

Christian started to pace, then spun round to face him. "I know I've cocked up but do you have any idea how fucking hurt I am? What do you think we're doing, Joel? We live together. Eat together. Argue. Fight. Have fun. We fuck all the time. I've never spent this long with anyone. I love you. I've loved you from the first moment I saw you but I knew that wasn't enough. I love Susie too. We're perfect as a three only now you think you can just walk out of our lives and we'll be fine. We won't."

"You and she—"

"I've already told you, there is no me and Susie. Not without you. I love you. Every time I look at you, it's as though I've been overwhelmed by this force, this compulsion to be part of your life, to make you part of mine. I wanted you to ask me to go with you to the States. I was waiting for you to say it only you think you're so fucking clever, leaving me with Susie so we don't mind you going. I won't lose you, Joel. I'm going to find a way to go with you. I can write as easily there as I can here. I can get a job with a magazine, no problem."

Something was happening inside Joel, only he didn't know what. Some emotion, something changing in his heart. "I want us to be together. I've been trying to find a way to make it happen."

Christian opened his mouth and then closed it.

"Only you let her see that story and now everything is fucked up because we've lost her."

* * * * *

Susie lay on her back under a tree. The noise from Greenwich Park faded as it emptied of mums and toddlers. The tourists had returned to their hotels and joggers to their homes. Cold seeped through her red, hooded top. An occasional leaf fluttered down and landed near her. Susie imagined all the leaves falling, covering her like a blanket, hiding her forever. Was that what she wanted? To return to her father and hide herself away? She sat up. Whatever else Christian and Joel had done, they'd shown her that she could be happy. She only had one chance at life and she wasn't going to waste it. Susie had done hiding, done thinking. How dare those bastards treat her like this?

She stamped down the hill. First, she'd go back to the house and tell Joel and Christian exactly what she thought of them. The more difficult part would be apologizing to her father. With no place to sleep, she had no choice. She'd never have mouthed off to him in the hospital if she'd suspected Christian and Joel might skip off and leave her.

By the time she reached the guys' house and saw the car in the drive, the lights blazing, the notion of turning thoughts into actions didn't seem such a good one. Her heart lodged in her throat and all moisture left her mouth. Was she brave enough? She clutched the key in her hand, turned it in her fingers and before thinking could stop her, she opened the door.

Christian came into the hall and his face lit up. "Susie, thank God you're okay, where have you—"

"Shut up," she snapped.

Joel appeared at his side.

"Where—" he began.

"You have no right to ask where I've been, no right to say anything to me." She looked from one to the other. "You both told me that you loved me. People who love one another don't treat them like shit." She turned to Joel and faltered. *What happened to his face? Had they been fighting?*

She composed herself. "You come over here, set your little game in motion, steal people's hearts and think you can just fly off again without anyone getting hurt." Then turned to Christian. "And you let him. You could have told me you were Raphael Strange. Why didn't you? Was this all a game? I'm one of Joel's pawns? Research for your book?"

"Susie—" Christian said.

"I haven't finished. I just hope you've learned something from this and you'll never play games with anyone else. It's cruel beyond belief…to…say things you don't mean. I know I'm naive but that's not an excuse to treat me like this. I have to go home now and apologize to my father, tell him he was right and I was wrong. Two guys loving me isn't so great after all. It's hurt me twice as much."

Before she started to cry, she fled. Susie stormed out of the house but didn't get far. Joel caught up partway down the drive and snagged her shoulder. He pulled her back and wrapped his arms around her as she struggled.

"Susie, don't. It's okay, sweetheart. I'm not going to hurt you. I only want to talk to you. Stop fighting or someone will get the wrong idea and call the cops."

Susie stopped struggling but held herself taut. Joel stood her in front of him, clutching her by the shoulders and then let her go.

"See? I'm not going to hurt you."

Susie didn't look at him.

"Angel," he whispered, "you've got this all wrong. Come back in the house."

"Why?"

"We need to talk. Lughead Christian has some apologizing to do."

Susie glanced behind Joel. Christian looked pale and worried.

"Please," Joel asked.

Susie stared up at his face. "Have you and Christian been fighting?"

"That was your brother Pete."

Susie's eyes opened wide in alarm.

"Come inside, darlin'. You belong with us. We belong with you."

"You don't want me," Susie said.

Joel sighed. "That's not true. I spent today trying to — well, as far as that book is concerned, there's a difference between fact and fiction. Christian mixed the two in his story, but the truth is we both want you, if you still want us."

He held out his hand.

Susie let Joel wrap her fingers in his firm grip. He pulled her toward him, looking into her eyes. Susie saw concern, raw hunger and love. Joel brushed his warm, velvet-smooth lips against her cheek, trailing them down along her jaw, and then nipped at her throat. Susie immediately felt the pull of desire. He held her tight as if he thought she'd disappear if he let her go.

His arm draped across her shoulders, Susie let him lead her back toward where Christian waited.

"I need you to do something for me," Joel whispered in her ear. "Hide the knives to stop me from killing Christian."

Chapter Twenty-Nine

ℬ

Christian breathed a sigh of relief when Joel and Susie walked back to the house.

"Sort things out." Joel left them standing in the hall and bounded up the stairs.

"It was just a story," Christian blurted. "What the three of us have has been so fantastic, I used it as inspiration. *Training Josie* was us and wasn't us at the same time." Christian took a step closer. "I finished the book before we knew about your cancer, before Joel dropped his bombshell about leaving. It was a BDSM novel, not a love story. I played up the dominance, the submission and the aggression, but not the emotion. I never meant to hurt you. I'm so sorry. Please forgive me."

Susie sighed and Christian took a deep breath. The cold slab he'd lain under for the last few hours began to lift.

"I'd never go to the States with Joel and leave you here. How could you think I would?"

"Because you love him."

"But I love you too."

Susie gave a little smile.

"I was sure I hadn't left the computer on," Christian said.

"You didn't. Bella came round to tell you she loved the book. She put two and one together and made four. A bit like me after I went upstairs and read the story. Not very successful at hiding your warped side and you picked a very *strange* name to write under. Maybe I should proofread from now on because you suck at endings."

Then her lips were on his and Christian fell into her embrace. He'd almost lost her twice. He'd ever let it happen again. Bella was history. It wasn't true that he wouldn't want Susie if Joel had left. It would be Joel's loss. Christian wanted the three of them together but there was no way he'd desert Susie. He slipped his tongue into her mouth and let it glide against hers. Christian dragged her closer, pulled her soft body into his hard one. Her hands moved to hold his head and it was Susie who deepened the kiss, filled his mind so he couldn't think beyond getting inside her, showing her how much she meant to him.

Christian broke off the kiss, lifted the red, hooded top over Susie's head, and dropped it. He chewed his lip as his fingers fought with the tiny buttons on her shirt. For each one he unfastened, Christian kissed her. He wanted to stick his hand down his pants and adjust his rigid cock into a more comfortable position, but touching Susie was more important and part of him welcomed the pain as a punishment for being a dolt, and not putting a password on his work, and not making her see how much she meant to him.

Dropping her blouse on the hall floor, Christian reached for her jeans. He pushed the button free and pulled down the zip, sliding his fingers over the top of her panties. Christian let out a noisy expiration of air when he felt how damp they were.

"You're so wet," he groaned.

Susie had his zipper lowered and her hand through his fly, tickling his balls. "So are you."

Clothes were shed in seconds and Christian stood in front of her, his hand grasping his cock. Susie sat on the stairs and stared at him.

"What are all those marks?"

His torso was mottled by circular bruises. "It appears I suck at paintballing too."

Susie sighed and pulled him toward her by the backs of his thighs. She looked up and smiled. "A lesson in how to suck in a good way."

Christian braced one hand on the wall and one on the banister as she drew him into her hot mouth. One long pull at the swollen head of his cock had him hissing between his teeth. Her teasing little tongue licked long and slow and she drew him deeper. Susie's eyelashes fluttered and as Christian watched her face, he felt the orgasm building in his head, his spine. He pulled away with a groan. Susie gave a mew of protest. Her need ratcheted him higher.

"I want to be inside you," he whispered.

He pulled her up, sat in her place on the stair and spread his legs. Susie lowered herself onto his cock and as she sank down, Christian felt the wash of creamy silk coat him in the tight channel. He grabbed her hips and kept her still. He needed a moment or he'd fucking come on the first thrust.

"Move," she urged.

Christian let out a strangled groan. "One minute, sweetheart."

"Thirty seconds," she panted.

Christian couldn't stop the chuckle and Susie flexed her hips, clasping around him, until the need to drive into her was so all-consuming and irrepressible, Christian had no choice. He tightened his grip on her hips and bucked, tilting her back as he dragged her down on his cock. Her eyes wild with desire, Susie thrashed her head and gasped for air.

Deeper, harder, faster—Christian drove them to completion. Her pussy contracted around his cock, the clench so tight the pleasure almost became pain. He pulled her forward onto his chest and held her against him as they unraveled and with every spurt of his seed, he whispered, "I love you."

Joel thought he'd been very patient. He'd stripped as he watched them, desperate to get in on the action. Seeing Susie ride Christian to a climax was almost too much for his cock, which jerked and pulsed in his hand. Joel had a tight grip on his balls so he didn't come but he almost lost the battle. The pair lay on the stairs, slumped in each other's arms, Christian's fingers running up and down Susie's spine before settling on her bottom. Joel leaned over the banister and gave a loud cough. They looked up. A smile played on Christian's lips and laughter lit Susie's eyes. Joel wasn't sure who he wanted more, Christian or Susie. Ah, both. He grinned.

"Are you going to work your way upstairs, doing something perverted on every step, or can I expect you in bed anytime soon?" Joel asked, and stood.

Christian eased Susie off his cock, her trembling thighs glistening with her cream and Christian's cum. A further jolt of lust struck Joel's groin, his engorged dick turning a darker red. When the pair of them began to crawl up the stairs toward him, Joel gave a husky growl. "Oh Jesus, look at you two."

When they reached the top, a glance passed between Susie and Christian, and Joel furrowed his brow.

"You promised to be my slave for a day, remember?" Susie asked.

Joel backed off. "I think that was a heat of the moment sort of thing."

"Oh no it wasn't. Stop moving. Stand right there and no touching us or yourself," she said.

Christian stayed back while Joel leaned against the wall. Susie brushed against him—the lightest of touches, a teasing caress. Joel wanted to reach for her, crush her in his arms but he didn't. She wiped her hand over the crest of his stone-hard cock, and Joel winced.

"How much teasing can you stand, slave?" she asked.

Not much was the answer and he was nobody's slave but then playing her game would get him what he needed.

Christian watched with a smile on his face. Susie ran her finger between her legs and put it to Joel's lips. He sucked and tasted her and Christian, kept sucking until she had to wrench her finger free.

"I feel like teasing you for hours, slave," she said.

Susie dropped to her knees at Joel's feet, wiped her fingers once more between her legs and then ran her wet fist along Joel's cock. When she licked his entire length, Joel nearly came on the spot.

"If you come before I say you can, I'll make you sit in the corner all night with your hands on your head watching me and Christian act out the karma sutra."

Joel opened his mouth and then shut it. That would never happen but no need to argue the point, and having Susie act so bossy was turning him on big-time. Susie nodded to Christian and he came to her side. Joel stood in the middle of the landing, every muscle rigid. Christian's tongue rasped down his cock as Susie licked up the other side. *Jesus.* As the pair of them laved and sucked, Joel felt like a volcano preparing to blow. Pressure building, organs melting, liquid heat rushed to his groin. The combination of Susie's soft, gentle lips and Christian's stubble was sheer bliss. When Christian took him deep in his throat, Joel hovered close to eruption.

"Share," Susie said, and Christian pulled back.

Joel looked down at their faces looking up at him, their eyes full of desire, and the slit in his cock peeped open to allow a large pearl of pre-cum to escape. Neither of them touched it and it hovered there for a moment.

"Please." Joel's voice was choked. "Both of you. One of you. Either of you."

"No." Susie smiled.

Joel changed his mind about a dominant Susie. She was too good at torturing. Christian's tight hand fastened around the root of Joel's cock and Susie pulled down on his balls. Joel's legs shook with the strain, his buttocks clenched and his breath burst from his lungs in jerky gasps. But the urge to come lessened. One moment's peace and then their mouths were back on him, tongues lapping, teeth nipping, fighting for possession. Joel longed to bang their heads together, yell at them to let him come and then he *was* coming and there was nothing he or anyone else could do to stop it.

Thick ropes of cum landed on Christian and Susie's faces. Some spurts made it into their mouths but most landed nowhere near. Joel's hand fell to his cock and he pumped what was left, a rough laugh rumbling from him as the pair fought to catch each drop. Christian licked Susie's face and she did the same to him, scooping up the trails of sticky juice with their tongues. Joel's knees gave way and he joined them on the floor.

"Have you any idea how sexy you two are," Joel muttered in between slurping Susie's cheek and Christian's chin.

Susie filled her mouth with Joel's semi-limp cock, suckling gently, and he let out a strangled gasp. He wove his fingers into her hair as Christian began to play with her nipples.

"We need a shower," Christian said. "Think we'll all fit?"

"If we stuff Susie in the corner and sit on her."

She let him out of her mouth with a plop. "Hey, I—"

Joel cut off her protest with a kiss, scooped her into his arms and carried her into Christian's bathroom. The shower was way too small but they'd manage.

Susie shuddered as Christian's teeth scraped down the side of her neck. Joel held her back against his chest, her hands locked at her sides. Water poured over them and Christian dropped his head to her breast and nibbled his way around her nipple. Joel's fingers were in the cleft of her bottom, sliding toward her ass. The sensation of them both holding her, both playing with her, sent a torrent of heat surging into her pussy.

Christian was eating her breast, devouring her—no pain, only pleasure, but Susie could barely stand the constant attention. Joel nudged her legs apart and his fingers seemed to be everywhere, one rubbing her clit, one buried deep in her pussy, one sneaking into her ass. Susie tipped her head back to his shoulder, gulped then coughed out a mouthful of water.

"The sweetest ass in the world," Joel whispered.

"Apart from mine," Christian lifted his head to speak before returning to torment her nipple.

Joel laughed. "And mine."

Then there were two pairs of lips on her breast, two tongues rasping. Joel's fingers moved faster and stars flashed in Susie's head as the orgasm ripped through her.

"Oh God, God," Susie gasped. "I can't—"

Explosions of biting sensation seized her, flung her higher and higher before she was allowed to fall.

She thought they'd stop but they didn't. Christian was on his knees, arms hooked around her thighs, his face buried between her legs. Joel held her twisted to his side so he could continue suckling at her nipple. Susie couldn't stand it, couldn't cope with more, couldn't breathe. The water was too much, the sensation too much. Her hips jerked as Christian's tongue slid in and out of her pussy while Joel had two fingers pressing in and out of her ass. Christian lifted her leg over his shoulder and his tongue delved deeper as Joel's fingers corkscrewed into her.

Pleasure fired along every nerve and Susie felt herself coming again. Joel's mouth slammed on hers and he pumped his tongue into her with the same force that his fingers pressed into her butt. Susie lost control of her body; she gave herself up to the ecstasy and screamed her release into Joel's mouth.

"Out of the shower," Joel said.

He kept hold of Susie as she began to slither down his body, and held her in his arms while Christian ran a towel over them both.

"No more," Susie moaned as he walked back into the bedroom.

"We've not finished with you yet," Joel said.

"I'm sick."

Christian caught Joel's eye and lifted his eyebrows. Joel dumped Susie on the bed.

"Nice try. The hospital said you were fine, you just had to rest. So don't do anything. Let us do everything."

"Pick on someone your own size," Susie mumbled, and the two men chuckled.

They settled on their backs, either side of her, and all three sighed together. A long, satisfied expiration of air. There was silence for a moment.

"Do you think I'm addicted to sex?" she asked.

They glanced at each other and laughed.

"I'm serious," Susie said.

Joel caught her chin with his fingers. "God, I hope so."

Chapter Thirty

ࡍ

The moment Christian heard Joel calling he was home, he dashed out of his study and raced through the house like a wall of water, down the stairs, straight through the hall and on into the kitchen where he slammed into Joel and sent him flying.

"Sorry." Christian pulled Joel upright. "Guess what?"

Joel took a beer from the fridge. "What?"

Christian glared at the lackluster response and waited.

Joel knocked the top off the beer and took a long drink. Christian knew he was teasing him.

"I guess something exciting has happened."

Christian nodded.

"There were no delays on London transport? Rain isn't forecast? You saw a flying pig?" Joel ducked the thump. "I give up."

"You'd never have guessed anyway. You're looking at the new feature writer for the *New York Times* and the London *Times*. Sacking Bella as my agent seems to have opened doors not closed them."

Joel's face lit up. "Hey that's great. Congratulations."

"The columns will be called *Metroman* in the UK and *London Eye* in the States." Christian was so excited he could barely get the words out. "I can still write the book for that publisher and the erotic stuff too. The *Times* are sorting out a visa, the *New York Times* talking about a green card. So I can go with you. We just need to sort out something for Susie."

"That's great, Christian. Where is Susie?"

Joel might be smiling but Christian knew something was wrong. He suddenly didn't feel so happy. "Susie's gone to see Mike. What is it?"

"Good news and bad news. I'd worked out a way of getting you a green card."

Christian sighed.

"But I can't get Susie over on anything other than the normal tourist entry. Three months max."

"But you said—"

"I said I'd do what I could and I have." Joel dragged his fingers through his hair. "I've explored everything. I can't even get her to the States on a longer student visa because she doesn't have enough qualifications to go to college over there. Three months is all she can have."

"No!" Christian slumped at the kitchen table. "But I had it all worked out."

The front door slammed and Christian shot Joel a despairing look.

The moment Susie walked into the kitchen, she knew. "You can't get me a visa?"

Joel shook his head.

"What about Christian?"

"He's okay. He's managed to land a job in the States."

Susie dragged a smile from somewhere. "That's great, Christian. Well done."

She felt her world falling apart again. They might not want to leave her behind but that's what was going to happen. Life would turn out a bit like Christian's book. She was too worthless to even deserve a visa.

"I won't go," Christian said in a quiet voice. He turned to Joel. "I can't leave Susie behind."

Susie felt panic surge inside her like a thousand moths had taken flight in her stomach. "No, you have to go. I'm not going to stop you being together. It's not your fault that I can't get a visa.

"I'll quit my job," Joel said. "I'll find something here."

Susie and Christian gasped, "No," at the same time.

"You can't," Susie said. "You have a great career ahead of you. I'd always feel guilty I stopped you being president."

Joel gave a quiet laugh. "We're fucked. Whatever way we play this, one of us ends up alone. I won't let it be you, Susie."

"And I won't let it be you. " She tightened her mouth so her chin didn't wobble.

Joel closed his eyes for a moment and then caught her jaw with his hand. "I need to speak to Christian in the other room. Stay here, don't move."

Susie knew it was hopeless. She'd thought of something they hadn't. Even though she was in remission from cancer, there was no guarantee it wouldn't come back and no guarantee she could have kids. She knew how much Christian wanted them. Someone had to be the grownup and do the right thing. She'd walked into their lives and she could walk out.

When they came back into the kitchen she spoke before they could. "You know what I'd like right now? No talking. I want the three of us in bed. Both of you inside me, loving me. "

"But—" Joel began, and they turned to look at him.

"But?" Christian and Susie said in unison.

Joel sagged. Susie knew they had something to tell her and she didn't want to hear it. One last time with them was all she wanted, all she could have. She took their hands and pulled them upstairs, past Christian's room and Joel's and on to the one they'd given her. Not that she'd spent much time in it since she'd moved in but Susie was touched they recognized she needed her space. They'd never made love in her room. First and last time.

By the time Susie had crossed the floor to draw the curtains and turned around, the pair were naked, their cocks fully erect. She laughed.

"Hey, you're not supposed to find our magnificent organs amusing," Christian said.

Susie laughed harder. Christian growled and pounced. A moment later, she was naked and wedged between them on the bed. They started slow and slipped to fast, twisting and turning her, arms and legs entwined, kissing, nipping, licking until Susie's heart pounded and her head swam. Joel pulled her over to face him, stared into her eyes and then kissed her, nibbling her lower lip before his tongue slipped into her mouth and began to gently pulse.

Christian licked his way down her spine and spread open the cheeks of her bottom. He planted an electrifying wet kiss deep in her cleft that nudged her deeper into Joel's embrace. Susie groaned as Christian's tongue swept along the narrow crease of her butt and then circled her asshole. Much as she loved the sheer wickedness of it, Susie still tensed. Joel pulled her on top of him, smothering her face with kisses as Christian pressed his tongue against her. Susie gasped into Joel's mouth as the relentless push of Christian's wet tongue triggered lightning bolts of pleasure to flash through her body.

"Oh God, Susie, I need some of your sweet ass too," Joel whispered.

Susie felt weightless, unable to focus or speak. Hands held her, stroked, soothed, teased. She watched Joel's dark hair moving as he slid down to lick between her legs. He glanced up at her, his mouth wet with her cream, and Susie felt every muscle in her pussy clench. Christian's hair rubbed her inner thighs. Their tongues sucked and tormented. Fingers in her ass. Fingers in her pussy. Hands pressing, stroking. The constant, relentless pleasure destroyed Susie's capacity to do anything other than respond. Tightening ribbons of pleasure curled through every limb, each jolt of delight finding a way back to her core, sensation building on sensation until she had nothing to do but come and come and come. Susie screamed as her body exploded, bursts of color detonating behind her eyes.

They moved her. Joel lay beneath her, his hands on her hips, Christian's hands on her hips as Joel's cock pressed at her pussy. The broad head nudged her swollen folds and then he circled her clit with the crown of his cock, sending waves of liquid pleasure running through her veins. The moment Joel slid a little way inside her, he sent her rocketing again.

"Jesus, Susie, wait for us," Joel said with a laugh.

He pulled her down to snuggle against his chest. Susie concentrated on breathing. It was all she could do and even that wasn't under control. Christian's slick fingers were in her ass, lubricating, readying her for his cock. She felt his tongue again and gasped.

Joel groaned. "Oh Christ, Christian, you bastard. Pack it in."

Susie felt Christian laugh and then his fingers replaced his tongue, pushing through the muscle barrier and she began to burn, fighting for every breath. Joel's hands cupped her face.

"It's okay, sweetheart."

"Need you," she gasped.

She felt the head of Christian's cock at her asshole and tried to push back, let him in.

"Now, now. I need you now." She wriggled between them.

"Susie, Susie. Take it easy. Breathe, darlin'. It's okay. We've got you." Joel stroked her hair, her face, kissed her.

Then Christian slid farther into her. Not far enough. Susie grabbed hold of Joel's muscular forearms and jammed herself down on the two men so they both sank balls-deep inside her. They cried out and Susie took a gulp of air. The sensation of being filled so forcefully sent her flying into space at light speed, hyper speed, warp speed. She gave a guttural cry from deep in her throat. Joel cursed over and over as he struggled to keep control.

"Fuck," Christian yelled. "God, you're so tight. Sweet Jesus, Susie."

Sweat trickled down Joel's face and Susie had the urge to lick the large drop that ran down his cheek. She was thirsty, in flames. Their cocks were burning her. Susie clamped down on both of them, a movement that elicited a chorus of grunts and groans.

Finally they began to move in their synchronized dance, Christian thrusting his hips against her backside as Joel pulled out of her. No time to miss the steel invaders before Joel jammed back inside her and Christian withdrew. Was it bad to like this, love this? Susie didn't care. Nothing felt this good. She had no idea where one orgasm started and another finished. Filled by their cocks, she felt more alive than she ever had before. Powerful spasms seized her muscles, kept throwing her over the edge for them to drag her back again.

Their bodies moved in perfect harmony, barely parting before they thrust again. Even the increase in pace came at the same time. Their cocks sped up, their gasps became more frantic. She felt everything. The slap of their balls, Joel's wiry hair, Christian's bristle where his hair grew back. Their strong hands holding her, their muscular thighs sandwiching hers. Their love. They loved her and Susie knew she'd have that forever in her heart.

Susie came again, wave on wave building into an orgasm she thought would rip her apart. She screamed, her hands bunched in tight fists. A spike of pain shot into her head. For a moment, she wondered if she'd die, if this was all too much. Susie remained trapped between their slick bodies as they worked in a tormenting rhythm. Each intent on pleasuring her, but also fixed on their personal journeys to implosion. Joel went rigid beneath her and Christian did the same at her back. They gave wild, guttural groans and Susie felt herself clenching over and over, ripples spiraling out to carry her to oblivion.

Saved the best 'til last, Susie thought, and gave a shaky sigh. For a moment none of them moved and then Christian withdrew, allowing Joel to slide her off his dick and lay her between them. Both embraced her. Joel buried his face in her shoulder while Christian's mouth pressed at her ear. No one spoke. No one could speak. All three were drenched in perspiration, their breathing hoarse and ragged. The musky scent of sex filled the air. Susie felt a hand from each man come to rest on her stomach.

"That was fan-fucking-tastic," Joel whispered.

"I can't feel...my legs," Susie said.

Christian's hand slid south. "Still there...don't worry."

"I may never move again," Joel said.

Christian groaned. "Not sure I really captured that in my book."

Joel chuckled. "Well, we'll have to keep doing it until you get it right."

"I got my bit right," Susie said.

They both laughed.

"Susie, you were perfect. You are perfect," Christian said.

Joel woke to Susie snuggled at his back and a male hand tightening around his cock. He opened his eyes and looked down to see Susie's hand clasping Christian's cock. God, the possibilities were endless. How could he even think of losing this, losing them?

A sweet mouth sought his and Joel turned into Susie's kiss, draping her leg over his thigh. He brushed his lips against hers, a whisper kiss. He wanted to go slow but the rhythm of Christian's hand working his cock drifted to his tongue and Joel began to fuck Susie's mouth, long deep plunges, stealing her air, reaching for her heart. As Christian's grip tightened,

Joel's hips arched and he groaned into Susie's mouth. His hand between her legs found Christian already there. Joel nudged him to her asshole so he could sink his fingers between her creamy folds. Christian's hand continued to pull and twist his cock and Joel's balls tightened. He dragged his mouth away from Susie's.

"That's enough," he choked.

"Never," Christian whispered, though to Joel's relief he let go of his cock.

Christian trailed a line of hot, wet kisses to Joel's nipple, which hardened under his abrasive tongue. Susie dropped her mouth to his other nipple, her tongue softer and hotter than Christian's. Had the pair planned this? Were they trying to drive him crazy? Joel thought he might die from an excess of sheer bliss. He moved his arms so that he embraced them both, his fingers stroking their shoulders.

He needed to speak. He should have said something before they'd come to bed only when Susie had said she wanted them, that was all he'd been able to think about. *Lying to myself?* What was he afraid of? Why was he even hesitating? He had the solution. Joel looked down at the pair of them lying on either side of him. Susie and Christian were his family, his life. He could have this forever. It was up to him to fix things.

"I need to say something." Joel pulled at their heads to move them away from his nipples.

Christian leaned up on an elbow. One of his muscled forearms remained on Joel's stomach. Susie lay back on the pillow and Joel nervously traced the line of her arm with his fingers.

"When I learned I was needed back in the States, I was going to leave you both behind. I told myself you'd be okay because you had each other. I thought I was being the strong one but I wasn't." Joel's heart raced. He swallowed to try to bring moisture back into his mouth. "Susie, I've tried everything I know to get you a visa and failed. But if you married me, you'd be eligible to apply for permanent resident status. I've talked it over with Christian and he's fine with it. We could all live together in my apartment in New York or we'd buy a house. Yeah, a house would be good. More room. You could go to college over there. There are loads of good schools. Maybe you can fix things with your dad before we go. We can't fight your battles for you, but we can help you fight them."

Joel hadn't expected to be greeted by silence. He reran his words in his head. It occurred to him he hadn't handled that very well, hadn't actually asked her to marry him. He reached for her hand, clutched it tight and looked into her eyes. "Susie, will you marry me?"

When she dragged her hand free, Joel knew this had gone wrong.

"No, but thank you for asking. Excuse me, I need the bathroom."

Joel sat up as she walked across the room. He turned to Christian. "What did I do?"

Christian glared at him. "You've talked it over with me? Like a business deal? Why did you tell her that?"

"I didn't want her to think marriage would push you out."

"But you made it sound as though it was a convenient way of handling things. You didn't say you *wanted* us to come with you or that you *loved* her. Christ, Joel, you're supposed to only get one chance to ask a woman to marry you and you cocked it up. Where was the emotion, the wanting to spend the rest of your life looking after her, having fun with her, making babies with her?"

"Shit." Joel looked at Christian. "What should I do?"

"Make it right."

Joel trembled. "I don't know how."

Christian levered himself off the bed. "Wait there."

Christian knocked on the door of the bathroom.

"Susie, can I come in?" he asked.

"Yes."

She sat on the floor in the corner, wrapped in a towel, her eyes bright with tears. Christian sat next to her. For a long while neither of them spoke.

"Forgive him. He should have let his heart do a spell check. He didn't say it but he *does* love you. So do I."

"Wouldn't you mind that I was married to Joel?"

Christian sighed. "I won't deny I wish it could be me but that won't solve our problem. I love you, Susie. I want to spend the rest of my life with you and if you marry Joel, it would be like you married me too, that's the way I'd think of it. I want to see your face when I wake up and I need you next to me when I go to sleep. I want you there to share the good times and the bad. And I want Joel there as well. Living my life without the two of you isn't an option. We can make it work."

"Can I try this again?" Joel asked from the door. "Only can we go back in the bedroom. When the kids ask how I proposed, I don't want to have to tell them it was while I sat on the toilet."

"I might not even be able to have kids," Susie blurted.

Christian hugged her. "We'll find a way."

"Please," Joel whispered.

Christian pulled Susie up, unwrapped the towel and tugged her toward the door. He had her fingers wrapped in his and he laid her hand in Joel's. Christian knew the significance hadn't been lost. Joel's Adam's apple shifted up and down. Christian followed them through to the bedroom. Joel sat Susie on the edge of the bed and then knelt. As Christian went past, he caught his hand and pulled him down on the carpet next to him.

Joel held one of Susie's hands and motioned for Christian to take the other. Now Christian had a lump in his throat that threatened to choke him.

"I haven't had an easy life, Susie," Joel said. "My mother left when I was seven. She took my sister, but not me. I'm used to things not being permanent in my life, partly because I came to want them that way. Less risky. You were right when you called me a coward. I'm afraid of being happy because the disappointment of losing that happiness is more than I can stand. So I was going to throw it all away, all I had with you and Christian, rather than take a risk on love. But I do love you, both of you. You make my existence worthwhile. With both of you by my side, I'm not afraid to face whatever life might throw at us."

He turned to look at Christian. "You are the most decent, loving guy I've ever met. If I could marry you I would. Maybe we can find some ceremony we can have between the three of us. Maybe we should make our own. You can write it. You're better with words than me."

Joel turned back to Susie. "Angel, you've fallen into our lives and I won't let you go. I'm not going to lie to you, this isn't going to be easy but you make me believe a future is possible."

Christian felt Susie squeeze his fingers. He shot her a little smile.

Joel took a shaky breath. "Miss Red Riding Hood, will you do us the very great honor of becoming our wife?"

Susie's heart had turned into a battering ram, pounding hard enough to break her ribs. They knelt before her, their eyes revealing how much they loved her. Time for her to take a risk too.

"I'd love to," she said.

Susie found herself flying backward onto the bed propelled by two strong males. Joel's mouth landed on hers.

He pulled back to say, "Thank you," and Christian pushed in and kissed her. "From me too," Christian said.

"God, we're so lucky." Joel kissed her cheek.

Christian stroked her cheek. "You flew off your bike and into our hearts."

"Sure you're not disappointed you didn't get Keira Knightley or Daniel Craig to answer your ad?" she asked.

"We turned them down," Joel said. "We made exactly the right choice."

Epilogue

ಹಿ

Susie looked down. This was the most beautiful thing she'd ever worn, which was as it should be. A long, strapless, off-white satin and lace dress that clung to her hips and then flared out.

"My little girl. You look beautiful. Your mum...I wish..."

Susie clutched her father's arm. A few yards away Pete and Mike stood staring back at her, smiles on their faces. Joel had gone to see her dad. Susie wasn't sure what he'd said but at least everyone was speaking without fists flying.

"How are we going to manage without you?" her father asked.

Shannon clung to Mike's arm. Susie hoped she was good at cooking.

Harry bent his head to her ear. "Not too late to change your mind."

Joel stood at the far end with Christian as best man. Joel looked petrified. Christian's hand rested in the middle of his back. Her guys—gorgeous in their dark suits, gorgeous naked. She smiled.

"You sure you've made the right choice?"

The truth was something just for the three of them.

"Yes," Susie said. "Exactly the right choice."

Strangers

About the Author

ဆာ

Barbara Elsborg lives in West Yorkshire in the north of England. She always wanted to be a spy, but having confessed to everyone without them even resorting to torture, she decided it was not for her. Vulcanology scorched her feet. A morbid fear of sharks put paid to marine biology. So instead, she spent several years successfully selling cyanide.

After dragging up two rotten, ungrateful children and frustrating her sexy, devoted, wonderful husband (who can now stop twisting her arm) she finally has time to conduct an affair with an electrifying plugged-in male, her laptop.

Her books feature quirky heroines and bad boys, and she hopes they are as much fun to read as they are to write.

ဆာ

The author welcomes comments from readers. You can find her website and email address on her author bio page at www.ellorascave.com.

Tell Us What You Think

We appreciate hearing reader opinions about our books. You can email us at Comments@EllorasCave.com.

Why an electronic book?

We live in the Information Age — an exciting time in the history of human civilization, in which technology rules supreme and continues to progress in leaps and bounds every minute of every day. For a multitude of reasons, more and more avid literary fans are opting to purchase e-books instead of paper books. The question from those not yet initiated into the world of electronic reading is simply: *Why?*

1. *Price.* An electronic title at Ellora's Cave Publishing runs anywhere from 40% to 75% less than the cover price of the exact same title in paperback format. Why? Basic mathematics and cost. It is less expensive to publish an e-book (no paper and printing, no warehousing and shipping) than it is to publish a paperback, so the savings are passed along to the consumer.

2. *Space.* Running out of room in your house for your books? That is one worry you will never have with electronic books. For a low one-time cost, you can purchase a handheld device specifically designed for e-reading. Many e-readers have large, convenient screens for viewing. Better yet, hundreds of titles can be stored within your new library — on a single microchip. There are a variety of e-readers from different manufacturers. You can also read e-books on your PC or laptop computer. (Please note that Ellora's Cave does not endorse any specific brands.

You can check our website at www.ellorascave.com for information we make available to new consumers.)

3. *Mobility.* Because your new e-library consists of only a microchip within a small, easily transportable e-reader, your entire cache of books can be taken with you wherever you go.

4. *Personal Viewing Preferences.* Are the words you are currently reading too small? Too large? Too… ANNOYING? Paperback books cannot be modified according to personal preferences, but e-books can.

5. *Instant Gratification.* Is it the middle of the night and all the bookstores near you are closed? Are you tired of waiting days, sometimes weeks, for bookstores to ship the novels you bought? Ellora's Cave Publishing sells instantaneous downloads twenty-four hours a day, seven days a week, every day of the year. Our webstore is never closed. Our e-book delivery system is 100% automated, meaning your order is filled as soon as you pay for it.

Those are a few of the top reasons why electronic books are replacing paperbacks for many avid readers.

As always, Ellora's Cave welcomes your questions and comments. We invite you to email us at Comments@ellorascave.com or write to us directly at Ellora's Cave Publishing Inc., 1056 Home Avenue, Akron, OH 44310-3502.

MAKE EACH DAY MORE *EXCITING* WITH OUR

ELLORA'S
CAVEMEN
CALENDAR

☥ WWW.ELLORASCAVE.COM ☥

ELLORA'S CAVE
Romanticon

Annual convention
for women who
refuse to behave

www.JasmineJade.com/Romanticon
For additional info contact: conventions@ellorascave.com

ELLORA'S CAVE
ROMANTICA PUBLISHING

Discover for yourself why readers can't get enough
of the multiple award-winning publisher
Ellora's Cave.

Whether you prefer e-books or paperbacks,
be sure to visit EC on the web at
www.ellorascave.com

for an erotic reading experience that will leave you
breathless.

CPSIA information can be obtained at www.ICGtesting.com
Printed in the USA
LVOW130744270812

296076LV00001B/17/P